Time & Place

Six Travel Stories

J. Lee Porter
Ed Teja

<u>nomadicgiant.com</u>

Table of Contents

Traveling Lives and Storytelling

As a lifelong traveler, my friendships are varied and start in curious and unpredictable ways. Lee and I first ran into each other virtually — on a traveler's website. Although we approached life differently, it didn't take many postings for us to learn we shared a lot of opinions and attitudes, especially on big issues, such as personal freedom and the joys of travel. Travel, moving from place to place, had always been a given in my life; Lee quit his job to travel.

Both Lee and I are avid readers. And I have been writing fiction since about the time of Gutenberg (Old "Gut" taught printing in my high school).

Ultimately, inevitably, we joined forces in the real world, taking trips together, writing together, sharing drinks, food, and ideas in new and fascinating places, and sharing our favorite authors and books.

And we shared cryptocurrency. As a programmer, Lee was very interested in cryptocurrency from the early days. We both appreciated the political implications, the personal freedom aspects of crypto and loved to speculate on how it has changed things and where that might lead.

Two novels have come from that so far. Some of the stories in this book involve implications of technology too, but the unifying theme is travel. Like Somerset Maugham before us, we write about the places we go and the people we meet, fictionalizing real people, real places, and real events.

At this moment, Lee is hunkered down in Merida, Mexico and I'm scribbling this in an adobe house in the mountains of rural New Mexico. Neither of us has a clue where the next adventure will take place, the next story will be rooted. Prediction is folly and our future locations and story ideas depend too much on the prevailing winds and the set of our sails. The next steps are joyously unknown and unknowable, or at least defined by uncontrolled variables.

But ultimately, travelers travel, some covering ground in wind sprints that take them across Europe in a week, others, like Paul Bowles, moving slowing across the face of the planet.

And writers write. So these stories, inspired by fragmentary glimpses of the world, sometimes in ways that took us outside our comfort zone, are shaped by our odd world views.

If we've done our job properly. each story in this collection will give you a different window into our experience and a taste of our love of this wild, wide, and chaotically crazy world.

Enjoy,

Ed Teja

. . . .

Cartagena, Colombia

When my brother Dan and I visited Ecuador in 2017, we met a lot of travelers who had recently been in Colombia. "It's better than here," a number said. "Cheaper."

As a result, when Lee suggested that we (he and I, plus Gigi, his wife, and his brother Brian) make a trip to Colombia, I was all for it. We flew into Cartagena where Lee had been once before. He was enamored of a particular restaurant that sat outside on the fortified wall of the old city and wanted us to see it. It was called Baluarte de San Francisco (Bastion of San Francisco) and I had agree that it was special.

Cartagena was overwhelming. We rented an Airbnb in the old city, and it was great, but it had too many tourists, too much of everything.

After a few days, we moved on to Medellin. It was there that the idea for a story that begins in that restaurant in Cartagena begin to bubble up. As we explored Medellin, we talked about story ideas... who was there and why.

We were writing a lot about cryptocurrency at the time, and we wanted that to factor in, and the protagonist had to be an expat. An expat remains longer in a place, and that gives him or her a different take on it than a tourist can manage, a view that usually involves a deeper understanding.

When my time in Colombia was running short, I flew back to Cartagena and visited that restaurant again, taking photos (including the cover photo), drinking, and staring out over the bay and the city.

Back in the US, Lee and I passed the story back and forth until it was right, until it told an interesting story that captured our sense of Cartagena.

Ed

INVISIBLE FORTUNE

(A Tale of Cryptocurrency)

"The whole point of Bitcoin is that you don't trust anyone else to tell you what the truth is."

— Andreas Antonopoulos,
Author of Mastering Bitcoin

A Bad Man

I met Daryl Saunders the way you often meet other compatriots when you are traveling. I'd gone to Cartagena, Colombia, taking a much-needed break from my job as a programmer in the states. It's a comfortable place, enough like the US not to be unsettling and yet a universe away from what passed for my normal life.

I'd been staying in the old walled city for about a week—long enough to find a few favorite places and get to know a few people. One of the absolutely best places I found to enjoy the sunset was a bar called El Baluarte De San Francisco. It is perched on the wall; it used to be a restaurant and still serves some overpriced food, but mostly it's an open-air bar with a great view.

The city is amazing. The Spaniards founded it in 1533 but it took until 1796 to build its walls, which were for protection from pirates. It was, after all, a key port for the export of Peruvian silver to Spain and for the import of African slaves. Now the old city is one giant museum and tourist attraction.

Sitting there in the humid evening air, enjoying a glass of 18-year-old Glenfiddich on the rocks and looking out over the city and the boats moored at docks is surreal. I could look down on 500-year-old Spanish buildings nearby, and with a small turn of my head see a new wall, one made of modern high-rise buildings. Right at sunset, the sun gleams off the metal and glass of new buildings gleam. Then, as the sky darkens rapidly, the lights come on. It's a glorious transition from shimmering modernity to a wonderland where everything sparkles.

And through it all, in the city below me, a horde of tourists, both Colombian and foreigners, are taking it all in, swarmed by vendors and hustlers selling hats, food, all sorts of souvenirs and promises of tours to magnificent beaches the next day.

Beaches can be nice, but I was content in my chair and watching it all. Diego, my waiter, smiled and brought my second drink without me asking. He was good at his job – the ice he'd put in the glass was a single large sphere. That minimizes the surface area of the ice and manages to cool the precious single malt without watering it down too quickly. That's important when you are outdoors in a heat that persists long after the sun sets.

As usual, I was drinking alone. Just as Diego had proven himself a good, no, an excellent, waiter, I had been an ideal customer. In appreciation of my generous tips, he made sure that I was seated well away from the speakers that would, at times, crank out raucous music, with the volume increasing as it got later in the evening. Unlike many who came there, I wanted to relax and savor my drink. For now, the music was soft jazz and I felt as mellow as the saxophone solo I could hear in the night air.

This is a crowded area and the ebb of the flow of the crowd brings different people in and out of your circle, your awareness. Given that, it was no surprise when a man came in, walked over to my table and asked if he could share my table. "The families are filling up the place," he said.

I looked up to see a man I guessed to be in his fifties. He was clean-shaven, medium height, and dressed in a loose shirt, shorts, and sandals – the uniform of the tropical expat. His request seemed reasonable, so I nodded. "Help yourself." As I said the words, I knew they were true. Suddenly, the idea of having company, of having an English speaker to talk to, appealed to me.

Conversation is a strange and complex exchange. I've often been amazed to find that expats and travelers who meet in some far-flung place will happily tell each other things that no one in their right mind would admit to if they were back wherever they escaped from. Perhaps it's a need to form bonds, maybe it's a way of staking out who they are. Perhaps it's the release of confessing (in some way) to a perfect stranger. Whatever it is, we all seem to become Chatty Cathy's when we are abroad and Daryl was no exception. He sat down, ordered a drink from Diego, who gave him a disapproving scowl that he ignored, and opened up to me.

In that flood of words, I learned a great deal. That's how I learned that his name was Daryl Saunders and that he was rich; that's how I learned his wealth was in Bitcoin. I hadn't asked, he just told me. I didn't care... not at first. What a person does with their money, even how they got it, doesn't interest me much. It's not that I'm not as curious about people as anyone else, but I was brought up to consider other people's finances none of my business. I didn't want to share anything about my finances either. It just seems unsettling to me.

Daryl came from a different world and had other ideas. He wanted to tell me, seemed to need to explain, how he'd invested in Bitcoin back in 2013 and made a bundle. He thought it was funny that because of that, now he didn't do anything with it at all. Once a month, to meet his expenses, he converted some of his cryptos to pesos. That was his work month. "It's like having a never-ending bank account," he said. "I stopped thinking about my money in dollar terms years ago."

I know that a lot of what people tell you in a bar is basically self-aggrandizing bullshit, but Daryl's story made sense. He told me about the huge house he had in town. "I renovated an old Spanish mansion," he said. "Well, I had it done." He smiled at me. "The locals do good work and I don't do any. It has old walls but a simple, modern interior. I bought another building, the one next door, and tore it down to make a garage."

"You need a big garage?" I was surprised anyone wanted to even own a car in Cartagena. The traffic was terrible.

A look of bliss crossed his face. "I need it for my collection."

"You have fancy cars here? In this traffic?"

"Motorcycles. Italian classics. I don't ride them. I'm not stupid."

Perhaps he wasn't stupid, but he was garrulous. His conversation amused me so I let him ramble on, and he drifted back to his favorite topic—his money. I'd read a bit about cryptos and was curious to meet someone who'd actually bought in early. So I subtly probed for a few details. "How do you sell it?" I asked. "We're in fricken Colombia."

"It's a global thing," he said. "I log into an account at a small exchange in Panama that caters to large Bitcoin holders. They cash out whatever I say, send it to my bank account, and my bills get paid automatically." He smacked his lips. "Shit, the little I spend these days isn't even coming close to pulling down the principle," he said. "That crypto shit is worth more every time I look at it. At this rate, I won't ever run out of money." He gave me a satisfied smile and rubbed his hands together. "It's my invisible fortune."

As I said, I absorbed the information, nodding at the right moments and listening politely. I can sometimes do that. When he paused we ordered another round of drinks.

"So you let the exchange hold your Bitcoin? Isn't that dangerous? Anyone who accesses the account could get your money – from what I read, Bitcoin is a digital bearer asset and whoever has the private keys controls the coins."

"No fucking way that happens," he said. "There is a ton of security. I have a separate phone that I use for getting into my account and it never leaves my office. It provides what they call dual-factor authentication. Without that phone... well, just say it's hack-proof!"

I wanted to explain that all that wouldn't keep his exchange from taking off with the money or the exchange itself getting hacked, but hell, it was obvious he didn't want any more advice from the likes of me. He was rich and successful, and I was just some guy in a bar.

"You asked me to let you know when your guests were arriving," a soft voice that came from behind me said.

I turned and was treated to the sight of petite, thin Colombian beauty in the flush of her early twenties. When she smiled at me, she was just being cordial to Daryl's friend, but, I'll confess that smile made me warm. That made the haunted expression in her eyes contradict the smile in an odd way. My impression was that this woman was unhappy, frightened maybe.

"This is Paola, my assistant," he said. "Not that I do any shit that really needs assisting, but I found her in Medellin and always wanted a girl Friday, so to speak." He gave me a sly, almost conspiratorial wink. "Now she's telling me I need to go to a dinner appointment. Got things to do and people to bribe." He stood up. "Good talking to you..." when he paused, I realized he'd never even asked my name.

"You too, Daryl," I said, just as happy he didn't know who I was.

When he left, with Paola in his wake, I waved for Diego to come over. I wanted another single malt.

"Your friend didn't pay his bill," he said.

I looked up at him curiously. Diego had been scowling and now he looked at me with a nasty sneer.

"He's not my friend, but I'll pay for his drinks, Diego. Put it on my tab and don't get all weird on me."

He tipped his head, looking as if he was deciding if he wanted to serve me another drink or not. That was serious. Diego was a young guy, with good English that made him popular with cruise ship guests who had zero Spanish. And he'd been friendly over the last week, so that puzzled me. I couldn't think of anything I'd said or done that had anything to do with him, and I don't like drama. So I called him on his attitude. "What the hell are you looking at me like that for?"

"You either have bad taste in friends or you are not a nice person either," he said.

"Nice?" I wondered if the man hated rich people. "And like I said, he isn't my friend. I just met that guy right here. He came over and sat down because he couldn't find another place to sit. Or so he said."

That surprised him. "But you let him sit with you."

"It seemed the civilized thing to do."

"He is a bad man."

"Bad? What are you talking about? How is he bad?"

"It isn't for me to say."

"But you *are* saying he is bad. If he is doing something, tell the police or some other people who are paid to give a shit."

"I can't go to the *policia*." I didn't like the sound of that.

"Why not?"

"Paola, his assistant, warned me not to. They will not help."

This was sounding worse all the time. "So you know the girl?"

He had a longing in his face now that told me he wanted to know her better than he did. That was something I could understand. She was a hot chica. "We talk sometimes when she comes into town running errands for the bastard. My house is near a store that orders special alcohol for him."

Then he remembered where he was and that I was a customer. "I'll get your drink."

I thought about what he said. Whatever was going on, it really bothered Diego, and I liked him. When he returned, I asked him the question that came into my head. "Would Paola tell me the stories about her boss?"

He shrugged. It seemed that the circumstances and my attitude granted me absolution of my guilt by association... for now. "She would talk to you if he was not around and you were a person willing to stop him."

"Like you?"

That question caught him off guard. "I can do nothing to stop him."

"But you want to."

He considered that. "I would do what I could."

I sipped the drink. "That's good to know." Even without knowing what Daryl was up to, my little programmer brain had already begun toying with ideas for ways to get to him. I was taking sides based on nothing. And I wondered what Diego meant by stopping Daryl... did they want him killed?

I wasn't sure I'd go that far, no matter what he'd done. But I was sure I could get to him in another way. "I'd like to talk to her," I said.

"I will tell her," Diego promised.

I drank my scotch and tried to put the entire thing out of my head, which naturally meant I couldn't think about much else. Whatever Daryl's vice was, apparently it wasn't just excessive drugs or orgies or something ordinary like that. No one would be interested in stopping him if that was all it was, especially not these two young people. If they went down that road, there were more candidates for stopping than you could manage in a lifetime.

A Chance Encounter

The next day, I had breakfast in a little cafe around the corner from the place I was staying. My room was outside of the walled city, in a picturesque neighborhood called Getsemaní that is a web of narrow one-way side streets and old-style doorways, with flower boxes hanging from second-floor windows.

I'd been to the cafe a few times and while I ate I chatted with a couple of local people who seemed to be regulars there. I asked them if they knew a guy named Daryl Saunders. They said they didn't and I figured that was the end of it. It wasn't.

"I'm sorry, but I overheard you asking about that rich man, Saunders," the owner said, coming over to the table.

"Yeah."

"Why are you asking about him?" He didn't sound pleased.

"I was just curious about him is all."

He gave me a hard look. "I'll tell you that he is a nasty piece of work."

"What do you mean by that? I asked.

He looked suspicious of me. Again I felt that I was being tarred with the brush of association. "If you didn't know, then you wouldn't be trying to find out more about him."

"Look, I just met him last night. He seemed okay enough, but then I was given the distinct impression that he's up to some kind of evil shit. Now, just because we sat at the same table drinking for a few minutes that seems to make me a bad guy. I'd like to know what's going on, is all."

"So you want to know what his vice is?"

"I just want to know if that's real—that he's some kind of creep. Like I said, I was told he was bad, but I'm not going to write him off just because of rumors, or rumors of rumors."

"In that case, I cannot help," the man said. "I only know rumors. But there are so many rumors that I am glad he doesn't come into my place. It wouldn't help the reputation of my cafe for him to come in here any more than it helps yours."

That attitude was unsettling and the intensity smacked of more than simple gossip. Clearly, talking with this guy about Daryl Saunders wasn't going to help me learn more.

After breakfast, I walked the old town for a time. The theory was that I could calm my mind with the tranquility of the beautiful buildings, large churches and street music echoing down the street. It didn't work. I turned back up toward the rows of stores, figuring I'd grab some snacks to take to my room. I wasn't getting anywhere, so I decided to watch a movie and see if I couldn't get my mind off worrying about whatever Daryl was up to.

That's when I walked into Paola—literally. She was leaving the store I was entering in and we crashed into each other in a head-on collision softened only by her small size. The impact knocked her bags onto the ground, and the groceries she was carrying scattered. A bag of detergent skittered under the counter and a bottle of aguardiente rolled in the opposite direction.

As we came out of the shock, she recognized me. "*Disculpa*," I said. "I wasn't looking where I was going. Let me help you."

She nodded, and we both squatted down to gather them back up and then stuffed them into her cloth bags. When we stood, I took her in, drinking the vision deeply. Her light cotton sundress hung low and since she wore no bra I had a grand view of the luscious curved brown flesh – the tops of her small breasts. They were covered in diamond-like tiny beads of sweat that seemed to curve up as if worshipping the sun. It took my breath away. As I lifted my gaze from those breasts to meet her eyes, I saw that the haunted expression was still there and she was trembling. "What's the matter?" I asked.

She shook her head. "Nothing. Thank you for your help. Now I must get back to the house."

"It was my fault. Let me buy you a *cerveza frio* or coffee to apologize for crashing into you the way I did."

"That's very kind, but Mr. Daryl..."

"Tell him you ran into the man he was talking to earlier."

"Why would I do that?"

"He knows that I've met you briefly. It would be only natural for me to delay a pretty lady, to want to talk to her and get to know her. There's nothing suspicious about that. You can blame being delayed on me."

"No, I..."

She wanted to leave. That was natural. She didn't know me, but she had seen me drinking with Daryl. Like Diego, she might have come to the wrong conclusion. But, with me holding one of her bags of groceries prisoner, she was in a bind. That stupid bag of groceries was my opportunity to let her know that I wanted to help. So I took her wrist and led her to a juice bar next door where I got her to sit down. "You need to calm down... pull yourself together," I said. "Listen, I know something is wrong – something much worse than dropping a few groceries. I want to help you."

She was confused. "I just need to do my job."

"Maybe if you told me what the problem is, the real issue, I could help fix things."

"The problem?" She seemed surprised.

"I was told that Daryl, your boss, is a bad man. I don't have any idea what it is that he is doing, or who he is hurting, but it clearly has you upset. Is he hurting you?"

Her eyes flashed for a moment. "Who told you these things about Mr. Daryl?"

"Diego, the waiter at El Baluarte De San Francisco."

"Aha," she said, starting to smile. "He worries about me." The idea obviously pleased her.

"He does and after he saw me drinking with Daryl he thought maybe we were friends and that I was like him. We'd been getting along and suddenly he was disgusted by me. I asked him, but he wouldn't tell me what the man does. Even when he realized I didn't know Daryl, all he'd say was that you wanted someone to stop him."

Her look became calculated; she was sizing me up. I couldn't blame her. For all she knew Daryl sent me to test her. "I don't care for people who frighten beautiful ladies and upset my favorite waiter. Tell me what it is and maybe I can help."

She was reluctant. "I should not talk about him." When she looked at me, those big brown eyes contradicted her words. She wanted to talk about him, but she needed me to convince her to do it.

"Anything you say would be between you and I. No one else. If I can help, I will."

She sat quietly, considering what I'd said, deciding if she could trust me. That made me wonder what kind of help she needed, what the job required. I'm not an intimidating looking person. I was a programmer who just got fed up with the rat race. I'd been burning out and was lucky enough to be valued by my employer. When I finished my project he'd ordered me to go on vacation. "I don't want to see your ugly face for a full month," he'd said. "I don't want you calling me, as it will only annoy me. I want you to go to... Mexico. Sit on some damn beach and drink yourself sick."

Being a dutiful type and always obedient, I'd come to Colombia and stayed the fuck away from the beaches. Who, after all, wants sand in their scotch. And get a few articles of clothing off a pretty girl and you get a better view than of one in a bikini at the beach.

So you can see that I was just a regular guy, in other words. If what she was looking for was muscle, maybe there was no point in telling me about her troubles.

After weighing the options for a time, unconsciously sucking her lip in a way that I found very sexy, she said quietly, "He does bad things to little boys. He hurts them, uses them. I cry myself to sleep for those children."

I'll admit that I hadn't expected that, yet somehow that particular bit of nastiness seemed to fit in with the character of the man I'd met. I hadn't suspected it at all, but I could believe it. "Why not tell the police?"

She laughed sadly. "Because he pays them money every month to ignore anything that goes on at his house."

"Right. We are in Colombia, not Des Moines."

"I thought about having him killed." She stared at me. "I truly did. But it would be expensive and then I would have no job."

"You are worried about losing your job? You want to keep working for that sleaze bag?"

Her smile was thin. "No, but without the money I send home, my family would starve. I should quit but just quitting the job changes nothing. That would just be me running away."

She was on the verge of tears. "He pays off the police?" I asked.

Her nod confirmed it. "He sends it to the chief personally."

That certainly complicated the idea of righting the world's wrongs, at least in Cartagena. "So he gets children and does sexual things to them."

She nodded. "He finds orphans, street children. Sometimes he even gets them from orphanages in the interior by offering them money they desperately need."

"He keeps them prisoner?"

"None now, but he has a room in the house where he keeps them locked up. Usually, he has one there, sometimes two. I don't see them, but I fix their food."

"What happens to them when he's done with them?"

She shook her head sadly. "I have no idea."

Child abuse was a sickness that made my stomach churn. This guy was living out his evil dream, of being one happy asshole. It galled me that he was using his invisible fortune to keep from paying the real price. Money insulated him from the human toll.

There had to be a way to get to him, to stop him. I turned the situation over in my head. I wanted to help Paola stop him, but I wasn't a killer or even a very threatening person. I couldn't intimidate him and I wasn't sure that would work anyway – not if he had the police in his pocket. All I did have was tech. I knew tech and thanks to Daryl's verbal diarrhea I knew his vulnerabilities. Suddenly, I had some rather dark ideas about good ways that, with a little help, could turn him from being a rich, sick fuck, to a poor one. That would at least slow him down. "I might have an idea," I told her.

Her face brightened. "You can stop him?"

"I think so, but I'd need your help."

She looked joyous. "Of course if you could..."

"Can you come back to my place?"

She tilted her head, regarding me curiously. "Your hotel room?" Her smile said the idea intrigued her, but in the context it was confusing.

"I have an idea that we might use to set this all right, but we shouldn't be discussing this in public."

She nodded. "You are serious?"

"I am." The truth was that I was serious about several things at once and, for a change, none of them had a thing to do with coding. I was serious about finding a way to stop the creep and bed the girl. That was a win-win scenario in my book. Even one out of two wouldn't be a total loss.

She hooked her bag of groceries over her arm and looped her other arm through mine.

"*Vamonos.*"

A Room With a View

As we walked the few blocks to the hotel, my focus on the problem at hand was compromised by the fact that her thin white sundress left little to the imagination. The bright tropical sun shone right through it, silhouetting her sweet body. I ran my eyes over her curves, seeing everything I could and imaging the rest with the result that I was having a hard time keeping my pounding chest in check. She had to know that.

When we got to my room, she gave it a quick look the way women do that makes you think they are imagining moving in. Then we put the cold things she'd bought into my minibar so they wouldn't spoil or wind up warm when she got home. While she put the things away I watched her bend over to load the fridge, catching sight of her lacy pink panties pulled taut over the curve of her ass. It made me sigh.

I forced my mind back to the issue we were supposed to be discussing. "He told me, Daryl did, that he has a second cell phone. Do you know where he keeps it?"

"Si. It is always in his top desk drawer. He never uses it except once a month when he pays bills. He calls me into his office to let me know he has sent my salary to the bank in Medellin and it sits on his desk."

"And could you get to it?"

"The phone? Yes, but if I took it, he would know. He has security cameras in his office."

"Does he look at the cameras often?"

She laughed. "Never. They are there in case something goes missing. He makes sure we all know they are there."

"Dummies," I said.

"What?"

"My guess is they are fake. He wouldn't know how to find what he's looking for. Better to buy cheap dummies and make people think he's protected."

"But he's rich."

"And a cheap bastard who skips out on paying for drinks. Some rich people are like that. But I need to know something. This is important—in that office of his... does he use a laptop or desktop computer?"

"A desktop. The computer is under the desk and it has a monitor and keyboard on top."

That was good. "And he doesn't lock his office?"

"No." Then she gave me a guilty smile. "Well, yes, he locks it, but it is just a latch that can be lifted with a butter knife."

I had to admire the crafty admission. She'd already been looking for some way to get to the man, something to use against him. "Do you always get paid the same day of the month?"

"Yes, it is always on the first day. He is rather..."

"Anal?"

She smiled. "Fixated was the word I was thinking of. *Obsesionado.*"

I thought about the timeline. The first was two weeks away. I was pretty sure I could line things up in time. Not alone, though. "If you are willing to help, I think we can stop Daryl Saunders."

"Yes?" she clapped her hands with delight. "Tell me how."

"You'll need to take some risks. You have access to the things we need. I have the knowledge, but if we are going to stop him, I need you to take those chances."

"Tell me what to do."

She was on board. "I need to work out some details. There are a couple of technical things and the timing needs to be right."

"And then we can stop him?"

Her excitement was contagious. "Not only can we can stop him, but doing what I have in mind will solve your problems, your family's problems, and even my problems."

"Your problems?"

"Yes. Mine."

"What problems do you have?"

"Mine are small. I hate my job. With money I can quit. I'm bored. With money I can travel. You can quit working too. You won't need to work anymore."

"How can that be? Any of it?"

"Because, Paola, we, you and I, are going take all of this bastard's money. We will steal his invisible fortune."

"Take it? How?" I saw a light come on in her head. "Not having money would stop him, but..."

"I know how to do it. All that is left is to put it in motion."

"And we will have money? His money?"

"Not in one chunk. We'd have it, but we couldn't suddenly just put it in the bank. If either of us was suddenly rich, that would arouse suspicion. I intend to set things up so that we each have more coming in each month than you can imagine," I told her. "You and I, Chica, will have enough to do whatever we want."

The look I saw covering her face was incredible. It was glowing with hope. Now I needed to come through on my promise. I'd set myself up to be her white knight and I intended to be just that – I'd never been anyone's white knight before and I liked the way it felt. The idea of becoming rich wasn't bad either. To pull it off I needed to do some research. That wouldn't take long. And right now, while she was caught up in the idea of an exciting future for the first time, I had another item on my agenda. I was determined to claim her.

She understood all that and probably much more as well. I saw that on her face now. "So we will be partners?" she asked.

I almost gasped at the heat in her smile, a lushness in her lips, and the sensual way she said that single word, 'partners.'"

I stood up and so did she, turning to look out the window. I had a nice view, but that wasn't why she'd turned that way. She was in profile, pretending not to understand what was building between us.

She was being coy. So I took the initiative. I moved closer to her and caressed the soft, curved mound of her ass. She didn't flinch and the heat I felt through her panties was intense. I leaned down and kissed her neck. She froze, arching her back, as I ran my other hand up inside her sundress. "Partners, I said. My hand slid easily up over her sweaty body, reaching her tiny breasts. I cupped them and let my fingers play with her nipples.

Paola let out a small moan that excited me because it was the sound her being aroused. "*Dios mio*," she gasped as I caressed her. She slumped against me and the smell of her, the feel of her warm body against mine was incredibly arousing. She looked up at me, stared into my eyes, and my lips were drawn to her lush mouth. We kissed, clutching each other, our tongues intertwining.

When we broke the kiss, I slipped my hand under her legs and scooped her up. The look on her face was of expectation and I carried her to my narrow bed.

When I put her on her back, she stared up at me, her brown eyes dilated, her mouth slightly open. She lay there as I began to undress her, revealing that lovely brown flesh. The sight of her was intoxicating, and when she was naked, I stood there undressing, then moving between those long legs, feeling the warmth of her body against mine, and then the magical way she enveloped me. Her legs tightened around me as I entered her; she held me, touched my face as I took her with a fierce passion.

Then, when I was spent, I moved off her to lie beside her exhausted. She curled up on me and put her head on my chest, listening to my heart slowing. My hands explored her back. "We will take his money?" she asked, looking for some certainty.

"We will," I said. "And I will take you again once more before you have to leave."

"Because we are partners," she said.

It didn't really matter, but I had begun to wonder who had seduced whom.

Planning

The next day required some planning, I spent the entire day with a close friend of mine named Jack Daniels. Fortunately, he travels well and, as I drank my friend into extinction, I thought about how my scheme could play out. Periodically my mind drifted off into warm and exciting thoughts of Paola, but mostly I was good and managed to quickly refocus on the task at hand.

Panama, I learned, has three crypto exchanges. I'd need to determine which one he used. Next, I needed his user ID and password. With those, I needed his phone or his SIM card. Whenever the exchange receives a request to move or convert crypto, it sends a text message. It's called a dual-authentication factor—it's a way of making sure some hacker doesn't get your coin.

I like to confirm things, make sure I understand what I'm doing. In this case, I turned to someone more informed, better qualified. His name is Vihaan and he's been a good friend for years. We met back in the late 90's. Vihaan was part of the first big wave of Indian programmers who came over to the US, recruited to deal with the panic surrounding the y2k bug. It was much ado about nothing, but Vihaan did good work and made a name for himself. He'd become a top security consultant for various fortune 500 companies.

The first time we worked late together, after we finally called it a night, I produced a bottle of single malt from my desk and offered him a glass. It was his first taste of such high-end liquor and he adored it. Then, the next time we put in a late night, once we finished work, his wife made Chicken Tikka Masala for us. It was the beginning of a long friendship.

Vihaan told me that his name meant 'dawn of a new era', it was certainly true then and again now. The bank we worked for at the time had no Y2K issues with the New Year of 2000, but the server techs did complain about the pungent smells of curry and scotch in their frigid humming domain.

Years ago, Vihaan showed me an inline keylogger. "A keylogger?"

He grinned with his nerdy enthusiasm. "You put it between a desktop computer and the keyboard," he said. "It records every keystroke made—until the memory is full, of course." He thought it was a clever gadget. "It would be a bit obvious in a data center," he said. "You'd notice it easily, I suspect."

You would see it there, but not in a home, where no one would be looking for it. That's why I was so happy when Paola told me he had a desktop computer. When he logged onto his account, the information would be captured.

"Do I want to know why you need this?" he asked. "I assume it has to do with a sexy girl."

"It does," I admitted. "Her name is Paola."

"Cute."

"She has a thing for high-tech shit. That will impress the crap out of her. She might bring a friend over if it is exciting enough."

He laughed. "Then I'll send it tomorrow." He knew I was lying, of course, but he didn't really care, either.

"Can you send a hardware wallet too?" I thought quickly. "Actually, I need two of them."

"Sure. Anything else? An ice cream cone? The left fender for a sixties Ford?"

"Wise ass."

"You are the one asking strange favors."

"Haven't I always been? Isn't that why you have friends?"

"I don't know. I only have you, and only your word for the fact that we are friends."

"Shut up and send the shit."

"Consider it sent."

With that done, I walked downtown to a small tienda, a little cell phone shop, and asked for a SIM card for one of the services that worked most of the time.

"*Passaporte*," she said, holding out a hand. She was supposed to collect the information from my passport, sort of communications Know Your Customer thing. Fortunately, this was Cartagena, not Miami.

"*Lo siento, no tengo conmigo,*" I said, telling her that I didn't have it with me. At the same time, I handed her 100,000 Pesos, which is about $40. That earned me a smile.

"*No importa,*" she said. It wasn't important... after all, we'd just become old friends and she knew me well. She pointed to the keyboard of her terminal, indicating I should type in my personal details.

For the name, I entered: "Chester DeMole Ster." I couldn't help chuckling to myself. Believe it or not, the name was part of my plan. Nothing necessary, just frosting on the cake.

I bought a cheap phone as well. I wanted a burner to use for the transfers. I was being overly cautious, but I'm a bit of a coward when you get down to it and this was cheap protection. Then, with my new SIM card in my pocket, and the information I'd accumulated buzzing in my head, I set off to get a cold Aguila beer.

I wished I could see Paola, but until this was over we had agreed to keep our meetings casual and public. We couldn't risk any rumors reaching Daryl's ears that she and I had gotten friendly and were spending time together. He might suspect something.

We did meet though. I needed to explain to her how crypto worked, so she could understand what we were doing. She'd need to learn to use a cold wallet and how to access funds later on. Fortunately, she was a quick study. I was also able to send her a couple of ebooks on how to use them and a link to a YouTube video that would walk her through the setup.

She picked it up fast and asked good questions. That gave me a good feeling about what we were doing—what we were getting into.

"This is gratis," Diego said, putting the cold beer in front of me without me asking. I mean, it wasn't a huge guess that this time of the day I'd start with that.

"*Por que?*" I asked. "Why do I get a free beer?"

"Because you are doing the right thing."

I wasn't so sure about that, but if he thought so, I was happy to bask in his good favor. I took a long, refreshing sip, and wondered if I should have an on-call masseuse come to my room. Without Paola around I was getting kind of kinked up.

I stared out over the walled city and decided that was a really good idea. A hard-working guy needed some relaxation, after all and a massage would help me stay on track.

Into Action

Time dragged by as we made our preparations. The goodies Vihaan had promised arrived and I eagerly set up my wallet.

Paola came by my place after doing her shopping. I was glad to see her and I knew she needed to be reassured. "What do I do?" Paola asked me. "These days pass slowly and I am going crazy."

I was too, but not in the way she meant. I longed to screw that wonderful woman again. I handed her the keylogger that had safely arrived. I'd already told her about it and now, as she looked at it I told her how to install it. "That sounds simple," she said.

It was simple. "Just make sure to put it so that it isn't in sight."

She scowled. "I'm not an idiot."

Her nerves were making her a little testy. "No, you are not an idiot. I'm just being careful, making certain."

I gave her the hardware wallet I'd gotten for her. "Your money will be stored in this," I said. "Get it set up the way you've learned so that it's ready."

She clutched it tightly, gratefully. "What else can I do?"

"When you are in the office check his desk for anything about Panama crypto exchanges... a name would be helpful. Write down what you find, don't take anything out of the office."

She scowled. "What if there is nothing there?"

"That just slows me down. It isn't important."

"Then why bother?"

"If we can find out it will help. Knowing what exchange he uses will let me prepare—take a look at it, maybe even open an account. Then I'll be used to the user interface, how it works, and that will let me do things faster."

"But even if you don't know that, you can still get the same information?"

"From the SIM card."

Her face brightened. "So I steal that instead of the telephone?"

"Exactly. After you are sure he has paid his bills, the first chance you get when it is completely safe, you will change his SIM card with this one." I handed her the one I'd bought. "That will give us everything we need," I said. "We can authenticate the transfers."

The smile she gave me was exciting. "*Simplistico.*"

She was right. The best part of the plan was that is wasn't complicated. When Daryl paid his bills, we would take his money, and he wouldn't have a clue until the next month. "It is simple, but don't take chances. If we have to wait a few days after he pays the bills for you to have a clear shot at getting the SIM card and retrieving the keylogger without him there, that's fine. Be very serious. If we aren't serious about doing this, if we don't understand the risks we shouldn't even try."

"I understand it all," she said. "The risks and rewards are very clear." She licked her lips. "But I need to be sure you are certain, that you are actually going to do this."

"Why wouldn't I?"

"In my experience, when it comes to the moment of truth, many men change their minds," she said. "So I offer a little reminder of the rewards that aren't included in his invisible fortune. With that, she dropped to her knees, unzipped my shorts, and wordlessly used her tongue and mouth to show me just how serious she was.

It certainly gave me a reminder that there were many good reasons for going through with this plan, regardless of the risks.

When she stood up again, wiping her chin, her eyes sparkled. "And that is just a teaser," she said. "I want my partner to be eager to do this."

I was and that eagerness was for more than Daryl's money.

She left right after that and I felt strangely alone. Something about her was different than other women I'd known. I'd always been glad when a woman left. I'd done well alone and there were always other women.

This time was different.

Two days later she called to tell me that the keylogger was in place and to give me the name of the crypto exchange. "He has a printout of his account information taped to the bottom of the desk drawer," she said. "I think he watched too many spy movies. Fortunately, so did I. It must be the same ones."

I'd seen that movie, or those movies, too.

"Good work," I said. "So, one other task for you when you go into the office to get the SIM card back is to go to his browser and delete the username and password for that account."

She made a humming sound, thinking it through. "To keep him out."

"Right. I don't want him checking it randomly. If it isn't there, he might think someone messed with his computer, but it won't suggest he's been hacked. It's all to give us time to get away."

"Excellent."

When she hung up, the room felt even more empty, or maybe it was that I felt hollow without her there.

Was I in love? If this was love, it hurt in a strange way. I felt more vulnerable than I'd ever felt in my life.

The Moment of Truth

You have to appreciate predictable people even if you don't like them. It's comforting, knowing that you can count on them to live up, or down, to your expectations. Daryl was a prime example, at least in his financial habits.

On the morning of the first day of the month, Paola called me from town. "He is doing it now," she said. "He went into his office as I was leaving to get him cigarettes."

"Get back there and make sure," I said.

"You relax. He is clockwork man," she said. I knew what she meant.

"The problem is that I don't have you here to relax me," I pointed out.

She laughed. "There are other girls around." Then she hung up.

From that moment on, the plan depended on her. All I could do was wait for her to find an opening, swap the SIM and retrieve the keylogger.

The next morning I found her standing at my door, looking gorgeous and holding out a SIM card and the keylogger. "Thank goodness," I said, sweeping her inside. For once, my intentions were tightly focused.

I got out the cheap phone I'd bought, put in the SIM card and looked at her. "Here we go," I said.

I plugged the keylogger into a new laptop I had bought when I was sure that we were going to do this. I didn't want any record of these transactions on my regular system. Then I connected an external keyboard to it. She watched over my shoulder as I opened Notepad and typed the code that would access the keylogger.

Although he'd logged in several times that day, probably paying individual bills, the username and password weren't hard to find. The login details for all his accounts were cached in his browser so he hadn't needed to enter those. But, because Paola had deleted his Panama PrivEx credentials from the browser cache, he'd had to type them in manually.

I wasn't worried about that alerting him to trouble. He'd be a bit frustrated by the hassle, of course, maybe have to look up the password, but computers had glitches. A fault in his computer, a localized screw up wasn't something to worry about. The computer never left his office, after all, and no one else used it. Even if he was tech savvy he would probably just double check the URL and, seeing that it was correct and that he wasn't the victim of a phishing attempt, he'd assume that a renamed text box or page name on the site was forcing him to re-enter his credentials. It would have been a pain in the butt, but not something that would alert him to trouble. When he'd tried to log on the site had forced him to enter the login information. Now, when I examined the key logger's record, the information I needed was right there, gleaming like cut diamonds.

With the username and password written down, I went to my laptop and navigated to the Panama PrivEx where I logged in. Moments later the dumb phone I'd put Daryl's SIM card in lit up. "*Un mensaje no leído*," it said. "One message unread." I checked the message, entered the code in the DFA popup, and held my breath.

It worked. The vault door opened and, without any fanfare at all, except for a tiny, "Welcome Daryl," notice in the top bar, I had my eyes and virtual hands on his account.

Daryl hadn't been lying. He had just over 730 Bitcoin in that exchange. At the time that amount was worth just about ten million US dollars. That would buy a lot of empanadas.

"*Dios mio*," Paola said when I told her how much money Daryl had had, how much we'd be sharing.

"Now the fun begins," I said. Her spicy warm breath warmed my ear as she watched me plug my hardware wallet, the cold wallet that would store the loot offline, into the laptop and authorize a transfer to it. One half of the available bitcoin floated in digital limbo for a time, with the transaction listed as "pending." It was an anxious time.

"Why so long?" she asked, nervous now.

"The transaction has to be verified. It's one of the weak parts of the blockchain. Needs to be fixed. So it's slow but sure."

I got up and went to my fridge and got a beer for each of us, but she shook her head. Fine, more for me. I took a sip and stared at the screen some more, urging it on. Go Satoshi, do it for us.

Finally, it was confirmed. I verified the coin in the wallet and unplugged it. Half of Daryl's money was gone... it was mine.

"My turn," she said, handing me her cold wallet. "You have the codes—the seed, safe?"

She nodded. I plugged it in, got the receive address and went back to the exchange to transfer the remaining coin to her wallet. When it read pending, we both sat back and stared at the screen. I sipped my beer and Paola ran her hand over my shoulder and back.

When it was confirmed, I unplugged the wallet and handed it to her. "So now you are rich," I said.

"More important, he is poor," she said.

"Yes. But remember about not converting all the bitcoin to cash, you need to..."

She laughed. "I've heard this so many times, from him, from you... I just convert what I need and try to hide the trail of the money. Yes, yes, yes..."

I hoped she did understand.

At that point, there was no way that Daryl could ever find the coin, much less access it, or even know where it went. That felt good. Paola kissing my cheek and rubbing my shoulders felt good too.

She kept it up as I erased the computer history, all the passwords, wiped the disk, and took out the drive and smashed it for good measure. It probably wasn't all necessary. Maybe none of it was, but being cautious never cost me any sleep.

"With luck, we have a month before he notices his money is gone," I told her. "You need to tell him someone in your family is sick and you have to go see them. Don't tell him you quit. And then you need to really go. When he learns he's been robbed there is no telling what he'll do."

She smiled. "My family wants me to come home, to Medellin."

"Perfect. I need to return to work. So I'll do that."

"Won't the police come after us when he reports being robbed?"

It was my turn to smile. "Even if he suspected you, the beauty of an invisible fortune is that he can't prove he had any money for anyone to steal. The worst thing he could accuse you of is swapping the SIM card out of his phone. And he has no leverage. He won't have money to pay the police to do anything to us. In fact, I will pay the police to arrest him for abusing the children."

She laughed. "I think that will make them happy too. The *jefe*, chief Alvarez, doesn't like him and would like to put him in jail."

Just not at the cost of losing their current income, of course. But now that it was going to end anyway they'd at least get a little something for wrapping up a bad guy. Seeing clearly makes a person cynical.

She stopped. "If you pay the chief... well, they will wonder where you got the money and why you care. They might think you have the money that he had. They might not get it back for him, but they wouldn't mind taking it for themselves."

"I'll have to use an intermediary."

She liked that idea.

"My careful lover," she laughed, running her hands down my body. I pushed the remains of the cheap laptop onto the floor. She stood, pulling up her sundress and showing me that she was naked underneath.

"Speaking of which, bring that over to my bed where we can be comfortable."

This time our lovemaking was so much more sensual and relaxed that it felt, rather eerily, like love.

As we lay in bed I said, "Now you should go back to the house and tell him you need to go right away."

"He will be angry."

"Maybe, but you no longer have to care. And if you leave without saying anything he might check his phone now. We want to have time to put space between the events."

She nodded. "*Bueno*," she said and as she stood in the doorway, almost out of it, she stopped and looked at me. "Can I come back here? For the night? I will tell him I am leaving tonight and spend it here. Then tomorrow I will leave to join my family." I could tell her brain was still reeling from the reality of her newly found wealth.

"I'd like that," I said.

I listened to the sound of her footsteps as she walked the one flight down to the street. Then I went to watch her from the window, enjoying the graceful way her tiny ass swayed on her way back to give Daryl the news.

I felt good. Daryl was going to be stopped. Paola was coming back to my bed. And I was rich.

I sat back and wondered what would be a suitable donation to a child-protection organization. I assumed there were such things. I needed to research that.

Loose Ends

Paola came back that night. Daryl bought her story, even been sympathetic. So she'd packed and left. "I want you to remember me," she said. "In an exciting way."

That, she did. She said her goodbyes in a way that guaranteed I would never forget her or remember her badly.

In the morning, she was gone. Despite knowing she was leaving, it still came as a shock to wake and find that she wasn't there.

I knew she'd be all right. I was still amazed at how quickly she'd mastered the way crypto worked. She'd taken to it and was running with it. Whatever happened next, the money had freed her to thrive or crash and burn. We'd been partners and now that was over.

I had a couple of days left in Cartagena and I spent them drinking and taking home girls who were pretty and sexy, but who only made me miss Paola more.

On my last night in town, as I was sipping my fifth single malt, I got a WhatsApp message from Paola on her new phone letting me know she had returned to her mom's house safe and sound. She sent a picture of her view of the city of Medellin at night. "The view from Santo Domingo," she wrote. "But we won't be here long."

The view was spectacular—the city was all modern high rises and penthouses. The problem was that she and her family could be found there. Yet I knew that with her resources that wasn't going to be a problem. It's easy to get lost when you have enough money.

I felt good. Paola was safe and moving forward. By the time anyone discovered anything had happened, she would have covered her tracks. All that was left was for Daryl to pay the price for what he'd done. I went back to the bar that night and took Diego aside. "You did a good thing," he said. "Perhaps more than you know."

"But there is unfinished business," I said. "Daryl Saunders is helpless and needs to be struck down. I need someone to pay the police to take him off the streets."

Diego shrugged. "That's possible. They, however, might want a great deal of money to do that."

"How much are we talking about? What is a great deal of money?"

"To arrest him they would want a great deal. There is so much paperwork and a gringo would mean media attention they don't want. To eliminate him would be much less expensive and far simpler."

"That's a point. You mean just have him killed?"

He looked askance, unwilling to say the words. "Without the police on his payroll, he can easily be stopped. There would be no interference, no one looking for him. But to do that—the police are an unnecessary complication."

"If you have the right connections. I don't."

He gave me the friendliest smile he'd ever shown me. "Yes, you do. You have me. You were willing to trust me to bribe the police. I'm suggesting that you trust me to handle his... retirement from his bad behavior."

That made perfect sense. "I was prepared to offer the Jefe of police fifty thousand dollars," I said. "And I was going to give you five thousand for being the messenger."

That part I'd planned in advance. I liked the life I'd found here and intended to be in and out of Colombia on a regular basis from now on. With that in mind, I'd opened an account at a local bank to make access to money easier. I contacted my brokerage account and closed my retirement account. I'd instructed them to wire seventy grand to that new account. I figured I was set. "I can go to the bank and get the money tomorrow."

Diego grinned. "Amigo, you overestimate the efficiency of my compatriots. Tomorrow you will find that there will be many reasons they cannot give you that much money—not in dollars or pesos. They have your money and wish to use it for a time."

"Shit." He was probably right.

"But for men like us, a little banking confusion should be no problem, amigo."

"No?"

"I understand you have cryptocurrency."

"I do." I wasn't sure how he knew, but of course, he talked to Paola.

He handed me a slip of paper with an address and a QR code. "Send the amount in bitcoin to this address," he said, enjoying my surprise. "I can't afford a hardware wallet, but paper wallets are free and easy to use, and safe."

I laughed. My pride in being clever with tech was catching me up once again. "I can do that when I go back to my room."

"And I will tie up the loose ends in this rather pleasant operation."

I was certain he would. I was also certain the less I knew about how he dealt with them, the better off I'd be. I put the paper in my pocket. "Given that you are being such a help, I'm guessing that you won't be here the next time I come back."

"That is unlikely. With this money, even after hiring the necessary help, I can begin a new career somewhere else," he said. "No offense, but I've had my fill of tourists." He looked out over the yachts. "I am not enamored of this city anyway."

I understood. "I'll go send the money now."

"And I will solve the problem."

We shook hands and I left, stopping at the liquor store to get a bottle and then going to my room and sending the money to Diego's crypto wallet. It amused me to be doing that—sending Daryl's Bitcoins to his assassin. Who would've thought it? Here I was, down in the wild world of Colombia, tying up loose ends with crypto payments to a waiter. This world was becoming a braver, if slightly off-kilter, new place.

Home Again

When I got back to the United States, I surprised myself by actually returning to the office. I hadn't been sure I would. Now that I had money enough for several lifetimes the work I'd been doing seemed pointless. But part of me wanted to see how things played out down in Colombia before I did anything dramatic.

I wanted to go back down there, permanently this time, but not if my name was showing up as someone wanted in an investigation of any sort. I haven't heard good things about Colombian prisons... or any prisons.

As I got back to work, I scoured the Internet for stories from Cartagena searching on Daryl's name. I found one that said he'd been reported missing. On a routine check, the police found his house abandoned. It had been looted. I doubted that it had been looted until the police found him missing, but no one had asked me.

I searched for news using Paola's name too and struck paydirt there. I came across one of those do-gooder stories. It seemed, according to the article, that some anonymous benefactor had established a new foundation to build an orphanage near Bogota. He'd funding the entire thing and part of the charter was that he had put Paola and a guy named Diego in charge of building and running it. They had nice salaries, but apparently, their benefactor had provided three or four million dollars to build the place and keep it running. I wondered if that would be enough.

I shook my head, just as my boss came in. "Bad news?"

"Far from it. Surprisingly good news." I seemed to always be underestimating Paola and Diego.

"Well, we have some issues to discuss."

"Do we?"

"Whatever happened on your vacation, it didn't make you come back all refreshed and energized—at least not about work. Your mind is somewhere else."

I looked at my boss for a minute trying to get the nerve up to tell him. He'd been good to me and I was going to have to lie. "You're right. My mind is on other things these days. I really liked living down there."

He laughed. "We aren't planning to open an office in Colombia anytime soon... probably never."

"Not to work. I'm sick of programming, at least doing these repetitive tasks."

"That's what pays the bills."

I smiled. "All mine are paid for a long time out. Except one and I intend to take care of that."

"What are you telling me?"

"That I can't do this anymore; that I don't have to do it anymore, so I'm quitting."

"That's a drastic step. Did you inherit some money?"

"I did, as a matter of fact." In a manner of speaking, I had.

"Colombia's a dangerous place," he said. He liked working with me and didn't want me to go.

"So is this one."

"Did you hear about the American guy they found who fell out of a helicopter?"

That got my interest. "What happened? How would he do that?"

"One of those tours over the beaches on the islands off Cartagena or some shit like that. Apparently, during the tour, he fell out and no one noticed. How does that work? Anyway, it happened a few days ago and they found his body this morning. It was on television news. The cops down there were looking for him because they thought he'd been kidnapped and he turns up squashed on a beach."

I smiled. "Well, things happen everywhere, like I said. And for a number of strange reasons, that just makes it more important that I quit and go down there."

"How does that work? Some guy you don't know dies and you have this sudden need to see where it happened or something?"

"No. I don't care where he died. I'm actually going to go to a place near Bogota. Some friends are building an orphanage and I ought to check it out."

"An orphanage in Colombia?" He scratched his head. I thought I knew you but I guess I was wrong."

"I'm still learning about me, so don't feel bad," I said.

I wasn't sure what I'd do or how life was going to go, but I could give Paola and Diego an additional donation to their work and still have enough to live on, very well, for the rest of my life. And I was starting to look at some of the alt coins. Even not needing the money, I was intrigued by the idea of trading. And I had a perfectly good account available at the Panama exchange.

And it was all invisible. It was also tangible and secure, if I was more careful than Daryl. And it was the start of a new existence.

THE END

Time & Place

Phnom Penh, Cambodia

Early in 2020, before it was official news in the west, covid was a very real thing in Cambodia, my wife and I had been in the capital Phnom Penh in a penthouse overlooking the King's Palace during the Chinese new year, Ed had just left Phnom Penh to return to New Mexico, people were becoming nervous, worried about foreigners, the masks started appearing, we took off for Chiang-Mai Thailand to find a good apartment to stock up with the essentials, but the great tourist exodus of South East Asia had begun.

Once settled and stocked up for a few months in Chiang-Mai, we got word they didn't want tourists to extend visas, they wanted tourists to return home, as we didn't have a home at the time, we were at a disadvantage, where do we find our bolt hole for this covid thing to blow over? Well, we went right back to Cambodia, but this time we decided to go to Siem Reap, less people, good infrastructure, and plenty of great rental houses left as the tourists fled the city.

We ended up in the city a couple days before the lockdowns, and the airport closure. The night walking street was still open, enough tourists had left that we were basically the only customers anywhere we went. At the hotel, the remaining 4 foreigners were busy making hurried return travel plans to Australia, Germany, and Canada. The tickets were astronomical in price, we decided we would rather use the same amount on a year lease of a nice house and pool, as again we had nowhere to retreat to.

The last expat to leave the hotel was a man from Germany, we struck up a conversation due to his Bitcoin shirt, he had been traveling around southeast Asia and made a living playing in underground card games.

The stories he shared over 50-cent beers and spring rolls became the inspiration for this story CAMBO HUSTLE

Enjoy,

-Lee

CAMBO HUSTLE

This story was previously published as A Calculated Gamble

NEW IN TOWN

"If you don't gamble, you'll never win."
— Aldous Huxley

I stepped out into the warm night a little after eleven, walking away from the room I'd rented at a small guesthouse near the riverfront. I walked away from the Tonle Sap, heading down a street filled with girlie bars. The waterfront in Phnom Penh, the capital of Cambodia, boasts a lot of nightlife but tonight that wasn't what had me hitting the streets.

It was still early for the area. Things were just getting started. The bars had spilled out into the street the way they do at night, with the proprietors setting up tables outside their establishments, and the bar girls, dressed in tight shorts or short skirts and halter tops, taking their places.

Walking those streets was a bit like walking a gauntlet. The girls, prowling for prey, the neon lights, the music charged the atmosphere and gave the very air edge. Whenever a man walked by, one or more girls would begin their long-range assault, waving and calling out encouragements, urging him to come into their bar and buy them a drink. All of their words, their movements, promised the lucky man with some ready cash a sexy and fun evening. All he had to do was enter their lair.

The street was alive — loud and raucous, projecting a scene that would look right in an old movie but with the vibrancy of a carnival sideshow. The girls, needing to make money, played the role of show barkers, doing their best to make it seem that everyone inside was having a boisterous good time. "Step inside, touch the naked ladies."

Walking by at a steady pace earned me disappointed cries and a few insults born of frustration and desperation. Few of the girls chose the career of a bar girl and would prefer to get on with the night's work, earn their money, and get it over with. I have nothing against those places, but that evening, I was headed for a specific destination — a particular bar among these so-similar venues, that boasted the strange name of <u>SNAKE GIRL</u>. In a place where most of the bar names implied sex or hot females one way or another, it seemed odd. The bar I was walking by, which a neon sign informed me was called <u>HOT PUSSY</u>, at least made some sense. But SNAKE GIRL?

Perhaps that was the point — to stand out however it could.

The girls along my route offered the usual mix of ages and beauty, or a lack of either quality. The majority of the girls had delicious brown skin, but the miracle of modern hairstyling meant I saw the gamut of blondes, redheads, and whatever it is you call girls with purple or green hair. Even the ones who had that lovely lustrous black hair I associate with Asia, had it cut in a variety of styles that were probably modeled after Western movie stars. I wouldn't know much about them — movie stars, I mean.

While they waited for lonely customers to stop in and appease their thirst and lust, the girls sat in plastic chairs in front of the bars. They idled the time away, playing with their cell phones, calling out to passing men, and eating noodle dishes, all the while chatting nonstop with each other.

If you are going to play the bar girl game, buying the girls the special, overpriced, nonalcoholic lady drinks so that they will spend time with you, whether you want to screw them or just have some company, Phnom Penh is an inexpensive place to do it.

A man could do worse than to sit with a girl, getting to know her. And if you are looking for more than company, getting to know her a little is probably a decent investment. It lets you know what she's like before you pay the fee that management gets to let her leave, her bar fine, and take her home.

That worked for the girls too. Even if she didn't strike your fancy and you moved on to another, at least she earned something from her cut from the drinks. It wouldn't thrill her that you passed on the idea of spending the night or even a short time with her, but she could feel she hadn't totally wasted her time. With the financial incentive plain and out in the open, the girls were eager to compete for prospective clients. And that was exactly what the bar owners wanted, too.

I walked the few blocks of this amazing yellow brick road of the night world, smiling and nodding at the girls while ignoring the cries of "buy me a drink," until I came to it — SNAKE GIRL Bar. Wedged in between BAD GIRL BAR and PUSSY PALACE, it was small and didn't stand out and it seemed odd that one girl sat outside, alone. She was on the phone, texting happily, but made the effort to get up to follow me inside.

I made my way straight to the bar and took a seat next to a girl wearing tight shorts and a tighter Black Sabbath tee-shirt that emphasized her breasts. "Slow night?" I asked as I sat.

She glanced up to stare at me, giving me a feeble smile that stunk of sullen hopelessness. I wanted to see that smile blossom. Her lovely brown face looked wrong with that look on it. Her mouth opened slightly as she started to say something, then she changed her mind.

She glared at the girl who had followed me in. I suppose it was a territorial glare because the other girl turned and, staring at her phone, went back outside.

"Help you?" the bartender asked, emerging from the back. He had a noticeable German accent.

"I'll have a whiskey, something Western, please. The local shit almost killed me once."

"The local shit is shite." He chuckled at his own joke. "I've got Jack, if that's okay?"

"Jack Daniels is fine. Let me buy you one, too."

He grinned. "Thanks."

I nodded toward the girl. "Give our Lady of Perpetual Sadness here a lady drink."

He nodded and grinned at her. "Chatty Kathy, you are in luck."

"You nice," she said, brightening.

"I am at that," I said. "And I am also terribly modest, which makes me even nicer."

Her puzzled look pleased me. Undeterred, but encouraged by the glass of colored water and the token the bartender gave her, she began stroking my leg. Clearly, I'd miscalculated. By rewarding her for being indifferent to me, I'd encouraged her to do exactly what I'd wanted to avoid. Live and learn... or was the appropriate saying: "no good deed goes unpunished"?

The bartender was watching me. "What kind of name is Chatty Kathy?" I asked him.

He grinned. "A nickname. Westerners can't or don't want to bother saying her Khmer name."

"Chanthavy," she said.

"Rather than stumble over it, they renamed her Chatty Kathy. They thought it was funny and it stuck."

"Chanthavy means 'as beautiful as the moon'," she said as the bartender poured us each a whiskey. She flashed a seductive smile that totally ruined an attempt at an aloof expression.

I tore my eyes away to speak to the bartender. "And your name is Becker, right?"

Surprise flickered over his face, then he smiled. "It means 'as macho as the sun'," he said. "Do I know you?"

"No, sorry. Arnold in Penang told me to look you up," I said.

"Arnold? Which Arnold?" he asked, giving me a blank smile.

"The Arnold you owe fifty bucks."

"Me, skip on a debt?"

"He said you never paid your share for some whores and dope you two enjoyed last March."

He scowled. "Oh, that Arnold in Penang. The man's got a memory, that's for sure."

"Hey, it's about sex and money."

"You aren't American."

"Dutch," I said.

"Then you aren't Arnold's cousin, Dudley. I was afraid—"

"No. I'm Aaron... someone who met him at the Rouge in Penang."

"Is he still dealing blackjack?"

I laughed. "If Arnold were dealing cards, it wouldn't be at the Rouge. No, he is still pimping out of that room over the old lady's store."

The German grinned. I'd passed his test. "I don't have his money if that's why you're here. This dump doesn't pay for shit so it will be some time before he gets it."

"No. I'm not after your money. Arnold owed me a favor. When I found out I was going to be here for a bit, I asked him who he knew. He said you were the only person he knew in Phnom Penh who knows where things happen."

"Things? That's a broad term." He nodded at Chatty Kathy. "You got girls right here."

"I'm looking for a poker game."

His eyes narrowed. "Well, you are in luck, moron. We've got an entire fucking casino across town. It's called Naga

World. It will be the delight of any tuk tuk driver on the street to take you to their front door."

Another whore, with red and green hair cut in a sculpted diagonal, walked up and put her hand on my shoulder. The one stroking my leg glared at her but said nothing. I gave her a smile and sipped my drink.

I looked at Becker. "I mean quiet games. Private ones. The games where people lose their money quietly, drink quietly, and then lose more money."

"Quietly," he said.

"I'm thinking of places that don't involve people with guns or houses that take a huge cut of the pot."

"Boy, you are fucking picky." He grinned. "I'm not sure such places exist in Asia." He refilled the drinks. "Arnold sent you to me?"

"I made him. He owed me. I'm a professional poker player and I want to find a game."

He nodded. "Why in Phnom Penh? They have better games in Penang."

I sighed. If I expected his help, it seemed I was going to have to tell him everything. Not that my reasons were secret, just embarrassing. "I hadn't planned to come here at all and now I'm winging it. My departure was rather hasty and totally unplanned."

"Rushing is a bad idea. A person needs plans."

"My plan is to play a big poker game in Singapore a month from now. It's an invitational and the buy-in is big by my standards. I need to play it, partly because it's hard to get on that list of players. In Penang, I was playing steadily so that I could raise enough money for the buy-in."

"Makes sense."

"After a game the other days, some guy, I don't even know who, turned out to be a sore loser. Unfortunately, he was a well-connected sore loser. He decided to take out his bad fortune on me, personally by sending some thugs after me. I got tipped off. I managed to get out with my bag before they grabbed me. I went to see Arnold for contacts. You were the only name in Phnom Penh he could give me."

Becker considered that. "So, what do you need a name for?"

"To find more games. Shelling out for an extra plane ticket and entry visa, plus abandoning a room I'd paid for in advance emptied my wallet. Not that I'm low on money, but because things unraveled so fast, so suddenly, I'm short on ready cash."

"But you have money."

"Yes, but not enough for that big game. I had a way to go before I finished accumulating my stake. So now I need to get going on that again. I'd also like to earn enough to cover living expenses here for a few days. I'm meeting people in Vientiane in a week and my visa for Laos isn't good until then."

"How are you going to play a game without money?

It was a valid question. "I've got money. It's just that I'm hesitant to convert my assets to dollars just to cover living expenses. They dropped recently and will come back up, but for now —"

"You have to pay for essentials like booze and whores," he said.

"Right."

"This is just being nosy, but what kind of assets do you have?"

"Cryptocurrency. Bitcoin."

"Another gamble," he laughed.

"A calculated risk. I approach poker and investing the same way — rationally. I try to use skill and trust luck only when necessary. Part of my long-term strategy has been to convert my winnings into Bitcoin, just holding back what I need for current expenses. That keeps my wealth safe and transportable. Under normal circumstances, when I need money for travel and to pay bills, I wait for the Bitcoin price to peak and sell enough to live on for a time."

"And that does what?"

"If things go my way, over the long haul the value of Bitcoin keeps going up relative to dollars. It doesn't always do it in the short term, of course. There aren't any sure things. But I did my research and think that if I'm patient, one day I'll be able to live off it."

"Live off it?" Becker shook his head. Disbelief was heavy. "How the hell do you live off something like that? From what I hear it's just computer code."

"It's a secure blockchain. Without getting into it deeply, it's just computer code used to create a ledger. Outwardly it's no different than the one that gives you your bank balance, but it's private and safer."

Becker laughed. "I couldn't live off my bank balance."

"No, because they pay you crap interest and they store your money in dollars or euros. Those don't have any investment value and can't actually appreciate except one compared to the other. And as long as governments keep printing more, over time you'll lose the value. Bitcoin is a finite resource. That makes it more like gold or silver, except I can sell it or move it around easily on a memory stick or over the Internet."

"No shit?"

I smiled. "It works like this. Say I save ten thousand dollars and buy Bitcoin. If I'm right, and other people decide it's a good investment, by the time I need it, it's worth one hundred thousand. And if I save a hundred thousand... you get the idea. But this has been a rocky year, to say the least, and now, when I needed cash, the price was down. You can't live for long off the principle if you are taking advantage of depreciation — the math just doesn't work out. A professional poker player is nothing if not someone who trusts math."

"But you put too much in Bitcoin."

I nodded. "In hindsight, I got too eager and depleted my emergency fund. If I'd known I was going to leave Penang when I did, I'd have held back some cash."

"So, you need a big deal game?"

"Ideally."

While Becker considered what he was willing to tell me, the whore behind me spotted a guy walking to a table outside the bar.

Her hand slipped from my shoulder, and she rushed over to him, leaving a cloud of cheap perfume in her wake. I wasn't much fun and Chatty Kathy hadn't relinquished her claim.

"I haven't been here that long," Becker said. "Over time, like a hotel concierge, I usually do get to know who is doing what in a town, but right now, I can't do much for you."

Chatty Kathy let her hand move up my leg to a more intimate place. I assumed she thought I was ignoring her. I had been, but I wasn't now.

Experience had taught her well. With a heterosexual male, her attention-getting strategy was rather foolproof. I looked at her and she sighed. "Mr. Chan's," she said. "Every Wednesday he has a poker game for some Excellencies."

"Excellencies?" I asked.

The German laughed. "She means VIPs — rich Khmer fucks. The Khmer call anyone who might be important an excellency. I think that's just in case they really are important. They might get insulted if you don't know who they are."

"Yes," Chatty Kathy said. "It is important not to insult them. They can make big trouble. Bad trouble is bad."

"So, the excellencies play poker for big stakes on Wednesday... and this is Sunday." That gave me time to make something happen. "Do you know where the game is?" I asked.

She frowned, sizing me up. "It's for excellencies."

"Could you get me into it? I want to play."

She scowled as if she thought she might see into me; I saw intelligence in those eyes that I felt sure she'd been masking. "You need plenty money to buy into a high-stakes game like Chan's."

"If I had the money, though... could you do it?"

She made a sour face. "Chan doesn't let unknown people in. You need a sponsor."

Becker, the German, rubbed his chin. "I'd forgotten about that game. Chan keeps it exclusive. Lots of security." He looked toward the door. "Are you any fucking good at the game?"

"Yes," I said, again exercising my famous modesty. "I'm exceptionally good. Why?"

"I won't even charge you for this information, because it is small beer, but tomorrow night there's a small game," Becker said. He nodded at Chatty Kathy. "Wang's is tomorrow, right?"

"Chinese monster Wang," she snorted. "Sure."

"Chinese monster Wang? Curious name. Is he a bad guy?"

She laughed and held her hands up, palms facing each other, about eight inches apart. "Not bad. Big."

"I hear that Wang likes to get _barang_ into his game if they've got the buy-in," the bartender said.

"Barang?"

"Foreigners. He thinks having expat money at the table will pull in a few richer Khmer. Everyone wants to move up."

"But the stakes are low?"

He nodded. "It's an introduction to the local scene. You might meet someone who knows of a bigger game and is willing to make introductions. And, if you win a little money to cover expenses while meeting people, it's all to the good."

He was right, and it sounded promising. Even if I only won enough to meet my immediate needs, I'd be playing poker.

"That sounds like a decent idea." I smiled at Kathy and ordered another round. When my self-appointed date pressed her body against me, I asked her outright. "Can you get me in Wang's poker game tomorrow night?"

She considered it. "Yes. If you have five thousand. Can do."

Getting that much wasn't a serious problem. I could get a cash advance on my credit card. If the cards were good, I could pay it back immediately. "I can get it tomorrow."

She smiled and rubbed my crotch. "Then tonight we go make love."

"We do?"

"I like you. You pay me for a long time. Tomorrow you get money and at night I take you to Wang's. If you win, I get fifty dollars. Extra."

Becker and I laughed. "She's a tough negotiator," the German said. "I should point out that if you keep her for a couple of days, it's only fair that you pay her bar fine for both nights."

I doubted anyone in the history of hiring bar girls had ever done that, but Becker was covering his ass. It wasn't that much money, and if it earned me a friend in Phnom Penh, it was a bargain.

I liked cultivating good contacts and I never knew when I'd be back in Phnom Penh again. "Fair enough. I can handle that."

Chatty Kathy, now happy Chatty Kathy, let her hands get familiar with my terrain.

"You ready to go?" I asked. "We stop for dinner on the way."

"Buy me another drink first," she said.

"You haven't finished that one," I pointed out.

"I'm not thirsty."

"So why buy another drink?"

"Getting you to buy me drinks is the job I do when we are in the bar."

The German was grinning at me as I dug out my wallet. He found the education the girl was providing me amusing. Arguing with Chatty Kathy wasn't smart or profitable.

"She eats like a horse," he warned me.

"Good food too," she said. "No junk."

"She's not the cheapest date," Becker said, sounding like the voice of experience.

"Seems not." I gave myself a moment to savor the irony that I was spending money on a whore, food, and booze when what I wanted was to build my stake. But you have to spend money to make any. It was a calculated gamble.

WANG'S GAME

The next day, after breakfast and a trip to the bank, we sat in rattan chairs on a restaurant patio on the Riverfront while Chatty Kathy made a couple of calls. Khmer is a musical language and made no sense to my ear.

"Okay," she said when she hung up. "Wang says you can play if you got cash and I work."

"Work?"

She wrinkled her nose. "Chinese monster Wang needs a waitress for the game. He doesn't pay good, but gamblers tip okay." She ran her tongue slowly over her lips. "You won't need me until after it is over."

It was a good plan. It would keep her out of my hair while I played. As a bonus, her being the waitress could be useful to me. "Will you be the only waitress?"

"Of course. Chinese monster Wang too cheap to have more than one. And he tends bar himself because he doesn't trust people."

"Then, when I am playing, I'll order whisky."

She grinned. "But you don't want whisky."

"I want a clear head. Bring me ginger ale and bitters. Will Chinese monster Wang keep that a secret?"

She rubbed her fingers together. "Twenty is plenty for him to mind his own business," she said, chuckling. I could see that my asking represented an opportunity and Miss Entrepreneur of the Year didn't hesitate to take advantage of it. Still, I handed her a twenty. That earned me a laugh. "You know everyone does that. Yes?"

She was right.

That night, after dinner, she led me on a meandering walk through the dark back streets and alleys of Phnom Penh. I would never have found the place on my own, but she knew exactly where to go.

When we arrived, we climbed outside stairs to a room above a shop where some people were setting up for the game. She introduced me to Wang, an overweight Chinese man with a greasy smile. "She says you good player," he informed me and pointing at Chatty Kathy.

"An enthusiastic player, at least," I said. "What is the game?"

His fat face wrinkled in a smile. "In Wang's place, we only play five-card draw."

"I'd prefer Texas Hold'em."

"That game is popular in some places around the city," he said. "Not here." His dismissive tone made it clear that I was free to go to any of those inferior places.

"Five-card draw is fine," I said as a slim and lithe Cambodian girl came walking up to us.

"Sophi," Wang told me. "She is the dealer."

I gave her the long, lingering look she deserved. Sophi filled out a Chinese Chong Sam like it had been poured on. This was my idea of classic Asian sexy. But she was all business.

Wang opened a small lockbox and gave it to her. She put it on the table, then got a cup of tea before sitting down and opening the box. It held ten or twenty sealed decks of cards. She examined them and put two decks on the table, then returned the rest in the box. She checked the chips and folded her hands on the table.

When we sat down at the table, there were four other players: a bald Brit in a stained tee-shirt, a well-dressed Cambodian who introduced himself as Chea Pran, and two other young Cambodian men in shirts and slacks.

As we each handed Wang the cash for our buy-in, Sophi slid a neat stack of chips to sit in front of us.

I can't say much about most of the players in the game. None of them was there to socialize really, so there wasn't a lot of chatting, although the Brit and I bantered a little about the upcoming World Cup. Spain had just beaten the Netherlands badly, and naturally, he wanted to rub that in.

Chatty Kathy took our order for overpriced drinks and when she'd served them, we got down to business.

Sophi opened a sealed deck, took out the jokers, and shuffled it seven times, as professionally as I've seen in any casino. Then the Brit cut, she burned a card and dealt the hand.

The opening salvos were muted. I like to lay back a bit in the beginning and get a feel for styles, but none of the four seemed to have much of a method to his playing.

I tossed in a few hands early on, willing to pay to see which of the other players liked to push his luck and who didn't trust the cards.

Once I settled in, I started winning. The two Cambodians in suits were easy to bluff and made it far too easy to tell when they had a decent hand.

From the way he played, I figured the Brit was there because he enjoyed the game. He stuck with a few hands I'm sure I would have folded, but he was smart enough that he only did it when it was a cheap bet. He stretched out his money.

Chea Pran was the only one who appeared to have anything close to deep pockets. Unfortunately for him, he had no card sense. A truly rotten poker player and frequently reckless, he relied on luck to take care of the trivial tasks like filling inside straights.

It was fun to watch him try to maintain a poker face of some sort. When he looked at his hand and a thin smile flickered over his lips, I figured it was time for some fun.

Earlier, he'd been dealt two pair at this point and he'd smiled then too, but this was a different smile, a new tell. I was guessing he had three of a kind.

That would have been a problem, but I had three aces.

When Chea Pran made a healthy bet, I was certain he had three, and that they were probably face cards.

After a furious bit of swearing directed at his cards, the Brit dropped out. He'd gotten stuck with a hand that had what we call "potential." Maybe a possible straight. He didn't have the guts or money to find out if his cards could live up to their potential, which was probably smart.

One of the other Khmer players dropped out too, but the other grimaced and stayed in.

Chea Pran threw in two cards, and when the dealer sent him two new ones, he picked them up and a beautiful smile lit up Chea Pran's face — a look of delight let us know that his dreams had been answered.

Compared to the first smile when we were dealt the cards, this was the sun going supernova. In short, he was acting.

I took one card, to keep everyone guessing. The other Khmer took three.

Chea Pran bid a hundred dollars.

I raised him another hundred.

The other Khmer clearly hadn't gotten his wishes fulfilled and threw in his hand. Leaving just the two of us.

Chea Pran studied my face, studied his cards, studied the pot in the middle of the table, and then ordered a drink. I smiled. He was sweating. While he waited for his drink, which was gin and tonic, he studied the same three things again, in the same order — my face, his cards, the great stack of chips in the pot.

After taking a sip of the drink that Chatty Kathy handed him, he raised me another hundred.

"So much study deserves a reward," I said, and I called.

My three aces beat his three queens.

I raked in the pot and Chea Pran sighed. "That's it, for me," he said.

The Brit was pushing his chair back too. "I'm done," he said.

The two other Khmer players blinked but said nothing. Wang cashed us in, and the Brit and the suited Cambodians slipped away. "I need a drink," I said.

"I'll buy," Chea Pran said.

Chatty Kathy poured me a whisky.

I looked around. "Everyone is going home," I said.

Chea Pran nodded. "Wang is in no rush to close."

Chinese monster Wang unsmilingly nodded. I'd call his look inscrutable but pleased. Chatty Kathy was cleaning things off the table and Sophi was putting the unopened decks back in the lockbox.

I graciously sipped the drink.

"You are skilled at poker," Chea Pran said.

"I always like hearing that," I said. "Too bad the take-home pay wasn't better."

He scrunched his face up. "The others didn't bring much money for you to win... or they decided to take it home with them. They could tell you were too good for them."

"I was lucky tonight." I was being careful, not humble. Somehow, the idea that you are skillful at poker all too easily gets misconstrued into the idea that you are cheating. Being good suggests an unfair advantage. I suspect that is because no one wants to think that they could play better if they took the time to learn.

He waved a hand. "There are better games in town if you want to win serious money," he said. "I'm not good enough to risk them, myself." He laughed uneasily. "You showed me that much this evening."

"As much as I like the idea, cash is a bit short at the moment." I held up the few hundred I'd won. "Even if I had a connection and could get invited to a game like that, I don't think this will be nearly enough to get me in."

"No," he said. "But the point being, you would like to play in a game where the players are better and the stakes higher?"

"Especially if they were playing Texas Hold-em."

Chea Pran stood and handed Wang some dollars. "Can we meet for breakfast?" he asked me. "I need to do some checking, but I might have a proposition for you."

"I have one for you tonight," Chatty Kathy said.

"A late breakfast would be good. More of a brunch."

"Where are you staying?" I told him. "I will send a car for you. Would ten be all right?"

"Perfect."

Then as Kathy led me back through the winding corridors of the back streets, I found myself wondering what this rich man wanted from a poker player.

"He is an excellency," she told me. "Or wants to be one."

"What could he want?"

"Something that will make him richer or more powerful," she said, her voice flat. "He will gain something from whatever it is."

"Am I making a mistake by talking to him?"

She laughed. "How can you get ahead except by letting the powerful people use you? Just make sure you are well paid for doing his bidding. What else matters?"

Her worldview was amazingly consistent and free of any irony. When you were born into the bottom of the heap, you did what it took to climb higher. If that helped someone else's agenda, what difference did that make? She was helping me out because it suited her. It was good for business. That meant she had no more guilt about being a whore than I did when I took some chump's money from him.

You didn't survive life by worrying too much about the other person. Kathy and I shared that view. You didn't cheat people, you didn't take what wasn't yours, but you couldn't worry about the consequences of other people's decisions.

Maybe Mother Theresa did, but then I read that the woman had an incredible ego herself. Kathy and I did too, but I was sure that's where the similarities ended.

"We stop and get food, then a bottle of whisky to take to your room," she said.

Kathy was either a great actress or she loved her work. At the end of the day, it was likely a mixture of the two. No one said you had to be totally consistent or all one or the other. And the balance of that mix didn't matter much when we got to my bed.

AN OFFER TO REFUSE

A dark SUV picked us up in front of my guesthouse the next morning, right on time. The burly, overdressed Khmer man with dark glasses got out and stared for a moment before walking over to where Chatty Kathy sitting at the outside table with me. "I'm here to pick you up," he said.

I didn't feel like playing nice. "Picking us up."

He went rigid. "My instructions are to bring you — just you," he said.

"Then you were told incorrectly," I said. "She hasn't had breakfast yet either."

"Just you," he said stubbornly.

I gave him my most cheerful smile. "Sorry. I understood the invitation to include my chief of staff. If that's not correct, then you'll have to tell your boss there was a misunderstanding because the current arrangements are not at all satisfactory. Another time, perhaps. I'm taking this lady to breakfast."

He stiffened, then glanced around, giving himself time to consider his options. Chea Pran didn't seem to be the sort that would want his minions improvising.

I had a hunch that when it came to alternative courses of action, smacking me in the head and tossing my inert form into the car ranked high on his personal list of favorites. The trouble was, he probably had no idea how important I might be to his boss. "Very well," he said, finally.

The restaurant wasn't far, just a few blocks that we could have walked easily nut Chea Pran's thug seemed content to drive.

He let us out in front. "Second floor," he said. We went in and found Chea Pran waiting at a table on the second-floor balcony, overlooking the sluggish brown flow of the Tonle

Sap. He scowled at the sight of Chatty Kathy. "Why is she here?"

"She is my chief of staff, my adviser on local-knowledge things. I don't go anywhere without her."

"And I'm hungry," she said.

Chea Pran made a face and cocked his head at a waiter. We weren't asked what we wanted, but as we sat down at the table the waiter set a place for her and then brought out plenty of food.

Watching Chea Pran's mobile face, my uneasiness about him came back. I wished I hadn't come. Something underneath the surface told me not to trust him. In the daylight, he seemed more self-assured, more confident of his position.

"I have a job for you," he said over coffee.

"I'm not looking for work," I said.

"You were working last night," he said.

"I was playing cards."

He smiled. "But you are a professional player. I want to hire you to play cards."

That surprised me. "That's a new wrinkle."

"Perhaps."

"How does that even work?"

"I provide the stake and the leverage to get you into a high-stakes game. The one I have in mind is tomorrow night."

The idea of playing with someone else's money sounded nice, but it is one of those things that only holds up in fantasies. In the real world, it is just asking for complications.

"If you can afford it, why not play the game yourself?" I was trying to figure out his angle. I certainly couldn't work as a ringer, playing in his stead. Glancing at Chatty Kathy didn't help. She was staring at the waiter and pretending not to soak up every word as she ate her breakfast.

"You are laughing at me."

"No. I'm trying to figure this out."

He waved a hand. "That's all right. It must sound odd. The truth is that I was invited to play. While I like the game, as you well know, I'm not good enough to play with high stakes. I don't mind losing, but I could easily lose too much."

"But you want me to play?"

He nodded. "For me."

"Why?"

"Because of a man who will definitely be in the game."

Something clicked. "You want me to play against someone you don't like?"

He nodded and his eyes rolled up and to the right. I study faces and could tell that the image of a man's face had filled his head.

"A man named Alex. This man thinks that he is a great poker player, but he is just a cheat. Recently, he cheated me and embarrassed me in front of important people. Now, I want him to lose face. I want you to show the other players his foolishness."

The logic of that stunk. "Is it that such big a deal? How will my beating him help you regain face?" I knew a bit about the Asian idea of face, but there were many nuances.

The man's face turned dark and he forced Alex's face out of his head long enough to glare at me. "To me, beating him, having it done, means everything. I owe this Alex payback."

"I see." I nodded, stalling. "But what, exactly, would you expect from an arrangement where I play him with your money? I mean, even if all goes well, you can't be there watching and witness his defeat."

"But the word will go out. The rumors will spread. And besides the satisfaction of arranging it... I will share in his money." He nodded, agreeing with himself. "I provide the buy-in and when you return my investment, you keep half the money you win."

That was the first part of this entire deal that had any appeal at all. "What's the game?"

"Texas Hold'em."

That was good. I held up a finger. "One, important question: What happens if I lose your money?"

"Don't think negatively, Aaron," he said. "You are a professional. You won't lose."

"That doesn't mean —"

"You will win. I have every confidence that you will win."

"So, you will simply hand me the money to play? You trust me?"

The man sat back. "Trust isn't necessary."

I laughed. "Since when?"

He sat back and took out his phone. Before I could react, he snapped my picture. "Before I hand over the money, I will add a photo of your passport to my little album."

"Making a Facebook post, are we?"

He smiled. "For my friends in immigration... people who owe me favors. They'll post it at every checkpoint. It's a small country and there aren't many border crossings or ways out. If you were to steal my money and run, you'd never manage to leave."

"Trust is overrated... especially when you've got tech," I said sourly.

Kathy put a hand on my knee and squeezed it. Probably reminding me not to sass an excellency. Every moment I spent with this man, the less I liked the idea of working this game. Not only didn't I like his strong-arm tactics, but I also had the feeling that he wasn't telling me everything.

"Do we have a deal?"

"Some of this doesn't sound right," I said. "I play a fair game."

He shrugged. "If you can win that way, it's fine with me."

"And what if I can't? This is a challenge you've presented me with. The cards don't always cooperate. Winning honestly could become a problem."

His smile made me shudder. "I doubt it would be as serious or difficult a problem as your imminent deportation."

I stiffened at the threat. "What deportation?"

His attempt to look casual was almost funny — a caricature of feigned indifference.

"If you don't agree to my little scheme, this afternoon immigration will take you into custody based on an anonymous tip. You will be jailed for a time and then deported for violating the terms of your visa. Although I haven't checked, I'm sure you arrived on a tourist visa, and yet you worked last night, playing poker."

"No one gets deported for that."

He smiled. "Unless someone with connections wishes it."

I glanced at Kathy. The look in her eyes told me she was damn sure he wasn't bluffing. I had to bow to her experience. Being jailed in SE Asia was never a good thing. I knew people who'd had the misfortune to experience the hospitality it afforded. "Deported to where?"

His hand waved again, floating across my blurred field vision. "To wherever you arrived from. It will be easy enough for my contacts in immigration to determine that from your files. Then I will ask my people in Malaysia to make inquiries about your activities there. They know other gamblers in Penang and perhaps they can contact some of your friends in the city so they can meet you."

The man was either a cynic who thought the worst of everyone or he had read between the lines and assessed my situation with uncanny accuracy. Either way, the prospect was chilling.

I didn't know what the situation was back in Penang. I'd hoped that if I stayed away long enough things would cool down. But this soon, any inquiries, any suggestion I was on my way back, might stir things up again. A grumpy loser willing to send muscle after me might have a long memory.

In short, being sent back to Penang didn't seem like it would ensure a healthy future for me. Worse it would cost me money for yet more plane tickets. I was losing options. In return for doing his bidding, the man offered me a chance to win the money I needed and avoid deportation.

The situation was exactly what Chatty Kathy anticipated. Excellencies use people, she had said. She thought the challenge lay in figuring out what you could gain from the situation. And there was potential profit in this for me. Besides, I had every reason to believe that if I defied him, he would do exactly what he said.

"I've never tried to target a single player, Prea Chan. Never even considered how it would be done."

That was true. I had trouble imagining how a person would go about that. Trying to win money in a game isn't the same thing as focusing on taking the money from one person. The very existence of other players complicated any strategy I could think of, of course, I wasn't thinking all that clearly.

Che Pran let an impatient hand brush away invisible insects. "No matter. You are skilled and clever. I am certain you can do it. You must do it. I'll give you the money and arrange for your name to be on the guest list."

"But isolating and beating one player—"

"How you manage the task is up to you. But you must clean him out slowly. Don't just take his money but humiliate him. I want you to show the other players how bad a player he is."

"You want him to suffer."

"A few hours into the game they usually take a break. I want you to call me and tell me how it is going. If you can manage without him noticing, send me a picture of him at the game. It will make a nice memento."

I could tell that 'if you can manage' wasn't as optional as it sounded. "That might be tricky. People don't like you to take pictures in those games."

He disregarded my objection. Another invisible insect. "Once we settle up, I'll release the flag on your passport. Then you will be able to leave whenever you want. If you are concerned about Alex, if you fear any repercussions he might decide to rain down on you, then I will take you straight to the airport."

The idea of this Alex character wanting revenge had occurred to me. I doubted going to the airport would help. That the idea seemed to amuse Chea Pran wasn't reassuring.

Regardless, the reality was that Chea Pran didn't need me to agree to his plan. He held all the aces. I agreed. I didn't see a way out. "So where and when do we meet to settle up accounts?"

"When the game ends, go down to the karaoke club. It should still be open. Give me a call and I'll have my man pick you up."

That didn't sound promising either. His man wasn't a friendly type and I couldn't count on Chea Pran and his muscle living up to their end of the bargain. Trust was, in fact, in rather short supply.

As I digested it, he sat back in his chair, watching me, evaluating. "I'll text karaoke," I told him.

"You won't be there long. Do I have your word? Are we doing this?"

More than anything I wanted to tell the man to kiss my ass. I didn't like him or his plan. There were too many ways for things to go wrong for me and not enough upside.

On the other hand, he waved a substantial stick. Being thrown in jail would only be unpleasant. I could manage that.

But being deported... in the best case, it could affect my ability to get to Singapore. The officials in Singapore didn't look kindly on anyone who had been in trouble.

Worse, if Chea Pran followed through on his threat to put out the word I was being sent back to Penang... that might mean I didn't live long enough to worry about Singapore at all.

I took a long breath. Playing, committing to winning, was also a calculated risk, but I didn't seem to have a choice. "I suppose we do."

Grinning, he reached inside his coat pocket and brought out an envelope, and put it on the table. "Then I need your passport." When I slid it across the table, he took a photo of the front pages with his cell phone.

"Now we are set," he said. He handed me a card with an address written in Khmer. "Here is the address of the game. It starts at nine. Have your..." He grinned broadly, "your chief of staff... that's what you called her, correct?"

"That's the job title."

"Well, have her take you there."

Kathy took the paper. "Here?" The man nodded, and she said something to him in Khmer. He laughed.

"Your whore thinks a fancy game should be held in a nicer place. She's right, of course, but Chan's game isn't authorized by the State, so he takes precautions."

I nodded, feeling numb and helpless. This was not the right way to get into a game. Not even close. I had no idea how to get around the trap he had set out. For the time being, he was in charge. He'd made an offer I knew I should refuse, but couldn't.

When we both stood, he smiled, actually looking happy. "I'm looking forward to this." And then he shook my hand and left.

Kathy and I watched him emerge downstairs. The dark SUV pulled up, and he got in. "He's an excellency," she said sympathetically. "Excellencies get what they want."

That had the ring of a defeatist mantra in the mouths of most people. Kathy just sounded resigned to it.

"He's a thin-skinned, well-connected asshole." Even as I said the words, I realized that somehow the man's very existence, his success, firmly confirmed Chatty Kathy's theories on life.

The idea saddened me and yet spurred me to the only action I could think of — I sat back down, signaled to the waiter, and ordered a whisky. It wasn't even noon, but he didn't even blink. "Chea Pran said to put it on his tab," I said.

That earned me a nod. He was a flunky. He didn't care.

Kathy poured herself more coffee from the pot. She stayed silent, sensing that I needed time to let the reality of the situation sink in, that I would have to accept the way things were.

"I don't know what to do," I told her when I finished my drink.

"Do what he said. You have to go to the game," she'd said. She let her hand creep into my lap. "And now you have to go to your room so we can make boom boom."

It was the best offer I'd gotten all day, so when my hands stopped shaking, we hailed a tuk tuk and I went to make boom boom with my favorite whore so that the day wasn't a total nightmare.

CHAN'S GAME

The next night, after a day spent enjoying my investment in Chatty Kathy's retirement fund and then enjoying a dinner fit for a king, I once again found myself letting Chatty Kathy lead me through the winding back streets of Phnom Penh.

She babbled at me as we walked, staying close to me as we passed the girlie bars where other women offered me encouraging reasons that I should dump her and enter their establishment to buy them a drink.

"You told Chea Pran you didn't like the place we are going," I said. She nodded. "What's wrong with it?"

"Chan has plenty money and the players are rich and his club is a dump," she said flatly, making me laugh.

"You are quite a snob for a bar girl."

When I saw her wounded look, I regretted my words immediately. "You think I'll always do this?" she asked. "I won't always be a bar girl."

"I'm sure you won't," I said. I meant it too. "What do you want to do?"

She let out a breath. "What I will do is make money and be rich."

"How?"

"A girl must be open to various possibilities and taking steps."

"Makes sense, but what kinds of steps?"

She ticked them off on her fingers, bending them backward, nearly to her wrist, the way Khmer girls seem to be able to do.

"A generous excellency might want a new mistress, or I might work as a madam or bar owner or run a front business for one of the many mafias or tongs. There are many ways to make good money and live well."

She knew her world and her options well. I admired that rather than spending her life resenting being born into a dung heap, she simply and matter-of-factly looked for a path that would take her to the top of that heap.

Walking through the noisy chaos, most of it playful teasing arising from an incurable optimism, there were darker sections where a sudden quiet would feel ominous. But Kathy knew the streets well and had a better-honed sense of danger for this situation than I.

I made myself relax. When I did, I found myself relishing the charm of walking through the warm night air, smelling the odors of a strange place. This, I reminded myself, was the essence of foreignness.

One of the fascinating aspects of foreign places, at least for me, is the smells. In a new place, the strange odors, from the smells of street food cooking to the rotting garbage, tend to be obvious at first. They can be delightful or disgusting, but they are new, and they sharpen the sense of being out of place.

I know that feeling unsettles some people, but it comforts travelers like me. A place that smells different promises new experiences, new things to learn and discover.

Unfortunately, those smells become the norm all too quickly, and it is as if you suddenly stop smelling them. Your awareness closes down just a little, and that sense of foreignness begins to ebb. Ask any traveler.

It is such a small thing, the smell of the streets, yet it drives me. I could play poker in almost any country in the world; I could pick a place I like and live well. But once I realized how smells worked, what they did for me, I also understood that regaining that sense of strangeness (being the stranger in a new place) was one of the many things that had kept me moving from place to place, never wanting a home. Or perhaps home was the road. I've heard that said. What it means must vary with the person.

Although the streets Kathy led me through were similar to the ones we'd traveled to Wang's club, when we arrived, climbing stairs that led above a karaoke club, we entered a much nicer place. That boded well for a high-stakes game.

It was cleaner, had a nice table, a well-stocked bar, and most everything you want for a serious game and nothing that might prove a distraction. Distractions are the last thing you want to deal with when you play poker. If you can't focus, it's hard to play your best.

Like Wang, Chan, the man who ran the game was Chinese. Thinner, better dressed, and with good manners, he was an upmarket version of Wang.

When I told him Chea Pran had arranged for me to play, he nodded and held out his hand. I handed him the envelope with the money, and he smiled.

"This is Ann, your dealer," he said introducing me to yet another lovely Khmer woman. Like most Cambodian women, she had the youthful look of a teenager — it seems impossible to guess their ages until they are ancient, and even then, all you can say is they are old. The way Ann handled the cards, and herself for that matter, was experienced. She projected a bearing that was calculated to instill confidence in the players.

At my instruction, Chatty Kathy chatted up the bartender, slipping her some money and explaining my drink order and then bringing us each a drink.

While Chan and Ann arranged things, we watched the other players arrive. Alex turned out to be a big man with an Eastern European accent. He dressed casually, introduced himself with a smile. The man was totally different from what I'd expected. I guess I'd expected a Cambodian who used a

Western name, an executive type. Alex had a blue-collar vibe. Not that it mattered.

Soon we sat down to play. As usual, I started off easy, trying to get a feel for the styles and characteristics of the other players' games. I was particularly interested in Alex, of course, but determined not to be obvious about my singular focus.

Initially, Alex struck me as a taciturn guy but watching him interact with people I realized that I had it wrong. He chatted with the dealer and the other players jovially enough. Flashes of humor danced across his hard face.

I sensed that Alex had the rare ability to take things as they came. His face simply reflected that equanimity clearly.

Once the game started, that impression proved even more correct. He played well, trusting his instincts and reason. I hoped his calmness might cover a tendency for bluffing. To test that theory, even when I had garbage hands and I had a hunch he was trying to buy the pot, and the pot was small, I called him even.

That turned out to be a waste of money. That placid face could have been watching paint dry. The only tic I saw was after the hand was over. His surprise at my weak hand barely caused the right side of his face to tighten in a half-smile.

That didn't help me find a tell that would let me know when he was bluffing.

When I took a break, one of the other players did too. He'd been silent at the table, so it surprised me when he introduced himself. "Brigadier General Bona," he said as I came out of the bathroom.

He was standing at the bar, holding out a hand. As I shook it, I took a good look at him, sizing him up. He was a tall, thin Khmer man, with dark eyes. "Brigadier General?"

He chuckled. "Most people take me for an accountant."

"No offense meant, Brigadier," I said. Clearly, he was an excellency.

"None taken. I wanted to meet you. I wished to speak to you."

"Why?"

"Because you seem intent on playing head-to-head with our Alex," he said. The idea seemed to amuse him. "I'm curious as to why that is."

Clearly, this was a close-knit group, and this general was an observant man. The 'our Alex' was the only disturbing, slightly ominous wrinkle.

Although I didn't like hearing that he'd spotted my focus so early on, he was clearly well trained. That made it inevitable and at least we were talking. The conversation had dangerous overtones, but it was friendly. "Is that a bad thing, beating Alex?"

He closed one eye and opened it again. It looked like a slow-motion wink. "Just difficult. I mean it is difficult to win, of course."

"He seems to be a good player."

The general cocked his head. "Good, yes. Most people aren't willing to discover if he can be beaten. Not seriously."

This man was able to make everything sound sinister. "Why?"

"Often people are intimidated by his... line of work."

"I can't be, because I don't know what it is," I said.

He nodded. "I suspected as much. You see, Alex is the local head of the Russian mafia."

"Fuck!" I said. The extent of what Chea Pran had omitted was starting to become clear. I wondered how much else there was to know.

"Exactly," the general said. "Once upon a time the big danger in Kampuchea was the Khmer Rouge. Today it is corrupt officials, through the police, and the mafias."

"I have no interest in trouble with either."

He flashed a thin smile. "If you intend to stay, and intend to engage in illegal gambling, I wish you good luck."

He returned to the table. I hesitated. The twin dangers he'd mentioned were exactly my current problem. Which was the rock and which the hard place, didn't matter, although, in my limited encounters with both, I'd always preferred mafia to corrupt officials. The mafia tended to keep their word.

More importantly, unless Alex decided I was cheating, I was probably safe. It wasn't my first time being in a card game with members of organized crime. My problem would be when he realized that I was less interested in winning in general than beating him. If he noticed and that bothered him, things could get dicey.

And clearly, I hadn't been as suave as I'd thought. The general certainly managed to notice. Alex hadn't given any sign that he did, but he had a damn good poker face.

I took a breath. I couldn't very well just leave. I'd lost some of Chea Pran's money and he'd have me deported. I needed to be very subtle and beat an excellent player without him being aware I was singling him out. I also had to hope the Brigadier didn't mention it.

No sweat.

I got a drink, a real whiskey, a double, and went back to the table for the next hand. When I looked around the table, Alex gave me a cheerful smile. The bastard knew something or thought he did.

It would be a long night at the table. I would play my best... I always did, but I had no idea if I could win the way Chea Pran demanded without cheating. The only thing I was sure of was that I wouldn't cheat. My mother always told me that my honest streak would be my downfall. Chatty Kathy seemed to have the same impression. Whatever, those were the cards I'd been dealt. I'd play them as well as I could.

A FINAL GAMBLE

The game evolved nicely over the evening. A few of the less-experienced players took turns having streaks of winning and losing hands. The few of us who knew the game well taking it in stride, the amateurs getting impatient or overly excited at the rise and fall of their fortunes.

If it hadn't been for my situation, the game would have been incredibly enjoyable. This was my element, my passion. The players were good and the money right.

It seemed that way for Alex as well. He played with a calm good humor that masked a steely disposition, a certain ruthlessness. I admired his ability to chuckle through wins and losses with nothing but a flicker in his eyes giving away his true feelings. He knew his eyes gave him away, and when he felt other emotions, he'd glance down at his cards or pretend to be counting the pot or doing something else to keep us from seeing his eyes.

It was subtle and I doubt most people caught it, but most people don't make their living in the game. As a result, his hiding his eyes served as a wonderful tell in itself. If he raised and looked away, it was a sign to call.

Spotting that tell cheered me, which was a good thing, because the cards I was getting weren't good at all. I'm good, but no amount of skill or practice can turn a pair into three of a kind, no matter how badly you want it. It took all my focus and best effort to stay in the game.

Watching Alex rake in a pot, it dawned on me that when I asked Chea Pran what happened if I lost, he hadn't answered. I had a hunch I knew, and I didn't like my guess.

After a few hours, everyone agreed to a short break. I took advantage of the time to consider the situation.

My clever analysis was that I was in deep shit. I'd lost half of Chea Pran's money. Nights go like that and normally, I'd just write it off to the slings and arrows of outrageous fortune, but I was on a mission.

I'd been right to think playing with an agenda beyond just winning as much as possible was a bad idea. Unless the universe decided to tip slightly to one side, the side that favored me, it didn't seem likely I'd win that money back, much less clean Alex out.

The problem wasn't just that he was a good player, but that there were other decent players in the game too. When Alex had crap cards, inevitably, the way the cards were running, it seemed another of them took over. I was the one out of sync with the game.

I've learned that when things don't feel right, when your gut tells you that you are in the wrong place or time, the best thing to do is quit. Sure, sometimes you can push ahead, keep your eyes open and maybe you can figure out where you put a foot wrong. There might be a path you didn't see, a door you didn't open, couldn't have known about.

Poker can be like that. Most things are like that. But with poker, no matter how much or well you plan, ultimately, the cards decide things, have the last say. In an honest game, no one controls the cards and their power can feel absolute, especially when it's being used against you.

This was one of those times. The pressure of the mission and the bad cards were getting to me and I had started making stupid mistakes.

I was glad for the break.

I went to the bar and got another whisky. As I sipped it, I saw Alex looking at me. He was assessing me, trying to figure me out. I decided to confront his curiosity. I asked the bartender to give me a drink for Alex.

"His usual," I said, then I took it over to him and held it out. I saw his quizzical look. "You are very good at Texas Hold-em," I said.

He took the drink. "You know your way around the table yourself. I expect that with a bit more luck, better cards, you might be formidable."

He scowled. "If I were getting cards like yours, I'd be tempted to call it a night and try again some other time. That you are sticking it out has me wondering why."

He was right. Cutting your losses was the way to go. "I'm afraid this is my one shot at giving you a run for your money."

His eyebrows peaked. "That's a shame. Are you sure you can't come next week? I'd see that Chan invited you back."

"I appreciate that, but I'm leaving the country. I have a visa for Laos where I'm meeting friends."

"So, go meet them. You could come back here afterward. Give me a call and I'll arrange things with Chan and perhaps the cards will be more favorable."

"I'm not sure that's possible, " I said. "If I leave, I'm not sure I'll be able to return."

He raised an eyebrow — just one this time. The other was unmoving. "No? Why is this?"

The question was honest and sounded sincere. Seeing things falling apart, being forced into this situation, I decided to lay it out for him. "When I tell you, you might not want me to come back either."

He smiled. "Now I am really interested in your story. You must tell me."

I shrugged. "It has to do with a gentleman named Chea Tran."

The name earned me a scowl. "He is not a gentleman. He is a cheap crook." Alex put the emphasis on the word 'cheap.'

"He got me my invitation to this game."

A finger touched his nose. "I see."

"He also fronted me the money for the buy-in."

That elicited a flicker of a smile. "The money you are losing is his?"

"Yes."

"I must say that I like that part of your story, but why would he give you money to gamble with?"

"Apparently, you wronged him somehow and I'm supposed to avenge the dishonor."

"Why you? Are you a friend of his?"

I shook my head. "I barely know the man. We met at another game. After I beat him, he contacted me and decided that life would be perfect if I came to this game and took your money."

"Ah." My story made more sense to Alex than to me. "He hoped to regain face. He must think highly of your abilities."

"When we played the other night, he jumped to conclusions about my skill and how much that might matter in terms of ensuring I could win."

"I've noticed that part of his downfall is that he doesn't seem to understand that the cards have a lot to say about winning and losing." Alex sipped his drink, then stared into my eyes. "But you know this. Why did you agree to this foolish and possibly dangerous plan?"

I coughed. "I was forced to leave Penang. Chea Pran knew that or he guessed I didn't want to return. At any rate, he threatened to have me jailed and then deported back there."

Alex nodded. "I believe you. That's his style. But you aren't doing well. In that case, I'm sure he expected you to cheat, and apparently, you haven't done that."

"No. I told him that if I could do it playing fairly, I would break you. I don't cheat. He did, however, make it clear that the terms of our agreement obligated me to win, regardless of what it took."

It was Alex's turn to laugh. "His grievance with me is that I caught him cheating. He was rather obvious. Chan banned him from the game."

"So that is his loss of face."

"That, plus recently I arranged citizenship for some business people of my acquaintance without paying him tea money. He fancies himself as well connected."

"Tea money?"

"A bribe. *Tek tay*, in Khmer." He gave me a hard look. "You've screwed yourself by telling me, you know."

"I was screwed no matter what."

"And I'm sure he flagged your profile in the immigration database. He's a crazy bastard, but he can be thorough. If you tried to leave with his money you'd be arrested."

"That is pretty much what he said. He wanted to save me from the trouble and embarrassment such a misunderstanding might entail."

Alex nodded thoughtfully. "If I were you..." he pursed his lips. "... I'd be thinking of getting on a flight out of the country the first thing in the morning. You might wish to go home now and pack."

I laughed. "And be arrested at the airport before breakfast? Or grabbed from my room tonight? Either way, he'd have me beaten and I'd spend time in jail before being deported and then possibly killed?"

"Not a good option."

"I still have some of his money. You haven't won it all yet. I don't suppose asking you to give it back to him would please him."

Alex waved a hand. "You should keep it. You deserve payment for what he has put you through. Besides, I would imagine that he would consider getting part of it back, and his mission not completed, the same as stealing all of it."

"True enough. Unpleasant, but true."

He cocked his head. "You mentioned going to Laos... I hear it is nice this time of the week."

I sighed. "The two problems with that plan are that I'll never get through immigration and my visa isn't valid for Laos for a few days yet."

Alex nodded. He pulled a business card and a pen from his shirt pocket. He put the card face down on the table and wrote on the back of it, scribbling rapidly in Khmer. He paused to read his work, then signed it with a flourish.

I didn't read Khmer, so when he handed me the card, I looked at the other side. "Kremlin Imports," it said. "Alex Rubbovich, General Manager for SE Asia."

I held up the card and gave him a puzzled look. "And this does what?"

"It solves your first problem. Think of it as an unofficial, but amazingly effective onetime exit visa," he said, his mouth twisting in a self-satisfied grin.

I nodded. "Sweet."

"It's only valid for early tomorrow morning." He nodded toward the table. "There isn't much point in staying to finish this game, so I suggest you go home and pack."

"I can do that, but Prea Chan expects my call at break and to meet after the game. And he knows where I'm staying."

"You are supposed to call him?"

"Yes. He said the group usually takes a longish break late. He wanted me to call and give him a report," I said.

Alex's eyes widened. "Chan!" Then he shouted out some Khmer. Chan and the dealer began clearing the table. The Brigadier nodded and began herding the other players down the stairs.

"What's going on?"

Alex touched my arm. "This is a setup. Chea Pran is arranging a raid. Gambling is illegal, except in casinos and then only for foreigners. That isn't a big deal normally, but some of his friends would be happy to make it sound like no one ever gambled in Phnom Penh before this."

"Shit! What do we do?"

Alex rummaged in his pocket for another card. Fancy Guesthouse, it said. "It isn't far, just over by the Silver Palace. You need to move there right now. Pay in cash and use my name. When you get to your room, book the first morning flight to Bangkok. Stay there until you can go to Laos."

"What about all of you?"

He waved at the empty table. "We are just friends having a night out. While you leave, we will go downstairs for some entertaining karaoke. After you check-in at Fancy, call him and tell him that it's going well and I'm down ten thousand. That should trigger the raid. It will be amusing to watch."

Chan came over and handed me money. "For your chips," he said.

I nodded and waved the first business card Alex had handed me. "How do I use this?"

"Get to the airport early, well before the flight. When you get to the departure area, keep to your right. Go only through the immigration booth on the far-right side... as you face the booths. Only that one. Wait for it if you have to. When you hand the official your passport, make sure the business card is tucked inside next to your visa. I recommend you add a twenty-dollar bill as well."

Bribery was escalating things a bit more than I liked, and this required that I believe Alex wasn't setting me up for something. I found I trusted him a lot more than Chea Pran. "And that's it?"

"That's it. The grubby little man who works there will be delighted to stamp you through regardless of any flags our friend has hoisted. That card will be of more value to him than turning you over to immigration officials and the money will help soothe his conscious, if he has one."

I stared at his face, but I couldn't read it. Was he bluffing? Suddenly, I decided to take everything he said at face value. It was a gut play and there was no logic to it, but his confidence, and everything I'd seen and heard about the influence of the Russian mafia in Cambodia, throughout Asia, made me think he knew what he was talking about. This was golden. "Why are you doing this?"

Chatty Kathy came over and stood beside me, smiling at Alex. In the chaos, her survival sense had kicked into overdrive. She'd helped Ann and Chan clear away any sign of gambling. Now I was sure that she had worked out that I'd be leaving. She was ready to move on and she liked the look of Alex. The woman could smell a serious player a block away.

Alex smiled back at her. "I'm helping both of us. You see, I've decided I like you and admire your directness. Also, I would like to play poker with you again under different circumstances."

"Different circumstances?"

"If I left you to the mercy of Chea Pran, I'm afraid that might not be possible. Besides, your story has prompted me to deal with that insect once and for all. This foolish attempt to entrap me is so typical of the man and his futile power plays... he has been a nuisance for some time. I don't pay him much attention normally, but this I can't ignore. He dares poke the bear." His face lit up, picturing that. "He needs to learn that doing so will get his hand bitten off."

I could imagine Chea Pran if Alex came for him. He'd tremble in fear, his confident facade couldn't hold up against that stare. "You are going to take him down."

"After you are gone."

I was starting to like Alex. "Odd, but now that you mention it, I feel a sudden urge to travel. I'll call our friend later this evening and let him know his arrangements are working out splendidly. You are furious at how badly your evening is going and determined to win your money back. We could be here until morning."

"Excellent."

Alex ordered another drink and turned his attention to Chatty Kathy. When he held out a hand, she moved to him in a flowing, lithe, cat-like drift from my side to his. I recognized it as a definitive statement of a shifted alliance. I winked at her.

"Of course. Leaving this lovely, sassy *shlyukha*, this whore, with me will let you carry out our plan." He gave me a sly grin. "I'll see that she is taken care of properly. Your flight should be early."

"I should get some sleep. Chatty Kathy isn't big on sleeping at night."

"In the morning we sleep," she said.

I left the building and wound my way through the narrow streets until a tuk tuk driver, desperate for a last fare called out to me. He said he knew the guest house I was staying in.

Naturally, he asked for double the fare. I agreed to it. Overpaying was better than getting lost in the winding streets. I gave him the card for Fancy and told him I'd need him to take me there in a few minutes. He scowled, but I knew I was making his night.

On the way to my room, I thought of Kathy. She was landing on her feet and I was glad. I liked her. A lot of whores were just about getting you off for money, but Kathy moved into your life. She'd never be happy as a man's wife, as she preferred being a short-term rental, but she had a good sense of fun. She made me feel that she might actually like me.

The tuk tuk pulled up outside the guesthouse. Three whores were standing around out front. None of them were smiling. This late, they didn't have much chance of finding business. Under other circumstances, it might have been interesting to see if they'd go for a two-for-the price of one deal. But I did need to sleep.

If Alex were telling the truth and I made it through the airport, tomorrow I'd be in Bangkok. Whatever awaited me there, I'd be out of Chea Pran's trap.

FLIGHT PLAN

In action movies, an escape is usually dramatic. The bad guys are in pursuit and the hero makes a dash for freedom. He runs through the traffic of busy streets; he jumps turnstiles and topples vendors' carts to slow his pursuers.

A real escape through an international airport is different. You can't run. You can't even rush things. Jumping or toppling things is right out. In fact, the last thing you want to do is attract any attention at all.

As in the movie, there are heavies with guns everywhere, but some belong. You can't know whose muscle they are until it's too late.

As a result, the tension is internal, not cinematic at all. Your stomach churns with dread while you stand, as if you had nothing better to do, holding your place in packed lines, waiting for permission from armed goons to move forward.

It's a time of torment as well as patience. You are poked and prodded at their whim; you offer yourself to them — as docile as any of the other sheep. You feign indifference as they scrutinize you and your documents, and all the time you are waiting for the moment when it all goes sidewise, the instant they yank you from the herd.

And that's an ordinary departure. Nothing was ordinary this morning. This morning a hasty breakfast lay heavy in my stomach as I went through those motions, walked the multiple gauntlets of human and technological analysis.

Passing through the intense scrutiny, the glares of authorities who might be in the pocket of Prea Chan and all the time trusting my fate to Alex, of the Russian mafia, hoping his good will would protect me... the irony was not lost on me. But it wasn't funny either.

At every moment I expected to be grabbed by the collar and yanked out of line.

"It's you!" some muscled, well-armed thug in uniform would exclaim. Then the others would swarm me and take me prisoner.

My shirt was soaked with sweat and my hands shaking by the time I reached the designated immigration booth on the right-hand side and handed over my damp passport, complete with a twenty-dollar bill and Alex's business card tucked inside.

The promised grubby little man was a chubby little woman, but the sleight-of-hand she performed on those items without the slightest hesitation made it clear I was in the right line. She stamped my passport with a flourish, and then, without a trace of a smile, handed it back and wished me a pleasant flight.

I exited to the gates as quickly as an honest tourist who was not a fugitive would.

I was early for the flight. Waiting is always stressful. For someone who has influential people gunning for them, waiting in a wide-open public place takes the tension to a new level. Fortunately, a vendor at the gate sold cold beer in cans.

I gave a silent thanks to The Powers That Be and bought several.

I drank my beer and stood near the gate facing out, pretending to be interested in the vital work that airport mechanics and logistics people do, or the intricacies of planes, or whatever was out there.

All I saw were pictures of stormtroopers, in my head, fortunately, and a blur of men and women in uniform in my peripheral vision.

Finally, the flight was called. I had bought a first-class ticket and trembled as the attendant checked my passport against my boarding pass and ran the pass through the machine that represented the last chance for officialdom to scream "gotcha!"

I floated down the jetway, found my seat, and slumped into it. A charming Thai lady in an airline uniform offered me a drink. "Please. Whisky, straight up."

I sipped it as the others took their seats. I had passed all the gates, but I was far from free yet.

The engines rumbled to life. A haze of announcements and demonstrations floated around me. The plane moved away from the jetway.

I ached with the tension as the engines revved up, and then the plane began to roll down the runway and launched me to freedom.

"Thank you, Alex," I sighed.

"Sir?" the stewardess asked, her plastic smile firmly in place.

"Can I have a couple of these?" I asked, holding up my glass.

She winked. "Of course."

The drinks, being airborne, all made me relax slightly. I was weak from the tension.

It was time to consider my next moves. I took deep breaths trying to remember if I'd mentioned Laos to Chea Pran. I couldn't remember. I didn't know how connected he was, but if he knew I was headed to Vientiane then I probably needed to change my plans

I thought of a woman who ran poker games in Bangkok. I'd left her on good terms. She might be willing to let me play. I could stay there, or down in Pattaya. The idea appealed to me. I'd call my friends and tell them things had come up.

If I were gambling in Bangkok, there was no doubt that Alex would be able to find me if he wanted to. The town was lousy with Russians. But I didn't worry about him. Not this time.

Trusting him, trusting that he'd approve of me getting back to work away from whatever he was up to, away from Prea Chan, was a reasonable plan — a calculated gamble.

Cuba

This trip was a bit different. I had a good friend of mine ask me about accompanying him to Cuba as his wife was very Ill and he had asked her if there was anything on her bucket list she wished to do, Cuba was her answer, so a couple days later we found ourselves in Cuba, for me a 2-hour direct flight from my home in Merida, Yucatan. Ed was off traveling somewhere else, van camping, I believe and there wasn't time to arrange a trip, and the trip was never meant to be for the purposes of writing a book, this was just a pure vacation, two weeks in Havana.

Havana is an amazing city, the colors, smells, the contrast of tourist vs local life is an experience like no other. Our first night we were sitting on a porch 20 feet in the air, drinking a 7-year-old rum, smoking a Cuban cigar while watching city life and the classic cars below. The second night we ate at a local restaurant counter, a thin cardboard box of rice and beans "moro racciones" and the thin slice of meat on top than the high-end restaurants run by the government, the man running the Casa Familiar was upset we had decided to eat there, but I suspect the government asks them to push the tourists to the fancier establishments.

As I got my box of food, I pulled out a bottle of Yucatano XXX hot sauce I brought with me. I had heard that hot sauce, especially foreign bottled hot sauce, was not a normal thing to be had in Cuba. The ten or so people at the counter all looked at me, curious as to what I was doing, I passed the bottle around the counter, everyone tried some, no one liked it, and now I was the insane gringo once again. So it is.

Over the course of my time in Cuba, I spent most of it just walking around exploring Havana, it pulled me like no other city has, if you read my other books, you know that I am very much at heart an Anarco-Capitalist, and don't have a nice word to say about collectivists, but damn, if Cuba was pulling me in... how would my life be different if I was born on this beautiful patch of soil? The beautiful city, ocean, women, food, music... would my life have really been as bad as I had always imagined growing up in a communist government? If I could live day to day for 2 weeks, blissfully happy, perhaps longer, perhaps forever? And thus the seed of the idea for the book you are about to read "Visions of Cuba."

Lee

JAMAICA

Montego Freeport Anchorage

In the early hours of the tropical morning, he sat on the stern of the catamaran, facing out to sea, and watching the first rays of light creep from the horizon to back-light clouds on the opposite side of the bay, washing them in soft pink.

"Good morning, Carlos," a sleepy voice said from behind him. "You're up early."

He twisted to see Gloria stretching in the hatchway, watching him.

She scowled. "Did you have that dream again? About Cuba?"

"Yes, the one about Cuba." The one that caused him so much confusion.

The entire world seemed dark and warm; he thought he felt the night caress his skin—a pleasant sensation. People were talking anxiously, whispering in hoarse voices as a woman, his mother, clutched his hand in hers, half dragging him across docks that smelled of fish, moving through the crowd.

The smell of her perfume mixed with the salty smell of the water, fish odors, and the pungent smell and rumble of a diesel engine idling, all touched by the counterpoint of what he knew to be night-blooming jasmine. The rustle of her skirt made their motions seem urgent, and it brushed over his face as she hurried him along, moving toward something—a boat.

"What is it?" A man said.

"Gaspar said—" she started.

"It's you then. Hand this one up," a man said. "We have to move quickly."

She did, grabbing him under his arms and propelling him upward. The man took him, turning, handing him to someone

else, passing him from person to person into the crowded hold of
the fishing boat.

The shrill cry of a whistle shattered the night, followed by
loud cracks, and then screams. Moving quickly, the man holding
him passed him to a large woman who sat in the boat, then
turned back. "Now! Cast off now!" he shouted.

"But the others—" the woman said.

"They are coming," he said as the engine roared. The boat
shuddered, then moved forward, and the woman pressed him to
her huge breasts as the boat surged away.

He smiled at Gloria. "Yeah, that same dream."

"Which version?"

Her interest in those dreams both surprised and pleased
him, although partly she was drawn into the puzzle that was
his life.

"The one where I get taken away in a boat."

"Instead of the one where you are left behind. I wonder
why sometimes it's one and other times the other?"

Her question immediately put his mind into that dream,
the one she called the other.

It is the same night, but different in many ways. This time a
man is carrying him through the crowd and the woman, his
mother, is ahead of them, but he can't see her. He has his small
arms wrapped around the man's neck, his face buried against the
man's, smelling his aftershave, feeling the roughness of his
cheeks against his face. Again, they come to a boat alongside the
dock. The woman approaches it and hands something to a man
on the boat. There is a sense of anxiety, of being rushed, hurried.

Again, the whistle echoes through the night. The woman
turns to face them, fear filling her face. Again, those cracks,
sounds that might be gunfire, ring out, and people begin to
scream. The men around him shout; the boat's engine roars. Men
throw large ropes onto the pier and the boat starts to move,
lurching forward.

The woman, his mother, shouts something at the man. Her words are filled with tears, panic. The man grabs her hand. "Run!" he shouts.

As chaos overwhelms the crowd on the dock, the boat disappears into the night. They move away, rushing back toward the city.

People are running in every direction and men are shouting "stop" and he hears more shots. Beside him, his mother cries out, staggers, and then falls to the ground.

"Carmen!" The man cries, stopping, turning back to where she lies. Then he shouts something and falls too. Wrapped in the man's arms, he hits the ground, scraping his cheek on the concrete. He cries out, and feels the man's weight on top of him, pinning him down.

"Come," someone shouts. They roll the man off him and a woman scoops him into her arms. Then they are running, ducking into doorways, down alleys.

When they stop in some basement, the woman holds him clutching him to her tightly, almost too tightly, but he feels safe and falls asleep.

He smiled at Gloria, appreciating the way she always made the effort to understand. She couldn't, of course. No one could understand his dreams... what they meant or how they affected him—it had him confused. He'd only mentioned these dreams to her to explain his sleeplessness. He didn't let her know how many there were, or that each represented a moment that seemed to have been snatched from a part of a life that he didn't know. But even so, she'd noticed how the dreams twisted the threads into parallel traumas that destroyed his nights. Every event, every incident, came to him vividly, and always in pairs—matched sets, dual viewpoints on those moments.

"You know, when you say it that way, the one where I escape on the boat sounds better, and yet, both feel terrible. No, not terrible, but tragically sad."

"Either way, you experience a sense of loss," she said. "In both scenarios, you are deserted—left alone. The results are much the same."

"I suppose." *Were they?*

"Well, whatever it is, coffee will make it better."

To please her, knowing why she said that, he laughed. "Well, it is a glorious morning in the Caribbean, and now we have the boat all to ourselves."

She sat, crossing her long, bare legs, and let out a long breath. "They were nice enough people, but I was so glad to see them leave," she said. "That's one thing about running charters. Even when the guests are pleasant, two weeks is a long time to live with two other people in a 40-foot boat."

"Even my first time, I see that. It gets tiring fast," he said.

They'd spent their days rushing about, feeding them, taking care of them, arranging snorkeling trips and picnics, watching the weather and meeting the carefully arranged schedule so their guest could catch their flights back home.

All of that was complicated by the need to watch their guests carefully. The clients had known nothing about boats or sailing, and a sailboat had many things to trip over and ropes and lines that could be a snare if you didn't pay attention. Sudden gusts of wind could swing the boom violently, right at head level.

But guests didn't charter a boat to pay attention to such matters; they came to relax, to sip tropical drinks, to bask in the sun, and swim. They expected the crew to keep them safe and content.

Gloria smiled happily. "Well, having you with me made the charter much more fun than it would have been. How lovely that you were able to help me out on such short notice.

With Gustav still in Denmark settling business, I couldn't have run the charter alone." She shook her head. "But I would've had to. We need the money. You saved my life, Carlos."

"No problem. This has been a lovely vacation for me, catching up on old times, and old loves," he laughed. He and Gloria had met at the University of Miami, studying marine biology. They'd shared classes, and later a bed. He'd thought she was the one for him, but she explained that she was polyamorous and loved him well enough, but she had no interest in exclusive relationships.

Now Gloria's beautiful, sleek catamaran, LOFTY AMBITION, sat at anchor in Jamaica's Montego Freeport Anchorage on the north side of the island. Catching a glimpse of her out of the corner of his eyes, he saw her watching him as he stared at the horizon. She chewed her lip thoughtfully, making him wonder where her mind had wandered.

"What?" he asked.

"I had a thought," she said.

"I saw the smoke coming out of your ears."

"Do you know where we are?"

He laughed. "Jamaica. Montego Freeport Anchorage. Do I win a prize?"

"I looked at the chart yesterday."

"You look at it every day."

She ignored him. "We are about 240 miles from Havana. Taking it easy, with half-decent winds, we could be there in a couple of days."

"Havana?"

"At the front door of Marina Hemingway."

He hesitated, uncertainty flooding him. "Go to Cuba?"

She sighed. "That's where the answers are."

"What if I don't like the answers?"

"I can't see you ever getting a real night's sleep until you resolve things. Those dreams—"

"They are getting better."

"Think of it... Gustav plans to meet me here, but that's not for two weeks. We could take our time sailing up to Cuba. We'd get out of sight of land, put up the sails, strip naked and just have ourselves a grand time for however long it takes to get there. Then, we get a slip at Marina Hemingway, and explore the city."

"That sounds great, but what about the charter business?"

"Well, I can't do much until Gustav returns in a couple of weeks. He'll give me a heads up and I'll have to sail to meet him, probably on Exuma in The Bahamas. I'm free until then and you've got time before you start your job at the marine research center in Key West. So I'm suggesting we sail there so you spend some of that time tracking down the places you see in your dreams."

"You think that will help?"

"It might. Look around, enjoy the place. And you can use some of the time to search their public records and see if you can find out what happened that night. And what's the point of having a boat if you don't sail places? If you don't learn anything, you still can have an adventure."

The idea appealed to him. "Of course, I don't know that anything happened or exactly what night it was. It could be just a dream."

"Maybe. But you know you wound up in Miami when you were about five. So find out what happened that year that might not have made the news in the States. You can also search their records for information on your birth parents—find your birth certificate. Some part of that might help you find out why the dreams trouble you."

She was right, of course, and Carlos knew it.

"You know you are insane, right?" he asked.

"I run a charter boat in the Caribbean and expect to earn a living... that's proof enough that I'm crazy."

"The sailing naked part does sound irresistible."

She smiled. "You see. It's a logical plan if you are a hedonist."

"Am I?"

"We can let you into the club on a trial basis and see."

"Sounds good."

"You'll need some money," she said. "It's expensive to convert dollars there. Better get some Euros. You can convert them at the bank."

"Good to know."

She winked. "I know all sorts of wonderful things."

She did.

HAVANA, CUBA

The channel leading into the Hemingway Marina is narrow, with shallow water covering coral reefs on either side. The sailing directions recommend approaching in daylight, and it was late morning when we arrived.

"Perfect timing," Gloria said as the channel buoys came into view. She luffed up the boat, spilling the wind out of the sails. We lost speed quickly. She let go of the helm and released the mainsheet. The large mainsail clattered as it dropped down the aluminum mast. "Secure it to the boom," she said. "Flake it nicely for me."

As he followed her orders, Gloria turned on the engine, shattering the blissful silence they'd known for days. With it idling, she stepped to the UHF radio and hailed the port captain.

After a short delay, an answering call gave them permission to enter the channel. "You have a slip in Canal three," he said. "A line handler will be waiting."

"Keep a close eye out on the color of the water," Gloria called. "LOFTY is wide. There is plenty of room, but I want to be dead center of the channel."

Nervous, worried that he might miss something, not exactly sure what he was watching for, Carlos went to the bow. Things went perfectly, with Gloria skillfully motoring through the channel and around the headland.

The Hemingway Marina has about 400 slips, arranged in long channels or canals. The guidebooks said that most of the slips needed repair, but it all looked fine. As they approached, looking at the array of masts, Carlos guessed that less than a quarter of them were occupied.

"There seems to be room at the inn," he said.

"And we have a reservation," she called back. "Starboard side to. Get her ready, please."

"Right." Carlos went to the starboard side and began tossing over the fenders that would protect the hull from chafing against the dock. They were already secured so that they'd hang at the right spot, right where the rub rail might chaff against anything.

The gruff-looking older man standing on the dock looked bored. Carlos tossed him the bowline. He grabbed it in a practiced, nonchalant motion and held it, then leaned back, pulling the bow toward the dock as Gloria reversed the engine and parallel parked LOFTY AMBITION.

"I'll check us in," Gloria said, waving a plastic bag that held their passports and the ship's papers. "Make sure she's secure and that you use proper hitches on the cleats."

"Aye, aye, Captain," Carlos said. Gloria was a stickler for doing things right. "A few minutes' extra effort now can make sure you've got a boat the next day," she often said. He didn't mind being reminded of the basics. He was enjoying his role of the landlubber learning to sail as much as Gloria loved being captain and he hoped his marine biology career would mean spending a lot of time on boats.

As Gloria headed for the offices, the man on the dock tied off the bowline with a perfect hitch and walked away.

Carlos busied himself securing the stern line and spring lines to ensure the boat would stay put. When he straightened, he let out a long breath and took a look around to take in the moment.

So, this was Cuba.

After a cruise, there were always jobs that needed doing, especially on Gloria's boat. He turned his attention to taking care of the important ones. He opened a locker and dragged the ship's hose onto the dock where he connected it to a water faucet that advertised the water was not for drinking. "*No es seguro para beber,*" it said. He turned it on and found the pressure was good, so he began washing down the decks and the cockpit area, getting off the corrosive salt water. By the time he finished, Gloria was back.

"Good work," she said. "I'm ready for lunch," she said.

Carlos laughed. "Now that you've brought up the subject, I'm suddenly starving."

"Let's eat in town," she said. She jerked a thumb toward the parking lot. "I hired a taxi, and the driver promises we will get great food and the best prices in Cuba. And if you can't trust a cabbie hustling you in the marina parking lot, what's the world coming to, right?"

They locked the boat and headed back to the main area of the marina where a pink 1953 Chevy Bel Air convertible sat waiting for them. A large man, wearing a bright Hawaiian shirt and a straw fedora, smiled at them. "This is Felix," Gloria said, "and this..." she patted the car, "this is Lucille, the love of his life."

Despite the duct tape that held some of the chrome on the vehicle, Felix was obviously car proud. "To the Floridita?" he asked. "Only thirty minutes from here. You can have a drink there and then the restaurant is nearby."

He made the drink sound like a visitor's obligation.

"Travel from Hemingway Marina to Hemingway's bar for a tourist drink? Why not?" Carlos laughed.

"We will be near Castillo de los Tres Reyes Magos del Morro," Felix said as he drove along at a slow and steady pace through Havana. "You call it Morro Castle. This is the old section of Havana."

Carlos and Gloria sat in the back, enjoying the warm breeze on their skin and excited by the city tour. Because of global politics, because of the little he knew of his family history, Havana, Cuba itself, had a somewhat forbidding aspect to it that made the ordinary somehow exciting.

"The city is cleaner than I expected," he told her.

"Why did you think it would be dirty?" she laughed.

He shook his head, then laughed. "American propaganda? I knew it wouldn't be bleak—it's the tropics and the people are Latinos, so nothing Stalinist, but given that it's communist, it has to be something bad."

Gloria just grinned. "Americans."

The afternoon was glorious. Felix found a place to park near the intersection of Obispo and Monserrate and pointed out the bar. The daiquiris at the bar, Hemingway's preferred version of the drink, what became known as the Papa Doble, which combined white rum, maraschino liqueur, grapefruit juice, and lime juice got them in the right mood. Then it was off to lunch.

The food was exactly what Felix had promised—basic Cuban food that proved to be simple, surprisingly not very spicy, but delicious.

On the way back to the marina, Gloria got a text on her phone. "It's Gustav," she told him. She frowned, concentrating. "He picked up an extra charter."

Carlos sighed. He'd been looking forward to the ten or so days ahead, but he knew that Gloria needed the money a charter would bring in. "When do you have to leave?"

She counted days on her fingers and sighed. "I'm afraid I'll have to leave first thing in the morning and at that, I'll need to motor sail to make sure I get there on time."

Carlos knew that Gloria hated having to turn on the engine to do anything but enter and leave port. He shrugged off his own disappointment. "It sucks, but I guess I'll have to find a way to enjoy Cuba by myself."

She pursed her lips. "I feel bad, talking you into coming here and then abandoning you like this."

He shook his head. "The sail from Jamaica was not to be missed for anything. This entire time has been fantastic. You have nothing to feel bad about. Without you in the way, I'll find a place to stay and take the time to do a little research on my family."

Gloria leaned forward and tapped Felix on the shoulder. "Say, amigo, could you help Carlos find an inexpensive place to stay in Havana? He needs to be close to public transport so he can go back and forth to the Civil Registry?"

Felix waved a hand. "No problem. How long will you stay?"

"A week or two. I'm not exactly sure. I have to check with the airline about changing my flight. I was supposed to leave from Jamaica."

Felix pulled at his face, watching them in his rearview mirror. "I do have a room above my house I could rent you very cheap. It even has a small kitchenette. I run a Casa Familiar."

"A what?"

"It is a place that foreigners are allowed to stay. That requires the police to approve the place and the owners."

"You need permission to rent to foreigners?"

Felix laughed. "In Cuba, we need permission to wipe our asses." It didn't seem to bother him. "It's all for the good of everyone, of course."

"The rental... the price would have to be cheap," Carlos said.

"If you could pay in cash in advance, that would make it much cheaper."

Carlos sighed. He didn't have that much money left, but a hotel would be expensive. Better to pay it upfront. Then he'd know how much he had to live on. "How cheap?"

When Felix named the amount, Carlos did a quick conversion. It was cheap. Still, paying it wouldn't leave him a lot, but all he'd need would be food and transportation. He could squeak by. In a couple of weeks, he'd be in Key West starting that new job, anyway. This was a rare chance to put his dreams to rest. "I'd have to convert some Euros."

Felix beamed. "I know a bank that would be happy to help you with that."

"How early do you need to leave in the morning?" Carlos asked Gloria.

She scowled. "I haven't checked the tide charts and I'll want to leave with the tide, but I do want to make an early start."

"I will give you my phone number," Felix said. "When you are ready, you call me. I will come here and get you. We can go see the room. If you don't like it, then we will find something else. This is a slow time and there are many available. When you choose one, I'll take you to the bank."

It sounded like a decent plan.

"If you truly must leave Cuba so quickly," Felix said, "I could take you to some dance clubs this evening. For a small fee, I will take you to a restaurant for dinner and then to the clubs. You can hear the finest music in the Caribbean and drink the best rum."

"Spoken like a true, country proud patriot," Carlos said. "Dancing the night away sounds good to me if the captain is up for it."

"Hell, any decent sailor has to be able to sail her boat while nursing a hangover," Gloria said. "Felix, amigo mio, you are on."

MOVING ASHORE

Carlos and Gloria had a fantastic last night together in Cuba. They let Felix pick the destinations. He treated them to a series of wonderful clubs where the pulsing rhythms of infectious Latin music had them dancing long into the night, even long after they were tired.

Even so, when he got them back to the boat, Carlos was happy to find that they both had enough energy and were sober enough to enjoy a wild night in the master stateroom.

It was the next morning that things became awkward as well as painful. Goodbyes made his gut ache and the act of packing his bag made the separation real, tangible. Then, he tossed his bag on the dock and Gloria calmly made preparations to shove off.

He struggled through the motions of saying goodbye to Gloria, sending her back to Gustav, and suppressing the bittersweet sensations of envy and loss that rose with their adventure being cut short.

The situation, unavoidable and inevitable, and no one's fault, still hurt.

He stood alone on the dock with his bag at his feet, watching the lovely lady skipper skillfully maneuver her beloved catamaran out of the canal and through the channel, sailing away from him. Shifting his weight nervously on the dock he cringed as she shrank from view—even before she left his sight entirely, he missed her.

Outside the channel, the boat awkwardly headed up into the wind. Squinting, he spotted her shadowy silhouette as she hoisted the mainsail sail; he heard it crackle as it unfurled and filled with wind, growing taut, billowing out. As the boom swung out to starboard, Gloria ducked back down into the cockpit. LOFTY AMBITION turned to run close to the wind, her bow pointed to the east. Then, with increasing speed, the sleek boat began growing smaller, shrinking into a speck on the huge water and finally disappearing over the horizon.

Even though his own adventure lay ahead of him, her departure left him with a sinking feeling in the pit of his stomach, the sense of missing out on an adventure. Gloria had sailed off into the unknown, appearing to fall off the edge of the earth. Over the next few days, his path would take him indoors, out of the sun, where he'd sort through stacks of musty records to see what he could learn of his past.

The search wouldn't be simple; he had no idea how it might take to unearth any information about his family. It all seemed a bit pointless and dull. Still, Gloria was right. Knowing what really happened that night, the night he left Cuba as a child, was the only thing he could think of that might stop the dreams.

There was time ahead for adventure.

Picking up his bag, he walked to the parking lot where he found the ever-reliable Felix waiting patiently.

"We go see the room now?" Felix asked eagerly.

"Why not? If it suits, we can go to the bank and get some money."

The room Felix showed him was basic, but clean. "My wife, Elinda, will clean it every day," Felix said when he introduced Carlos to her and his two children. Felix didn't want any paperwork, no rental agreement, so the cash simply changed hands, giving Carlos a strange, vulnerable feeling. Vulnerable and light, as if his existence made no mark. Outside of Cuba, other than Gloria, no one in the world knew where he was. His adopted family still thought he was in Jamaica. They had always been good to him, but they were never that close. It didn't seem important enough to let them know about the change of plans.

A strange sense of being free, somehow, touched everything around him.

After he settled in, with the radio blasting more of the music he'd danced to with Gloria, Felix drove him to a bank. It wasn't crowded and a friendly senorita with a charming smile entered his information (passport number and so on) on a huge, old, green-screened computer that then converted his Euros into Pesos. Then another bank employee put the Euros in a wooden box and quickly walked them to the safe.

Thinking about his bank balance hovering near zero made him feel weak. It was good to be starting a job soon. His student loans wouldn't pay themselves, and even getting to Key West would cost money. He'd probably need new clothes for the job. The truth was, he had no real idea what he'd need. One of the nice things about the job was that he'd have a free dorm to live in.

Back in the car, he shoved a handful of pesos at Felix. A week's rent. It seemed significant somehow... not the amount, but the commitment.

"And now?" Felix asked.

"I'd like to see where the Civil Registry is. That's where the documents will be, correct?"

"Exactly! We must go to the Ministerio de Justicia," he said, as if he'd never been there before and looked forward to the adventure of it.

Along the way, amid his tour-guide spiel, pointing out famous places, Felix gave him a primer on the public transportation systems. "You can save money using the local cab system instead of the cabs the tourists use," he said, "but the drivers are restricted... some can run only north and south, others east and west."

"How do you know which ones are which?"

"You must ask. Talk to people. You tell them where you are going and people will help you get in the right car," Felix said. "There are no signs or schedules. Fortunately, although your Spanish is bad, your accent is more or less Cubano and they will understand you."

Carlos chuckled. He'd been damned with faint praise.

When they arrived, it was still early, so Carlos had Felix write down the address of the room he'd rented. "I want to check it out. I might as well get started right away," he said. "And I'll find my way back... start learning transportation too."

That pleased Felix. Nearly everything seemed to please him. "You need anything, to go somewhere..." he grinned. "Maybe you need to meet a CIA agent for a secret meeting. You don't take the cheap taxis for that. For such things you need Felix."

His hushed tone made his words sound serious, but the sparkle in his eyes said the comment was a joke. Hell, with all the paranoia in the States about Cuban communists, and the paranoia in Cuba about American influence, Carlos didn't think it was a stretch to think that any American visiting Cuba could easily be a spy. Or vice versa.

That made it more interesting.

The Registry, the place he would be doing his research, turned out to be a damp and dark set of rooms in the basement of an ugly and poorly maintained building. The rooms were filled with files stuffed into cabinets and left in stacks. Apparently, organization wasn't a highly valued commodity. He asked a harried clerk a few questions about the indexing system and got mostly a blank stare. It wasn't a language problem. Very little of the information had been digitized, and much was incomplete. Almost nothing was systematically catalogued.

As he worked, a thin, young woman in a business suit came in. Her jet-black hair was pulled back into a bun, accenting the thin, determined lines of her face. Carlos found her attractive—not beautiful, but charming to look at and pleasantly sexy. He watched as she sat at the big table with him, dragged out some books, and flipped through the pages, making notes.

He turned his attention back to his search for any records about the night his parents put him on the boat. He combed through books containing copies of death certificates, looked through news clippings, hoping to find any sort of public record, but came up empty.

"Ugh," he said, finally.

"You are having a problem?" the girl asked.

Her voice delighted him. Something about the way she asked made him laugh at himself. "Only that I can't find anything," he said. "You seem to know how this works."

"I'm Juanita," she said, holding out a hand. "And I have spent a fair time learning what passes for organization. Maybe I can help."

"I'm Carlos," he took her hand and shook it. "I'd appreciate it if you could shed any light at all on things."

"It is confusing," she said.

"More than that. Either I'm not understanding what I read, or a few days—the events that took place—are completely missing."

Her expression became serious. "They might be."

"Really?"

"Incompleteness is the single word that describes the records of certain periods, some of the more controversial things that happened." She smiled. "During the revolution, for instance."

He shook his head. "I'm looking for information about events from less than twenty years ago."

"Was there some particular... event you were interested in?"

"That's when I was put on a boat and sent to the US. Something happened, but I don't know what."

She pursed her lips. "There shouldn't be anything particularly eventful or controversial about that era. But then, these records have their own strange logic, or lack of it. Where the information you are looking for is kept might depend on what it is you want to know, and also—"

"What?"

"Well, truthfully, it depends very much on whether the facts you are looking for fit correctly with the official version of the events. Even that can change over time, which produces an interesting ripple effect on what we call the truth. From what I've seen, it happens everywhere, but in a small country such as this one, the results are more dramatic."

"Dramatic?"

"Unfortunately, it means some bits and pieces, some information, may never be found."

"That sucks."

She smiled. "Can you tell me what you are looking for? I have a lot of experience with these records, and I've finished my work for the day. I might be able to help."

That appealed to him on more levels than he wanted her to know. "I'd appreciate that. Is this what you do? This is your job?"

"She nodded. I work for a company that provides official records, birth certificates, baptismal certificates, all sorts of things for Cubans living in other countries. We locate the documents and then charge them to get certified, official copies."

"Then you might be able to help. I'm trying to find out what happened to my family. About fifteen years ago, at night, someone put me on a boat. I think it was my mother. The boat took me to Miami. I don't even know for certain what night it was."

"And you don't know much about your family?"

"Just some names."

He handed her a sheet of paper. "When I arrived in Miami, at least according to the State Department, they found these names pinned to my clothing."

She stared at the paper that said his name was Carlos and gave his parent's names. "Well, if there is anything to find, and there should be, we should be able to track it down." She chuckled. "I don't suppose you know the date you arrived in the US?"

"Only approximately. That's part of the difficulty in finding out anything."

She sighed. "Of course. Knowing that would make life too easy. Well, I can talk to my boss. He knows more than I about locating this kind of information. I'm sure he can offer ideas."

"I can't afford to pay the company to locate the data."

She grinned. "I will make sure Fernando knows that I am asking for a friend, not for business." She touched his arm. "Cuba is a place of relationships. We help each other."

The idea of being her friend, that she would call him that, pleased him. "Thank you."

"Will you be here tomorrow? I can let you know what he says."

"I'll definitely be here. I plan on being here a week and this research, learning about my family, is the reason I came." The idea of seeing her again pleased him too.

"I hope you will take some time to learn about us, the Cuban people while you are here."

"I want to."

"It is truly the only way our countries will ever overcome this distance and the walls that have grown up between us. I find it amazing and sad that we are closer to countries thousands of miles away than to one of our nearest neighbors."

"I hadn't thought of it that way, but I agree completely."

She held up the paper. "Can I keep this?"

He nodded. "Sure. I have a copy... several, in fact."

The day had been long and emotional, and Carlos needed to stop his search, at least long enough to gather his wits. "I appreciate your help."

She smiled. "I do this work all day long. If I can't apply what I've learned to help someone out, what good is it?"

Despite being exhausted, Carlos didn't want to spend an evening alone, eating in a restaurant that he didn't know, and then returning to his empty room. But the moment he decided to invite her to have dinner with him, as a thank you for her help, before he could speak, she glanced at her watch and made a face. "I'm afraid I must get back to the office. Every Wednesday we have a meeting of the staff after work."

"A bunch of hard workers," he said.

She smiled. "I'll see you tomorrow then?"

"Absolutely," he said.

A DAY AT THE OFFICE

The next day, Carlos braved the local taxi system. As Felix had said, people seemed delighted to help him find his way. It was still early when he headed down the cracked concrete steps into his basement 'office' and found Juanita already there. She was hard at work, hunched over a Chinese-made laptop computer, feverishly entering data from a huge stack of documents.

"What's all that?" he asked.

She straightened and smiled at him. "Good morning. This is just busy work, but unfortunately, it must be done."

"What are you doing?"

She laughed. "I told you that much isn't digitized. So, whenever we don't have a specific job for a client, the boss has us enter as much data as possible. He is building his own database. He hired programmers who are building search engines that will be optimized to find the kinds of information we provide clients."

"Ambitious."

"The government doesn't see it as a priority, but my boss won't be satisfied until the need to send people here or scramble around to church parish offices and so on to read through old records is a thing of the past."

"I can't blame him. This is damnably labor intensive."

"By the way," she said, holding out a piece of paper. "I found this."

He took it and stared in amazement. It was a birth certificate for Rudolpho Jesus Menores. He took a breath. "That's my father's birth certificate. How did you find that?"

"Proof of my boss's concept. I took a long shot and checked through the current version of our company database. I couldn't find one for your mother or you. Sorry about that."

"No, this is great."

"That is just a printout of a copy." She pointed to numbers at the top. "You can use those numbers to obtain a legal copy if you need one."

"No." He stared at it, struck by how having that single document in his hands made the idea of his father more real, more tangible. "This is fine for now. Thank you."

"I'm afraid I won't be much more help today," she said. "I have to enter all these names and dates and places. I'm spending the day as a typing machine but if you have any specific questions, I'll be here, chained to this beast."

He waved the paper. "You've already been an enormous help. This is fantastic." He glanced around. "I thought it might be useful to skim a chunk of the newspapers for the time when I... left the island. If something newsworthy happened then, it might give me a clue, another lead."

"Unless it was something bad, and had political implications," she said. "The press doesn't provide a lot of details on anything that makes the government look bad. Don't get your hopes up."

"Too late," he said. "Just coming here did that." Meeting her had been a big part of restoring his optimism, but he resisted saying that. It sounded creepy, but on the other hand, he liked her, and he needed to find a way to tell her.

"I'd start with Diario de la Marina," she said. "It's been around since the late 1800s and is well established."

"Thanks."

He went to the media room and got to work, grabbing the bound issues of the newspaper, and skimming through the ones for that year. He found a rich treasure of stories, most of them either domestic things, or telling how successful this or that economic program had been, how the crime rate had been almost eliminated with proper training in socialist ethics, and so on. There wasn't much about the outside world, nothing on boat people, or no indication that there had ever been any kind of dissent. If it hadn't been actively suppressed, at least the journalists ignored it.

He found a few stories of people killed on the docks or the police intercepting contraband of one sort or another, but again, nothing political and nothing about any mass gathering like the one he saw in his dreams.

But then dreams were always subject to interpretation and the crowd, the chaos, being handed into the boat, that might be all something his brain cooked up.

And yet... the smell of those moments clung to him—especially of his mother's perfume. That had to mean something.

By the end of the day, tired and unenlightened, he watched Juanita closing her laptop. "Off to another meeting?" he asked.

She shook her head. "No. Only on Wednesday. Today I don't even have to go back to the office. I already sent in my work over the Internet."

Carlos looked at her, hesitating a moment, before asking. "Can I buy you dinner?"

A pleased smile lit her face, giving him hope. "That would be lovely. I'd like that."

"You will have to pick the restaurant," he said. "I don't know any places, not anything good, and I'm not rich, but..."

She laughed. "I know many good, wonderful but economical places. Places the tourists don't know and wouldn't like because the atmosphere isn't much, and yet the food is good Cuban fare."

"Perfect," he said.

"And I have a car."

"You do?" That seemed unusual.

"In a manner of speaking," she said. "It's a Lada."

"The Russian car?"

"It's more of a Russian metal box with a motor in it, held together with good Cuban baling wire," she said. "We make fine baling wire. The car doesn't have a radio, which is not a problem because you couldn't hear it over the engine. What I'm saying is, it is cranky and uncomfortable, but it will get us there. At least, it usually gets me where I'm going."

"The journey is the adventure," Carlos said.

She snapped her fingers. "Exactly." She grinned. "Because she is reliable if reluctant, I named her Dapples."

"The name of Sancho Panza's donkey," Carlos laughed.

"A trooper," she said as she led him to a Russian metal box that was, indeed, dappled, spotted with primer and rust.

The noisy car was recalcitrant and sputtered as they went, but dutifully took them to a place in an area that looked familiar. Carlos barely knew the city, so he realized they weren't far from his new lodgings.

They sat at an outside restaurant and dined on beans and rice, with some meat in it. It was deliciously spiced. They ordered cold Cristal beer and chatted happily over the meal. Juanita trained a wonderful smile on him and asked questions. That combination made words flow out of him. By the time he wiped up the last of his meal with a piece of his baguette, Carlos felt drained. It was as if, by rattling on the way he'd done, he'd emptied out his life, telling her all about him.

And yet, although she talked, he realized he had learned remarkably little about her. "Tell me more about you," he said.

She shrugged. "What can I say about a life spent studying hard and then, on graduation, being given a demanding job that leaves remarkably little time for anything else?"

Carlos heard the bittersweetness in her voice. She felt lucky, yet as if she was missing out. For him, the good part was the implication that there was no husband or boyfriend in her world.

"An attractive woman like you should have a rich social life," he said.

Her smile was wistful. "When I have time, the men who interest me either turn out to be married or are impoverished and without any prospects."

He struggled to think of something to say, but then she said it for him. Her hand touched his across the table, and her smile warmed him. "But now you've come along."

"I won't be here for long."

She laughed, her eyes twinkling. "You can't know that. For all you know, you might end up living in Cuba forever."

"I leave soon to start a job in Key West," he said. "I told you that." *He'd told her every damn thing about himself.*

"You told me of your intention to take the job," she said brightly. "But now, you are here, and we don't know what tomorrow brings."

"Live for the day, you mean? Stay in the moment?"

"If not that, at least don't put all your hopes on an unforeseeable future." Her long, slender fingers wrapped around his, comfortingly, wonderfully. "And I think that this moment has a certain amount of charm to it."

He looked into her dark eyes and let his gaze take in the soft, beguiling line of her mouth, her brown cheek and jaw; he noted the way his pulse raced at her touch, and how the warm night air, carrying a strong floral scent, wrapped them in a sensual cocoon. The moment had more than a little charm to it.

It all seemed so good, so natural. He paid for their meal and she drove them to his small room in the rackety Lada. Later, he couldn't remember telling her where he lived, but words seemed unnecessary—an intrusion. They got out of the car and he went to her and kissed her. Then he took her hand and led her up the outside stairway to his room. Wordlessly, they undressed each other and when they got on the bed and made love, they made sounds, but still spoke no words. She wrapped him in her essence. He took her with a passion that did his Latin heritage proud.

Deep in the night, she kissed him and finally spoke again, making an apology. "I must go," she said. "An early meeting for work."

"When will I see you again?" he asked as he watched her dress, once again tasting the bittersweet emotion of seeing a lover depart.

"I'll be at the registry this afternoon," she said.

And she was. She was there and happy to share a meal and his bed again that night, but again leaving well before morning. "I wish you could stay," he told her. "I ache for you when I wake in the morning."

"I'll see," she told him, kissing him.

Each day he went to the registry, but every day his research came up empty. He found no records of any events that paralleled his dreams. In the evening, Juanita was with him. With her sleeping with him, she learned about the dreams, as Gloria had. Like Gloria, she seemed curious. "So, you have always dreamed of Cuba?"

"And what happened," he said. "Something must have happened. And it is confusing because of how I have the dreams of two different people blending together."

"Both a Cubano and an expat," she said.

That summed it up. "I see things from two perspectives. And it is so strange to have two different perspectives on a place I shouldn't know anything about at all."

"Two visions of Cuba. Just as if you were two different people."

"Yes."

"Are you looking for some sign of a thwarted revolution?" Juanita asked.

"Nothing political," he said. "The dreams just center on these things and I was hoping that it would lead me to learn something. Why was I put on a boat alone? How is it that I also have dreams of not making the boat?"

"So it is about finding out what you can about your family? Only that?"

"And, in the process, finding myself."

She nodded. "Write down your dreams," she said. "Give me any details you can think of."

Surprised, he did, and Juanita joined in the search. They found tidbits, mentions of people with the same names, but nothing important.

It was disheartening, but at least, every evening now, he had Juanita. After the third day, Saturday, when they got to his place, she pulled a ratty bag from Dapple's trunk. He looked at it.

"You asked me to stay the night," she said. She held it up. "If I'm going to be here with you, I need my things."

She stayed through Sunday, and took him around Havana, showing him parts that tourists didn't see. "This is fantastic," he told her.

"What do you like about it?" she asked. "It is poor and rather shabby. I'm certain our country is not as elegant as America."

"The people," he said. "The simplicity. In a way, it's what American used to be."

"Certainly not politically," she laughed.

"I don't care about that," he said.

She stared at him, weighing the words as if she could measure whether he was telling the truth or saying what he thought she wanted to hear.

"I came because of the dreams," he said. "Only the dreams."

"Would you like to live here?" she asked.

That stopped him. "I hadn't thought of that."

"Why?"

"Because it is impossible."

"Why?"

"I have to go earn a living. I owe money."

"What if you didn't need money?" she asked. She waved a hand at the people walking in the old neighborhood she'd brought him to. "What if you could earn plenty of money to live here, like this?"

"That would depend," he said.

"On what?"

"Would you be with me?"

Her laugh delighted him. "That would make the difference as to whether you stayed?"

"You are the one who brought it up, and the truth is, in my time here I've had a new vision of Cuba... and you are part of it," he said. "If it were possible, I might happily follow that vision."

"¿en serio?" she asked.

"Seriously," he said firmly.

That ended the conversation then, but thoughtful expression left him feeling like she'd learned something important, whether about him or his plans, he couldn't tell. For his part, the idea of living in Havana had taken on more than a little charm. He dismissed it. All dream visions, all fantasies about an ideal future had that quality.

And yet, the dream he was living there in Cuba, the routine they settled easily into, pleased him. Every morning, after breakfast she would drive him to the registry, sometimes going in with him, sometimes going to the office, but returning in the afternoon with that awkward-looking laptop. At night, they would go out for dinner, then to his tiny room and his bed.

"I don't know if I'll be successful," he told her. "I don't have a lot of time left."

"You have years," she laughed.

"I mean my time in Cuba," he said. The deadline for reporting to his new job, for starting a new life approached. "And I'm beginning to think my dreams are nothing more than that."

"We found proof that your father was real. Besides, the dreams that brought you here are something, not nothing," she said. "They brought you to Cuba, and they brought us together."

"That's true enough, but now it makes it that much harder to wake up. I have to return to a different world. I'll return with nothing more than what you gave me at the beginning— my father's birth certificate. I haven't made much progress since then."

"Perhaps that's enough," she said, wrinkling her nose. "At least we've proven you are really Cuban."

"You don't seem sad," he said.

She touched his face. "Carlos," she said. "Tell me, are you hurt because you think I'm not sad that you are leaving? Or are you hurt that I don't believe you are leaving me?"

"I'm leaving, Juanita."

"You intend to leave," she said. "There is a difference. You have a vision of leaving. Maybe that's just a dream too."

"You are a strange woman, Juanita."

"And you love me."

He did. "That just makes it all even more confusing."

DEPARTURE

The day before his flight was scheduled to take him back to Miami, Juanita took Carlos to the registry for one last time. From her manner, it might have been just any day, not his last. He envied her calmness but couldn't share it.

That morning, on a random hunt through the part of the database, he found something odd. Searching on his parent's names brought up the mention of a son. His heart pounded with the discovery and began searching for the new name: Luis Menores. There were many mentions of him, although nothing exceptional, nothing tragic. He won an award in school that got him a scholarship to university. Frantically backtracking through references, he found that Luis was exactly his age.

Excitedly showing it to Juanita, he was surprised to see her give him a wry smile. "Perhaps the dreams you have are his."

"What do you mean?"

"You assumed, everyone assumed that the names pinned to your clothing were those of your parents, but perhaps they are his—this other boy."

"That makes no sense," he said impatiently, certain that she was provoking him. "It said my name was Carlos, not Luis, and the records show he grew up in Cuba. His parents died when he was young. He had foster parents, as I did."

"Of course, and dreams are just dreams," she said.

He suspected she was angry with him for leaving, leaving her, leaving Cuba. Even though she wouldn't admit it, there was a tension and besides, if she loved him at all, then she had to feel something more than she'd shown.

"There can be many explanations," she said. "But you are only prepared to accept certain ones. If a person can dream about other people, why can't they dream as another person?"

"That sounds crazy," he said.

Her smile arrested him. "That doesn't make it wrong."

A frantic search through the rest of the afternoon found little more than occasional mentions of Luis Menores, the orphan Cubano, graduating from university with a degree in marine biology—the same degree and same year as Carlos' degree, simply a hundred miles (and a universe) apart from each other.

What did it mean that the people he thought were his parents were thought, by the Cuban government, to be the parents of another man, his own age? What did it mean that their lives bore these superficial similarities and probably a thousand, a million differences?

His head spun.

And all this confusion was compounded by the turmoil that came with yet another separation—one that certainly would be permanent. Once he was on his path in life, chasing a career, he doubted he'd ever return to Cuba and Cuba wouldn't wait for him.

That night his lovemaking with Juanita was intense. Passion gripped them both. And as he held her body against his, he admitted the truth.

"Part of me would love to stay here in Havana," he said.

"Then stay." She made it so simple. "If you love Havana and you love me..."

He did love her, she of the sweet brown thighs, the beautiful dark eyes, the sharp mind. And the climate and the tempo of life here suited him. Yet he didn't turn a blind eye to the problems, it was more that the shortages, the crumbling infrastructure didn't bother him any more than they depressed Juanita or Felix. Such things were fixable over time, and anyway, no matter where he lived, they were outside his control.

"This job is my future," he started to tell her but ran out of words before he could finish. He didn't know what that meant any more.

He accepted a job that seemed the answer to a prayer. Now, he understood that it was simply a doorway, a threshold he had to cross so that he could be taught the mechanics of his chosen profession. He knew the science, but he lacked practical knowledge of the world of grants, of networking, and of making a living. It was the open door to what he would do, not what he was.

A vague anxiety gripped him. Leaving meant giving up on Juanita, losing the quiet pleasure of this measured life. And what would he gain? He'd work toward becoming a scientist, but he had no idea what that even meant.

He'd come to Cuba for answers about the past, his past, his family. That search yielded only confusion, and not just about the past. It created a desperate uncertainty about the future, about what he wanted, a more intense anxiety than he'd ever known in his life.

Packing his bag to leave for the airport, his hands trembled.

Am I doing the right thing?

How could a man who didn't even know who he was answer a question like that?

THE AIRPORT

Although his flight was at noon, Carlos rose early the next morning, causing Juanita to give him a somewhat accusing glare from her bed. It took all the willpower he could muster to get through the morning. As he packed his bag, the concept of a doorway that lay ahead still intimidated him.

Get a grip. You always know what you are leaving behind and never enough about what lies ahead. That's just life.

He had come for answers and was leaving with only small pieces, incomplete and incoherent fragments of his past that he had tucked in a plastic folder—his father's birth certificate and the bits and pieces he'd found on the life of Luis Montero shaped into a vague dossier. He might never totally fill in the gaps of the dreams, but he knew that he might learn who the man was and how he fit into the puzzle.

And in a bittersweet way, the other world beckoned, calling to him to walk away from all this.

He'd said his goodbyes to Juanita; she'd given him a kiss and driven off to work in Dapples as if it were any other day. Then trusty Felix arrived to take him to the airport for his flight to Miami. "The Jose Marti International Airport is named for a great poet," he said as they rode. "We call him the Apostle of Cuban Independence for what he did to get freedom from Spain."

"You love your history," Carlos said.

"A person should appreciate what it took to create what we have. And now you have Havana too, so you must learn about it. It is part of you now."

"I'm sure I'll come back," he said, wondering if it was true.

"Perhaps you will never leave," Felix laughed, making him wonder what it was about the Cubans he met that made them think he'd have such a hard time leaving.

Felix dropped him outside the departure area. When Carlos said goodbye, the man shook his hand. "We will see you again soon," he said, leaving Carlos wondering as the man climbed back into his car and drove away.

At the airport, clutching his one small bag in one hand, passport and boarding pass in the other, he went to security. It wasn't crowded, and he tossed his bag on the conveyor belt, tugging at his shirt. It was hot and the air con didn't seem to be working. His clothes stuck uncomfortably to his skin, making him wonder how the security people stood it all day.

As his bag disappeared into the scanning machine, he put his wallet, phone, passport, and the folder containing his research into a blue plastic tray and put that through next. Then a bored female officer, dressed in a khaki uniform that included a short skirt, black lace stockings, and high heels, waved at him to pass through the tall scanner. It was definitely a more alluring look that he was used to seeing at airport security. Giving her a smile that didn't manage to penetrate her boredom, he gave up the attempt and walked through. Just as he arrived at the other end of the conveyor belt his bag emerged.

He yanked it off the scanner, grabbed up his things from the blue tray and strode off into the large main departure room. Happily, vendors were selling cold beer. He got one and went off to the side, tucking the folder under his arm and dropping the bag on the ground beside him. He took a breath and tasted the delicious beer. As he drank, the sound of birds made him look up. They seemed to be nesting. He gulped the beer down and thought about getting another. Before he could, a stern-faced officer in uniform walked up to him and pointed to the bag at his feet. "Is this yours?" he asked.

"Yes," he said, nervously. He knew there was nothing illegal in the bag; he was doing nothing wrong, but the spotlight of attention from the authorities troubled him, anyway. It always did.

"Do you have other bags?" he asked.

"No. Just the carry-on. Is there a problem?"

The officer nodded. "Papers," he said.

Carlos handed him his passport and boarding pass. The officer pointed at the folder. Confused, Carlos handed it to him. "It is nothing but public records."

"Grab your bag and come with me," the man said, starting to walk toward some offices that were situated off to the side of the hall.

Carlos followed obediently. There seemed little else he could do.

The officer led him into a bleak room... probably exactly like hundreds of other bleak rooms in international airports around the world. Old, gray acoustic tiles covered the ceiling and walls, except for a mirrored window. A rectangular table took up most of the room and there were four green plastic chairs. The seats of two of the chairs were badly cracked, and the officer pointed to one of the cracked ones. "Sit," he said.

Carlos settled into the chair, feeling it wanting to give away completely. The officer put his bag and the folder on the table a distance away from Carlos.

The door opened and a cheerful-looking man in a drab suit came in. The officer handed him Carlos' passport as he went to a chair in front of the bag and sat. Carlos noted he was careful to take a chair that wasn't cracked.

He opened the passport and squinted at it as if he needed glasses. Vanity or were they expensive here? Carlos had no idea.

"So, Senor Reyes..."

"Is there a problem?" Carlos asked. "My flight leaves soon."

The man clucked his tongue. "I'm afraid you might need to take a later one. I am sorry for the inconvenience, but I have some questions for you."

"About what?"

"About this," he said, holding up the passport. He held it up to the light, then squinted at it again. "It is very good."

"Good? Of course. It's a genuine US passport."

The man smiled and pointed at the passport. "Yes, it says that right here, doesn't it? But that raises an interesting question... if it is a real US passport, why does it have the face and birth date of a Cuban citizen? And why is the name wrong?"

"What are you talking about? That's my name and my passport."

"Then you must have more than one name. That is unusual, you must admit." He picked up the folder and skimmed through it. "This is interesting. What is it?"

"I was doing some research. On my family."

"So, you admit you were born in Cuba?"

"I never denied it. At least I was told I was born here. But I grew up in the US. In Tampa, Florida."

"Curious. And you grew up as Carlos Reyes?"

"Of course."

"Then why did the finest facial recognition technology in the world, technology provided to us by our brothers in the People's Republic of China, identify you as someone else?"

Carlos took a breath. This was insane. "I don't know! How would I know that? Maybe it was hacked. Maybe there is a bug in the system."

The man surprised him by nodding. "Ordinarily, I would say that was impossible, given the quality of the technology and the assurances of the Chinese technicians. But then I would have said that a forgery of this quality, one that scanned in perfectly and seems completely genuine, was impossible. You must have access to equipment and supplies of a quality we didn't imagine and, well, we can't have that, can we now?"

The door opened and a tall man, probably in his fifties, with a pock-marked face walked in. "That's enough," he said.

"What do you mean?" the cheerful man asked. "And who the hell are you? I'll have you arrested."

The newcomer took out a wallet and showed him a badge. "I am the person who is taking over the investigation," he said.

The drab man stared at the badge. "Dirección General De Inteligencia?"

"This is a matter of state security, and under the jurisdiction of DGI," the man said, sitting down.

Carlos flinched. He'd heard of the DGI... it was the Cuban equivalent of the CIA.

"What does this have to do with me?" he asked.

The drab-suited interrogator refused to bow out gracefully. "This is a matter of airport security. This gentleman has a bogus US passport."

The newcomer leaned back. "And how do you know it is bogus?"

The official scowled. "Because it cannot be authentic. Facial recognition identified him as a Cuban citizen, not as this Carlos Reyes it claims he is. If he is Cuban, then the passport is bogus." He looked pleased with himself.

"And what name did you come up with to match his face?"

The official looked again. "Luis... Menores." He picked up the folder Carlos had been carrying. "Not only did the system identify him as Luis Menores, look at this." He shoved the folder across the table. "He was carrying what amounts to a dossier on himself. There is even a copy of his father's birth certificate."

The man in the suit scowled. "And you are certain of this... you would swear that the man sitting here is this Luis Menores?"

"I am certain."

"I see. In that case, I think you've caught yourself a remarkable spy."

"What do you mean?"

"I mean, you are to be congratulated. You managed to capture a man whose skills are far above those of most spies. Not only can he produce excellent passports, but he can be in two places at once. A valuable quality in a spy, don't you think?"

"What do you mean?"

"Our people track the same facial recognition results that you do, although with more energy, amigo. And it is a matter of fact, recorded by the systems, that Luis Menores flew into this airport, arriving just an hour ago. It seems he went through America's airport security in Miami at the same time you took this man in custody."

"Impossible!"

"I prefer to think of it as remarkable. Needless to say, that event is not insignificant, and it set off flags." He waved through the window. "Now, because I am certain you do not believe me, let me introduce you to someone."

The door opened, and a neatly dressed man walked in. Carlos stared in shock. The man looked amazingly like him.

The official looked from this new man to Carlos and back again. "What is this? Are they twins? Is this some kind of test?"

"It isn't a test, amigo. And we are not entirely certain what is going on. But DGI knows that, despite what the system told you, the man you detained is not a Cuban national named Luis Menores." He pointed to the man standing erect, hands behind his back by the door. "I can be certain, because this is

Luis, and he has worked for me for a year now. Naturally, he has been thoroughly investigated, as are all DGI people."

"This is insane," the drab man said.

"Again, such hyperbole, amigo. Our office regards it as uncanny and remarkable. The resemblance is uncanny, and his possession of these documents is remarkable— remarkably rich with possibility. As such, this matter bears further investigation." He smiled. "By us. Therefore, I will take charge of determining the truth about the items you've collected and Senor... Reyes. You, in turn, will forget it ever happened."

"But—"

"It would be unpatriotic to assert that our security system could make such a mistake. I don't think you'd want to suggest that."

"No, but..."

Carlos waved a hand. "Hey, I have to get to Miami. I'm starting a job in Key West. You've already made me miss my flight."

"You have plenty of time," the man said calmly. Then he looked at the drab man. "You can leave now... and take the officer with you. You've heard too much already."

Sullenly, the man stood. He started to grab the folder, then thought better of it. Then, with a forlorn glance at the passport, he nodded at the officer and they headed for the door, with Luis Menores holding the door for the two men as they left. When he closed it the pock-faced man pulled a notebook and pen out of his pocket. He flipped through a few pages, skimming notes, then turned to Carlos.

"You arrived in Cuba by boat."

"Yes. LOFTY AMBITION."

"Which is not your boat."

"No."

He tapped the pen against his cheek. "Tell me: Why did you come here? To Cuba?"

"To see the place where I was born and learn something about my family."

"Nothing more?"

"What do you think I've done wrong?"

The man nudged the passport with his pen. "Pretended to be someone else."

"Who?"

"This passport didn't quite agree with the biometric data our facial recognition systems have collected to associate with this face."

"I don't understand."

"When you went to the bank, shortly after you arrived, the system flagged you. At that time, although the bank wasn't aware of it, the system cross-referenced this face, your face, to my amigo's identity—just as it did here at the airport. That isn't supposed to happen. We've been keeping an eye on you since then."

"But..."

"You see, we thought the same thing the airport officials thought—that someone was using a bogus identity. Worse, it was the identity of one of my men. You can see why that might raise flags." He chuckled. "Going around looking like Luis... in that sense, I suppose you were using a bogus identity."

"Look, I never pretended to be anyone but myself. I didn't call myself Luis Menores."

"What were you doing before you came here?"

"I was crewing a charter boat. You know that. We dropped off the clients in Jamaica and had time to kill. The Captain, my friend Gloria, suggested we come here so I could find out some answers that have bugged me for years."

"It was her idea to come here?" he glanced at his notebook. "... this Gloria Kaufman?"

"Yes." Obviously, they'd gotten details from the port captain.

"Not yours?"

"No. But when she mentioned it, it seemed sensible."

He toyed with the passport, thinking. "Tell me about this job you are supposed to start in Miami."

"Key West."

"What kind of job is it?"

"Nothing important. A low-level job at a marine research center. I just recently got my degree in marine biology. It's a chance to get a foot in the door."

Carlos found himself unable to keep his eyes off Luis Menores. Although he didn't spend a lot of time looking at himself in the mirror, he thought this man could pass for him easily. Apparently, the resemblance was strong enough to fool a facial recognition system.

"You've got a degree in marine biology too, don't you, Luis?"

The man blinked. "Yes. But did he know that?"

The official waved the folder. "His dossier is incomplete, but he learned a few things." He handed it to Reyes, chuckling. "Perhaps on your trips to America you didn't keep as low a profile as you thought, Luis."

Luis held his tongue as he flipped through the pages. Then he clucked and handed it back. "No. This isn't surveillance. It's all clips from Cuban newspapers." He handed it back.

"I found it all at the civil registry," Carlos said.

The man opened it again and slowly flipped the pages. "Interesting. You see, Luis, they sent this man here to learn about you." He pointed at the page. "I didn't know you won a chess tournament when you were young! How is it I didn't know that?"

The man cocked his head. "That was a long time ago."

"And do you know this fellow, this American who looks like you?" he asked, jerking his thumb at Carlos.

A sly grin flashed over the man's face. "I don't know him, and you damn well know that, Enrique."

"But he knows you."

Carlos raised a hand. "No," he said. "I didn't know he existed until now, until I came across it in those newspapers."

Enrique turned to face Carlos. "But why? Why did you dig up information on Luis; what did you learn from his father's birth certificate? What does the CIA want to know about him?"

Carlos held out his hands. "I have no idea what they want to know. I came here to learn about my parents." He pointed to the birth certificate. "That was my father's name, according to the information I showed up in America with. I couldn't find any mention of myself, but later I saw the mention of Luis as his son."

The two men exchanged glances.

"You don't believe me," Carlos said. Convincing them seemed impossible. There were just too many aspects of the situation that were wrong. His story sounded wrong, contrived, even to him.

"Actually, we do," Luis said. "We think you are telling the absolute truth, as you understand it.

The sincerity shocked Carlos, and he looked to see if he could detect sarcasm in the man's face. He saw none. "Then..." he couldn't think of the words to finish his sentence.

"You came because of the dreams," Luis said.

"How did you know?"

Enrique shrugged. "Luis has them too. Another thing you share."

"Is that a problem?"

"It's a relief, actually. We thought it might be a problem that he had dreams of a past in the United States that never existed. It's kept Luis from being sent out for serious field operations." He rubbed his hands together. "But now—"

"You didn't find the answers you were looking for in the files, did you?" Luis asked.

"Nothing. Just about you."

"It was a troubled time. Our parents stood on the wrong side of history and paid the price. You were lost. I was saved."

"Our parents?"

Enrique rubbed his hands together. "You two are twins."

Carlos sat back in his chair. The absurd statement made sense of things. "How—"

Luis rocked his head back. "I was allowed access to some very confidential records. Our parents were part of an insurrection, an attempt to overthrow the government. There was a meeting at the docks. The DGI and some troops put an end to it. Our parents were both killed. I was found and taken to a government orphanage."

"No one knew what happened to you. We knew a boat managed to escape with some people on it, but that was it. It would seem that the state department changed your last name to shield you from us."

"I was adopted and took the family name."

"Ah. Well, it worked out the same."

"Where is your adopted family?" Luis asked.

"They divorced when I was ten. I haven't seen my father since. My mother died last year. So you didn't know I existed?"

"Not really. One lost child wasn't worth a huge search, even though your parents were influential in the counterrevolutionary movement. But then we had one of their sons and were able to raise him as a patriot, a shining example that any Cuban is redeemable."

"Nice rhetoric," Carlos said.

"Thank you. It serves the purpose. As will you."

"Me?"

Enrique pointed at Luis. "We have here a young man who trained as a marine biologist, and also as an operative." He picked up Carlos' passport. "We have here, a genuine US passport that the facial recognition systems agree has a picture of..." he pointed to Luis, "our man on it. Modern technology, combined with two governments that don't share information, has created a situation where you two are somewhat interchangeable. This is too fortunate an opportunity to waste."

"An opportunity?" Carlos was trying to understand.

"Yes," Luis said. "I was just in the US learning about what it would take to establish myself there, to create a new identity. Now I don't have to. If I understand what my jefe is thinking, you've done the work for us. I'll simply take your passport, board the next plane for Miami, and take your new job."

Carlos started to object. "But I—"

"You can stay here," Enrique said. "Rather, you will stay here."

"What about my life?"

"You can have a good life... as a Cuban, the way you were supposed to. We will get you a job." He tapped the pen against his lip. "Yes, at the Guanahacabibes National Park, our marine sanctuary. It will probably be a better job than the one in Key West and it will serve the cause."

"You are swapping us?"

"Precisely. You see, without even knowing about each other, you and Luis have shared dreams, shared visions of Cuba. Now Luis knows the United States rather well, and we are going to send him out, as you, to help the dreams of our leaders come true. And you will have a chance to learn about the real Cuba."

"This will never work," Carlos said. "You can't just swap people without someone noticing."

Enrique grinned. "I think it will." Then he shrugged. "If not, if Luis is discovered, then our governments will claim he took the place of a CIA spy and arrange an exchange. After that things will be much the same as they were, except that you two will have answered this question of your dreams and visions that were not your own." Then he laughed. "Except that they are your own."

A NEW LIFE

Carlos never knew for certain exactly what had been involved in the process of watching him after that bank exchange. He suspected that Enrique had flagged him even before that and possibly both Felix and Juanita were part of keeping track of him. Although they would never admit to anything before he ever knew there was a problem they'd both hinted that he wasn't leaving Cuba. When he showed up again, neither of them seemed shocked to learn he hadn't left Cuba and wasn't going to.

He didn't worry about it though. The angst of leaving was gone. Now his new job would be here, and he let himself be convinced (by Enrique and then Juanita) that it was the best of both worlds. A sense of inevitability came with what he learned.

No one seemed surprised when they were told that he was now called Luis Menores and would be starting work in the marine sanctuary.

The way the discoveries about his life twisted the world made it almost make sense. It didn't even faze him to learn that his new job involved being the sanctuary's liaison under the Bilateral Marine Science Agreement with the US. It didn't even seem odd that he had to coordinate with the representative from the Florida Keys national marine sanctuaries — a Cuban American named Carlos Reyes.

Shortly after he settled into the new job, Juanita was transferred from her department to an administrative role at the sanctuary. They married that spring and spent their honeymoon staying at Fat Mary's, his translation of the name of the only hotel at the remote location, the Villa Maria la Gorda.

By the time he settled into his work, it all seemed natural to him too, even the idea that the US government thought that he (Luis Menores) was a DGI agent.

When he finally met up with his brother again, it was in Havana, at a meeting on the preservation of ecosystems. After a day of boring discussions, they slipped off for a quiet drink and to catch up.

"I was angry about you taking over my life," Carlos admitted.

"It was necessary."

"But it worked out. I have a different vision of Cuba now."

Luis chuckled. "Living in America is far different than I ever imagined... even with what I knew from your dreams," he agreed. "Experiencing it... well, yes it gives me a different vision."

"And the revolution?"

Luis, now Carlos, smiled. "I have a different vision of that now too. My task here might take a long time to accomplish. This damn job keeps me busy enough, anyway."

"Take your time," Carlos, now Luis said. "Take all the time you need."

He was in no rush to abandon the vision he had now.

"Do you still have dreams that are in Cuba?" one of them asked.

"You know I do," the other answered.

Rob Phelps, Gisteen Porter, LauraJane Phelps, and J. Lee Porter

A huge thank you to my travel partners for this trip to Havana (not to mention five other international trips!)

Also, a big thank you to our hosts, Maru y Tony, and their wonderful Casa de Familia. We hope to visit again once Covid restrictions are over.

Merida, Mexico

It's fitting that I write this at 3:53am after drinking a bottle of el Jimador blanco, but sometimes the cheap booze of a foreign country provides excellent insight. Due to health reasons, I retired at an age that most would consider very early, 37. Sounds nuts right? I was told by a doctor in my late teens that I would not live to see 40. It sobered me up, mentally at least. I worked two or three full-time jobs, usually 100+ hours a week until I could retire. I spent every free moment at my various jobs reading travel books to make mental lists of the countries I wanted to visit, the food I could sample, the various drinking options, and of course the exotic women I wanted to enjoy, etc... it became my life's obsession.

I was having financial problems a year or so after retirement, as that is what happens after a bad divorce and alimony, I ended up in Chelem, Yucatan at a nice house a block from the beach, and when the rent+food and utilities exceeded $1000 a month (a lot of money for a new writer), we moved to an even cheaper house in Progreso. As Progreso is a small town we met an Uber driver who became our friend and took us on shopping trips to Merida... oh my is Merida an amazing city, before setting off on my travels I had never even heard of the city of Merida.

What is it like? Hot. fucking hot, it's brutal, but I am a disabled giant with crippling arthritis, so, it's actually great for me. I made friends with a number of men whose names I will never mention, but one thing was always consistent, they knew people, worked with former presidents, worked at secret bases, on secret projects, and some had done secret missions, one took a grenade, one encountered a car bomb...

The more booze that is absorbed, the less the unwritten agreement of quiet service is observed.

I had done some work for an agency at one point and was visited in my normal bar south of Tallahassee by a non-regular that was very keen on the work I was doing. It was sensitive at the time but I stuck to my cover story... when I did, even while greatly intoxicated, he thanked me and winked, and left... It was also the last time during that project I allowed myself to visit a public establishment when imbibing. Sometimes it's safer just to drink at home.

No matter where you are in the world as an expat, it seems you are always sitting next to someone at the bar on the run, or on a mission, but always, always they have a good story. Buy the person next to you a beer and hear them out, and if their story sucks, buy them a bottle of cheap Tequila and let them make something interesting up.

I hope you enjoy the story that such people have inspired CANTINA EXPATS, based in my current home of Merida Yucatan.

Cheers,

-Lee

1.

Raquel Hernandez put on her apron and took a stack of small, carved wooden bowls down the shelf. She opened a large bag of peanuts she'd gotten at the mercado on her way to the cantina and began pouring them into the bowls.

Soon, after the lunch hour, her regulars would start arriving; they would begin drifting in, depositing themselves on the same barstools or at the same table they sat at every day. Not that Pisano, Raquel's small neighborhood bar in Merida, Mexico, on the Yucatan Peninsula would be booming, but she business would be steady, the demands on her constant, and this quiet hour was her time to get ready.

They came like clockwork. Of course, that's what made them regulars. They didn't just show up every day, they tended to sit in the same seats, drink the same drinks, and have more or less the same conversations.

There weren't many of them, just five she counted as regulars, and two more that qualified as semi-regulars. All seven were all retired, or at least unemployed gringos. They weren't a bad lot, and mostly she liked them. They came for cheap booze and local atmosphere in a place a far cry from the upmarket bars that catered to the tourists who came to Mexico to party in the same kinds of hotels and bars they had in the US and Europe. Her customers weren't particularly demanding and, happily for Raquel, they all drank steadily enough to pay her overhead. They kept her in business. That meant that the locals who came in for a beer or tequila were pure profit — except for Hector.

Hector was not profit, except when the gringos, who liked him, bought him a round. No, Hector was family, sort of. A *primo*, a distant cousin, the son of a cousin.

The gringos called him her shirt-tail relative, which made no sense at all. What did clothing have to do with *la familia*?

Whenever the gringos ignored him, Hector would wait until the times when she was busiest to order himself a drink. When he finished it, he would wait until another whirl of activity and sneak out. It was a game. He'd pretend he forgot to pay and she'd pretend she didn't notice that he hadn't.

She checked her stock and wiped her hands on her apron. After she checked her long, black hair in the mirror, she sighed. "*Estoy lista*," she sighed. Ready.

When the men started filtering in, they nearly always arrived in about the same sequence. She'd get them their drinks (almost always the same drinks), and then spend her day refilling their glasses and the bowls of peanuts, keeping track of their tabs (noting that Ricky needed to settle his soon. He was honest but forgetful) and watching and listening to them.

With her preparations complete, her afternoons were lovely. It was like having a private theater, only her actors paid her to perform their self-created roles, to write their own dialog. And, my, did they have grand stories to tell — stories of adventure and danger, or innovation and corporate intrigue. Typically, the one telling the story was forced to leave out significant details 'for security reasons' or because of nondisclosure agreements they had signed.

Ricky came in first, a toothpick in his mouth and a pack of cigarettes that she never saw him open in his hand. He went straight to the barstool by the wall and, as he'd done for four years now, folded his thin, almost emaciated frame onto it and leaned against the wall, with the top of his head brushing the bottom of the large, golden-painted frame that held her print of a painting of a statue of Francisco Pancho Villa charging on horseback.

She wondered if the pictures showed Pancho charging Blackjack Pershing or running from him. Or maybe running from the federales. If you believed the television, outlaws did a lot more running than robbing. It seemed a rather pointless life, but then most were. Still, she liked what Pancho Villa represented.

Chris came in next, with his ubiquitous newspaper tucked under his arm. Without seeing it, with no need to see it, she knew it would be The Guardian and that he bought it at the newsstand in one of the five-star hotels. Sometimes he had lunch there with a totally different crowd of friends. At least, that was what he said.

Just as she finished opening a beer for Ricky and pouring Chris a tequila (having him clap his hands with delight as he always did), a newcomer stepped in through the door. His entrance broke the rhythm of her day in a delightful way. It was always nice to have a new actor bring in fresh dialog and introduce new complexities to an otherwise rather slow-developing plot.

It was fun to watch a new customer come in, see other gringos and assume a pose — he wasn't posing for her. Not yet. When they came in a local cantina for the first time, expats saw the other expats first. And each had his own way of presenting himself to the other gringos.

The clothes he wore and the way he moved, hesitating cautiously and then walking in a calculated deliberate stride, were nothing new. She called this style of American "the spy." Everything seemed calculated to give him the air of a man with deep secrets. Another "if I tell you who I really am, I'll have to kill you" wannabe.

He brought it off well, though and his clothes were just that much more on target. That made him slightly different from her regulars. Where they favored t-shirts with Hard Rock Café or Tecate emblazoned on the chest, and ball caps, he wore a loud Hawaiian shirt and a straw hat. Otherwise, he favored the standard expat uniform of ratty jeans (an official option to cargo shorts), sandals, and expensive shades. But those differences worked well. He stood out by not standing out. And yet, clearly he was trying to look cool and different — just like the rest of them.

She found him relatively good looking enough that, while he checked out the room, checking out the patrons, she gave him a second glance. This time she noted other details, deciding that she liked that he hadn't gone for the silver Willie Nelson ponytail or shaved head, the most common hairstyle options among the expats. This guy was old school, with his fine brown hair cropped short. And he was clean-shaven.

It didn't hurt that was fit and younger than most of the regulars, maybe about forty. His deep tan suggested he hadn't just flown in from Seattle on vacation. No, he'd been bumming around the tropics a bit, or maybe Florida. Or maybe he'd sailed to Mexico on a boat from Texas or even Cuba.

When he finally completed his survey of the room, he selected the table she would have picked for him — the one at the back of the room, facing the door. If he'd asked, she would have said: "This is the one you want, Senor."

He sat and folded his hands on the table. Waiting.

Time to learn more. The first encounter. She walked to the table, letting her hips sway. "What can I get you, Senor?" she asked.

"Rum," he said.

That was different. "You drink rum in Mexico? Not tequila?"

"Rum. What kinds do you have?"

"We got two kinds, and both are shitty."

"No good ones?"

"Nope. No one ever orders rum."

"Then you pick the better of them for me."

"White?"

"Fine. Bring the bottle and a glass. A little lemon and sugar and ice."

She shrugged and went to the bar. The man hadn't flirted with her or tried to impress her. That impressed her.

When she brought his order, she wiped her hands on her flowered skirt and pulled her shoulders back. He was watching her after all. Good, he was human. "Been in Mexico long?"

"Just a few weeks this time."

"I haven't seen you before." And she would have.

"I was in Mexico City and Guadalajara until today. On business."

"Merida is much better," she said.

"Is it?"

"Cleaner, better."

"If you say so."

His abruptness annoyed her. She could count on the two regulars sitting at the bar to be flattered if she lingered and talked with them. With no encouragement, they would be more than delighted to regale her with their tall tales, filled to the rim with gringo bullshit. But she'd heard most of the good stories a few times now. They'd tell them sober, then get drunk and tell them again, sometimes with a different ending. That was fun, but new stories would be much better.

Men were such fools. Even Terry. As much as she cared about him, she couldn't understand him, getting himself in trouble the way he did. And that made her a fool because for caring about him.

"You don't know Merida?"

"Not really."

"Why come here then?"

"Like I said, I'm on business," the man said.

"Monkey business like the rest of these men, I bet."

He squeezed lemon into his glass, added a spoonful of sugar, then dropped two ice cubes in and poured the rum over them, filling it about half full. She wondered why he didn't just fill it to the top. Men had these things they did. Crazy shit.

He gave her a thin smile. "Real business. I'm looking for someone and heard he came to Merida."

"I'm looking for a man too," she laughed. "And I can give you a little tip, there are seldom any men in here. Not real men. We mostly get the Gringo Underground."

He gave her a puzzled look. "What is that?"

She nodded toward the bar, giving him a sly smile. "I mean those men and their friends. I have it on good authority that they are very brave men who have saved the world from destruction, often by themselves, but sometimes with others. They claim to be a team, but they all, every single one of them spent years doing undercover work, running covert operations, and arresting drug cartels, all the while working as a dentist in Salt Lake City and raising a family. They are amazing macho men, no?"

The newcomer laughed. "I see."

"The only reason they didn't win the Nobel Prize for peace and science is that they are too humble to let the world at large know their exploits. But I am more fortunate as they happily tell me of these things — many times over."

He sipped his drink, his expression sour. "I can't believe that you actually like to listen to the stories these guys spout."

She laughed. "It is fine and even amusing when I am bored, which is often. Serving beer and pouring whisky is not the most demanding task in the world and sometimes what they say amuses me."

"If you say so."

He didn't believe her any more than she believed the stories.

"Tell me about the man you are looking for. Perhaps he comes in here."

The gringo gave her a sideways look, then shrugged and pulled a photo out of his shirt pocket and handed it to her. "Sure, maybe you've seen him."

Guessing she already knew who was in the photo, she braced herself, not wanting to act as if she recognized him. She stared at the grainy image. It wasn't a great shot of him, but it was clearly Terry. Even his new beard wasn't nearly enough of a disguise. She handed it back. "Sorry. I don't remember seeing this man, but we do a good business here and customers tend to blur together," she said.

He raised an eyebrow, giving her a cynical smile. "You telling me all gringos look alike?" he asked, laughing.

"I didn't say that." She handed the photo back. "You showing a photo like that tells me he isn't a business associate."

"No?"

"I think you are hunting this man."

He grinned. "What if I am?"

"What do you do when you find him?"

The man tucked the photo back in his shirt pocket. "Depends a lot on him. He and I need to come to an understanding about some things, about what he wants to do. It's totally up to him." He winked. "Tell him that for me."

"If I see him, I will. What is his name?"

He took the picture out again and put it on the table face up. "The name of the man you don't remember? He's used many names since he left the states."

"That must be confusing, no? For him as well as you."

"I'm sure he prefers being confused to being caught. For me... I have this picture. His name doesn't matter."

"So you are the police? Or maybe a bounty hunter?"

"I'm a businessman."

"In the business of finding another man."

He shrugged. "Sometimes. Now."

She pursed her lips and bent over to look at the photo again. "He doesn't look so dangerous. Cute, but not dangerous."

"I didn't say he was dangerous. I'm not tracking an escaped murderer." He paused.

"Then why track him here?"

"There are people who consider him a danger of a different sort." The man sipped his drink. "I'm told that my associate has been here, in Merida for a few weeks now."

She nodded toward the bar. "You should ask them. They claim to see everything that happens in Merida."

"Being secret agents and all?"

She sighed. "Not all are field agents, Senor. That wouldn't be reasonable. No, one of them is a master forger. Ricky, the tall man, is the go-to man if you are in the market for a new passport or government identification."

He glanced up at her. "What kind of ID?"

She shrugged. "Some of them find the girls won't take their word for the histories they claim, so Ricky provides them with CIA credentials, things like that."

The man laughed. "Probably makes them on a laptop from a template he got on the internet."

She smiled. "Perhaps. Ricky does a lot with computers. But I bet you have a nice-looking government ID."

He sat back. "I told you—"

"I think you are lying to me."

He cocked his head. "You are something, lady. Pursuing that kind of thinking can get you in trouble."

She laughed. "I know. I hear this all the time. If I figure out who you are, you'll have to kill me, no?"

"No. I don't care if you know who I am. It doesn't matter. I'm just a worker bee. What's important is finding the man I'm after."

"Does he know you are after him?"

"Me? No. He doesn't know me, but if he doesn't think someone, maybe a few people are after him, he is dumber than I think."

"You think I can help you find him."

He licked his lips. "He has a reputation for charming ladies and telling... amusing stories about himself."

"Are any of the stories true?"

"Just the ones that end badly — for other people, so far."

"Now you want this one to end badly for him."

"No. I don't care about him. I only care about finishing this job so I can get paid. And if you help me, I would pay you."

"You should consider talking to those men."

He glanced toward the bar, appraising the men more carefully. "Those two? They looked like, what did you say, retired dentists?"

"That's Chris, the big man on your left. Had a dental practice in the Midwest somewhere."

"And the other guy?"

"Ricky. He claims to have run an IT business in Sacramento for many years. Says that he sold it for a small fortune." She laughed. "Moving here, it became a large fortune. According to Chris, Ricky's biggest clients were the state — the motor vehicles people and the records department. That's how he gets information... something called a back door."

He looked surprised. "If that's true, that means the great State of California has a serious security breach."

She touched her lips, hushing him. "If you say so, perhaps, but I wouldn't mention that. Who knows if it is true. If it is —

" she flashed him a dark look, "you might not want them to know that you know. *Verdad*?"

The man chewed at his lip as he picked up the rum bottle and refilled his drink.

Raquel wandered back to the bar to make sure that the regulars were kept happy. They'd understand her chatting with a newbie, and even would appreciate it, but drinking was serious business and their drinks were dangerously low.

"What's his story?" Chris asked her as she refilled his tequila, got Ricky a beer, and topped up the peanuts in the bowl between them.

"He's looking for a guy," she said.

"Terry?" he asked.

"Maybe."

"Name?"

She shrugged.

Ricky swung around and glanced at the man, then pulled out his cell phone. "Hector, *como esta?* I have a little job for you," he muttered into it. "This one is a catch and release. New guy in the bar now."

When he rang off, he smiled. "Your cousin will be outside so he can lend a hand with our research. We should know more by tonight," he told them. "Warn Terry. He better pack a bag in case he needs to go on a trip until we sort this out."

Chris slapped the bar. "Like the old days, huh, Ricky?"

He made a face, his eyes flicking toward Raquel. "What old days?"

She smirked. "Right. You can't talk about it." Except when they are drunk, which was every night after about nine.

"For now," Chris said with a glance at the newcomer, "we wait."

"And drink," Ricky said, taking a long pull from his beer.

2.

Ricky held up a gray, laminated ID card and squinted at it. "It says that his name is Drummond. Pete Drummond."

"Could be a fake name," Chris said. "Don't believe everything you read."

Ricky ignored him and flicked the card against his fingers, studying the patterns in the background. "I wonder what speedy print place got the contract to make these."

"Speedy print?"

"It's not a high-quality print job. Hell, I did more sophisticated wedding invitations when my sister married that asshole she's with."

"Then it is fake?" Raquel asked.

Ricky snorted. "Actually, no. It's real. Government issue crap. My tax dollars at work, or how they'd be used if I paid any taxes. Ever."

"What agency?" Chris asked.

Ricky read the long name of the issuing authority. "Some federal prosecutor's office in DC."

"That makes no sense," Raquel said. "Terry is a whistleblower. He is in touch with the people he provides information to."

Ricky pursed his lips, staring at the card. "Maybe he isn't giving them everything they want and they sent this hombre to revoke his free pass."

He handed the card to Raquel who looked at it. It was the guy's photo. "He should be back in soon." She carefully slipped it into the wallet Hector had brought her, ensuring she put it in the same slot it came from, facing the same way it had been. Who knew what the man might notice?

"How will you get it back to him?" Chris asked.

Ricky rocked his head back, eyes closed and picturing it. "Hector slipped it right out of the guy's back pocket and he never noticed. He promised he took nothing from it — not one dollar."

Raquel nodded. "He'll backtrack, looking for it, and when he comes in I will give it to him. After all, he left it here accidentally and I found it under the table after he left."

"Where were you when I was working, *mi amor*?" Chris asked her, sighing dramatically and giving her a bogus love-struck look. "We could have been a hell of a team."

"She would do the work and you would take the credit," Ricky said. "You know that's how it would go, Chris."

A heavyset Frenchman came in, the thick and pungent smell of Galois cigarettes preceding him. He went to a table near the bar, sat heavily in a plastic chair facing them, and leaned his elbows on the table. "Who is working and why are they doing that?" he asked. "I demand to know."

"Who do you think does the work?" Raquel asked him. "And for so little money, too."

"Claude doesn't like work," Chris said. "It makes him itchy."

"It makes me nervous," Claude said, smiling as Raquel brought him one glass containing a double shot of cheap whisky and another with water back. "Work is evil." He sat up and smiled at Raquel. "Bless you, my child. I hope you aren't working for these degenerates."

"I work all the time," she said.

"But this is intellectual work," Ricky said. "We are uncovering an undercover agent's cover."

"We think he's an investigator for a federal prosecutor," Chris said. "Or a bounty hunter."

"He after Terry?" Claude asked.

"Seems so."

Claude sipped his whisky. "Should prove interesting. What's the line?"

"The line?" Raquel asked.

"On how long it takes before we get rid of him. Can't be a long one, not more than a few days, right? I mean it isn't like he is CIA or one of those other bulldog types."

"He could still be CIA," Chris said. "It's not like he'd announce that."

"What would the CIA want with Terry?" Raquel asked. Chris shrugged.

"Might even be here freelancing, for all we know. Maybe after a bounty."

"There's a bounty on Terry now?" They looked up and saw that another regular, an ugly man named Ralph had come in to sit, as always, across from Claude. He had a portable chess set with him and put it on the table. "If there is, I hope it is substantial. My bank account is getting a little low."

"Who knows?" Ricky said. "And it's a two-fold problem. Is there a bounty, worthy of going after? And, if there is, how hard would it be to collect it?"

"I imagine that Terry might object to us collecting it," Claude said.

"I always thought Terry's story was shit," Chris said. "I didn't see him as a whistleblower."

"Even if he is, why would a real whistleblower hide in Merida," Ricky said. "He'd figure to be in witness protection in Omaha or something."

"Part of his deal?" Chris asked. "Maybe he hates Omaha or isn't popular there."

Raquel had been listening with half her attention, but now they were looking at her, waiting for her to explain things. "I don't know anything more than you," she said. "Don't mix me up in all this."

"You must know something," Chris said.

She needed to shut him up. "Terry said he has proof of some corporate wrongdoing and he's got to stay low profile for a time while the authorities verify it."

"Either Terry's story is bullshit, or someone leaked information about him to the wrong people," Chris said. "Someone is after him and their man is right here, right now."

"Very right now," Ricky said, nodding toward the door. The man was walking in, looking stressed.

"Lose something?" Raquel called out.

He let out a breath. "I can't find my wallet."

She held it up and his eyes widened. "I found it under the table. You must've dropped it when you paid."

"No, I—"

"I think you put it on the chair next to you when you put that photo you showed me back in your pocket."

"Photo?" Ricky asked. "What sort of photo?"

"A man he is looking for."

"It's business."

"Is he hiding from your... business?" Chris asked.

"He doesn't need to. It's to his advantage to talk with me."

"Show them," Raquel said.

Hesitating slightly, he took out the photo and handed it to Ricky. He gave it a thoughtful stare, puckered his lips, shook his head, and passed it to Chris. Chris did the same, letting Claude and Ralph have their turns.

"None of you knows him?"

"Can't say we do."

Chris put up a hand. "You know, I saw a guy, might've been him a couple of days ago. I was having lunch in the restaurant at the Hotel Victoria. A couple of gringos came in, and I think one of them was him." He shrugged. "That's not much help, I guess."

"I'll check it out," the man said.

"If we see him, if he did come in here, we could tell him to get in touch with you," Ricky said. "If we knew who the fuck you were and where you are staying."

He nodded, considering. "Pete Drummond," he said. "I do work for law firms. Serving subpoenas, chasing down witnesses, shit like that. I'm supposed to find this guy, get him to call the lawyers. I'm staying over at Hotel Maya Yucatan."

"Must be a cheap-assed law firm you work for," Chris said.

"I work freelance and expenses come out of my pocket. That's why I'm in a rush. I need to find this clown and get home."

Ricky tented his fingers, then looked at Drummond and picked up his beer. "What happens if you don't find him?"

"I don't get a bonus."

"To him?"

Drummond shrugged again. "No idea. Look, I don't know what the deal is, why they want me to find him. There's a shit ton of lawyer-client confidentiality stuff involved. Or so they tell me. My need to know is about zero, apparently. I'm supposed to get him on the phone with the lawyer."

Ricky picked up a peanut and dropped it in his beer. "Didn't float. I thought it would."

"It didn't the last two times you did that," Chris said. "Why would it now?"

Ricky stared at Drummond. We could help, but it would be a hell of a lot easier to convince someone to meet with you if they knew what it was about."

Drummond nodded. "I need to call in. I'll tell my boss that you mentioned that. See what he says."

"Have you got copies of the photo?" Claude asked. "We can put out the word. If he's dining at the Victoria, someone will have seen him around town, maybe even know who he is."

Drummond nodded. "Keep it. I've got a few." He took out a card. "Have a pen and paper?"

Raquel handed him the pencil she used for keeping accounts and a paper bag. The game was getting complicated, but interesting. He scribbled a number on the bag. Ricky took it, recopying the number and then tearing the bag apart, handing them each a piece, including Raquel.

Drummond glanced around. "I bought a local burner phone when I got to Mexico. You can reach me at that number. A lead that takes me to him is worth a hundred bucks."

"We will pass it around," Ricky assured him.

"I'll go check the Victoria," he said.

Raquel slapped the counter. "Wait a minute!" He stopped and looked at her. "My pencil," she said.

He handed it over with a sheepish grin, then he left.

"What a cheapskate," Claude muttered. "A hundred dollars for betraying Terry?"

"Better than being expected to do it out of patriotic duty," Chris said. "I never even got a bonus."

"Why would a dentist get a bonus?" Raquel asked him. "They charge so much that people fly down here to get dental work done."

Chris simmered a bit, but he'd get over it. He always did. It wasn't quite enough to forgive him for being a dentist, but almost.

"We need to do some research," Ricky said. "I'll go see what I can find on Drummond. Chris, have you got any leads you can follow?"

Chris gave them one of those half smiles where one side comes up and the other corner of the mouth stays put, the way it does when someone has had a stroke. "I'm going to check out Terry's story."

"If you could do that, why haven't you before?" Claude asked.

"No reason to before now. I thought it was just bullshit. Now, well, if someone is after him, there might be an interesting twist to it. Like, maybe the real story is better than the whistleblower."

"If his story checks, look for rumors about someone putting out a contract on him," Ricky said. "That Drummond looks special ops to me, not just some freelance investigator or messenger."

"Because he is fit?" Raquel asked. "Just because the rest of you can't be bothered?"

"Exactly," Ralph said. "A guy hanging out in Mexico who bothers to stay in shape has an agenda of some kind, or a need to be fit."

"It's hard work," Claude said.

"How would you know?" Raquel asked, immediately regretting the cheap shot.

He let it slide, and her band of regular customers drank up and left the bar depressingly empty.

3.

With the regulars gone, Raquel called Terry and told him what she knew. "Your gringo crew is researching to find out what the real story behind his appearance is," she said.

"My crew? I barely know those bums."

"Still."

"What are they doing?"

"Looking into who the guy is. They find his story shaky." And yours. But she passed on telling him what Chris was up to — investigating Terry's story. It wouldn't help his attitude. "Ricky asked Chris to find out if there are any rumors about someone putting out a contract on you."

"Shit. Those assholes will just draw attention to me."

"Probably." That did seem likely. "They plan to meet here tonight after dinner. You might want to come and hear what they've learned."

"Maybe," he said. "I'm having dinner with one of my contacts. Maybe I can find out something on my own. If the news is inconclusive, I'll come by. Otherwise, you can tell me when you get home."

"So the prosecutors do have someone here? I thought you said you called them and stayed in touch that way."

"They decided to send a go-between. I complained about how they are dragging their feet and told them I can't hide forever. They said they were sending someone to sit down face-to-face and tell me where we are on this and talk about the next steps. He flew in yesterday."

"Be careful. If the people in Washington sent him, this Drummond might know about him. That might be how he knew you had come to Merida. He could follow the guy to the meeting."

"Good point," Terry said. "There might be a leak. Killing a whistleblower isn't unheard of."

"I took a photo of his identification. The name might be fake, but it has his picture."

"That might help," Terry said.

The call hadn't improved her concern. Something in Terry's voice had sounded more disappointed than upset or concerned. That didn't make a lot of sense.

Before she could analyze it more, a busload of tourists 'discovered' the cantina. Primo Hector had convinced his Indian friend Ram, who owned the tour bus, to deliver ten middle-aged housewives and three overweight men to her door. They were guests at the Hilton who wanted to escape for a day. Ram took them around.

Ram would get a free meal for bringing the tourist to the cantina and Hector would expect a commission for arranging it, but Raquel would make good money, and he would deserve it.

Putting on her cheery 'welcome to Mexico' face she sat the tourists at four tables away from the bar. The noisy, happy people started in enthusiastically, drinking a lot of tequila, the men taking it straight and most of the women wanting Margaritas.

"Much better than some stinking museum, no?" Hector asked them.

They all agreed. They seemed to like Hector.

After an hour they were hungry. She called cousin Isabelle, who ran a restaurant next door. Isabelle was happy to prepare and send over six taco plates, chips, and salsa. Raquel would charge them twice whatever Isabelle charged her.

From a business standpoint, it was a brilliant day. Her nagging worries about Terry, about Drummond, slipped into the background until Ram told his herd it was time to go.

As they filed out, leaving excellent tips and flashing smiles, Ricky and Chris returned, taking up their designated posts.

"Whew, that was close," Chris said. "We almost got touristed."

"Yes, it seems my cantina was discovered," she said.

"Hector bribed Ram so he'd get a commission?"

She nodded. "It's the price of discovery when the online sites have never heard of you."

"You need a website," Chris said.

She ignored the ugly thought and put out drinks and peanuts for them, then set about cleaning up. By the time she'd cleared and wiped down the tables, Claude and Ralph were in their seats.

"Well, as we have a quorum, I call this meeting to order," Ricky said.

"What did you learn?" Raquel asked.

Ricky shook his head. "I've got people trying to use facial recognition to figure out who he is, but he isn't working for that prosecutor's office. No one by that name is."

"Someone clearly is bad enough at forgery to make a crappy ID card," Ralph said.

"That office doesn't have the authority to carry out an overseas operation. They'd need clearance from the State Department, and they don't."

"Doesn't mean they can't hire a guy off the books," Claude said.

"True. I can't understand why they would, but then if Terry is involved with the stuff he says, I sure couldn't find a record of it. It's either sealed for some reason, such as security, or he isn't working with them."

"He said a go-between was meeting him tonight," Raquel told them. Terry hadn't said to keep it quiet.

"What did you find, Chris?" Ricky asked.

"Crickets." He held up a hand, his thumb touching the tip of his forefinger. "Zilch is what I found out. There is nothing on the dark web, or in any chatter about a hit on Terry, or anyone like him, or even on anyone in Merida," Chris said. "If something is happening, it's being kept within a single agency on a need-to-know basis."

"Amazing," Claude said. "Even when they try to do that, people know."

"No one knows about this."

Raquel heard conviction in his voice. He sounded sure of himself. "What do we do?" she asked, making it an open question to all of them.

"We wait," Ricky said. "We can't make assumptions."

"Don't even know enough to make any," Chris said.

"We could have a chopper standing by to get Terry out of here," Ralph said.

They looked at him. "And go where?" Claude asked finally. "They seem able to find him. Moving around is risky. At the moment, they, whoever they are, don't seem to know where he is. If he starts moving, they have access to cameras, GPS, flight logs."

"I propose we have another round and see if anything new emerges," Chris said.

So they did, but no new information came up. Nor did it with the next few rounds. In fact, when they all staggered home, the only insight Raquel had was that she'd forgotten to press Ricky to pay his tab.

Thank God for the tourists Hector had brought.

Going home after closing, she found her little casita empty.

She'd half expected it. Dealing with a clientele of expats on a regular basis, she'd learned a great deal about their natures. Mostly, she'd learned not to expect them to be reliable. Not the ones who moved to Mexico and lived on the cheap, at least. They were the ones she knew.

She'd thought she'd known Terry... a little. But coming home and finding he wasn't there, his clothes and duffle bag gone, told her she'd been wrong. She'd never believed his story, but she'd never really doubted it, either. He came from a different world, and the things he told her were too far outside of her experience for her to judge them.

It was just his story. He'd been working for a high-tech company that stole information from the government and sold it to the highest bidder. It sounded like something those companies did. Terry claimed he had gone to the authorities and they told him they needed to check his story out. He had to hide.

For all she knew, even now, his story might be somewhat true. Whatever was going on, he didn't trust her with the truth and he was afraid. What he was afraid of, she didn't know.

4.

Drummond came in and sat at the table he'd taken the day before. She never understood the gringo penchant for sameness, but then, as with everything else, she was familiar with a small subset of gringos. Still, over the years she had known a few.

She fixed a tray with rum, lime, and sugar and took it to him, setting the things on his table. "He's gone," she said.

"Gone?"

"He left Merida yesterday."

Realization flooded Drummond's brown eyes. "Shit."

"I don't think he would have met with you anyway."

"Can't blame him." He turned his attention to fixing a drink and took a long sip.

"Why not? You said you didn't know what it was about?"

"I called the law firm and told them I needed to overcome the suspicion of people protecting him." He smiled, and she nodded. "Turns out, telling you probably wouldn't have helped. I was supposed to give him some papers. See, he is being sued for divorce and for fraud."

"Fraud?"

"He sold apartments in a new building that was going up. It was a real nice one and his price was irresistible. Unfortunately, he didn't own the building or have an arrangement with the owners. Before anyone got wise, he left the country."

"So he wasn't a whistleblower."

"It seems his wife was. She went to the feds, turned him in, and filed for divorce. One-stop revenge for him keeping the money a secret from her."

"Then he gets away with it?"

"No. The feds managed to find the bank accounts and seize them. The people will get part of their money back." His phone beeped and Drummond glanced at it. "Seems they caught him boarding a plane for Panama. They are taking him to Mexico City and he will be held for extradition."

"Then your work is done?"

"Seems to be. Time to be moving on."

"To another job?"

He nodded.

The regulars came in and nodded at Drummond. Raquel brought them their drinks and gave them the news.

"We heard," Ricky said. "If he's smart he won't fight extradition. He'll be safer in a jail in the US."

Her assessment of her gringo squad needed revision. They did have access to a lot of information, and they didn't get it from reading the Guardian or watching newsfeeds.

"Then that's the end of Terry," she said. She missed him already.

"Roger Wendall," Ricky said. "That's his real name."

And that was the end of Terry... for her.

5.

The cantina settled back into its slow rhythm. Raquel was lonely for Terry at times, but glad the drama was over. Terry's name slowly disappeared from conversations at the bar until the news broke that Roger Wendall had been shot.

"Only the Federales would transport him from one secure location to another for no reason," Claude moaned. "They probably announced it in advance."

"Neither location was ever secure," Chris said. "We knew about the Trotsky safehouse years ago. It was nice to have that in our pocket."

Raquel thought to cry for Terry, but it was confusing. Terry had disappeared and she didn't know this Roger Wendall. So she just raised the prices on the cantina's drinks, instead.

A hot and sultry afternoon a few days later, a newcomer came in. More like Drummond than her squad, but dressed all in khaki, as if he'd grown up on safari movies and confused Mexico with Africa. He sat at the same table Drummond had taken. Happily, he drank tequila. The markup on tequila was wonderful.

"I'm looking for a man," he said. "Maybe you've seen him?"

When he showed her a picture of Drummond, it barely registered on the surprise scale.

"He was here for a time."

"I know."

"Then you know he left."

"I hoped he'd be back here." He flashed dark eyes at her, drinking her in. "I could see he might want to."

"He said he was on to another job."

The man nodded. He took a business card from his pocket and put it on the table. "He's a very dangerous man. If you do see him, keep your distance and call me. That number will come straight to me."

She looked at the card. Trace Munrow, CIA, it said. It also said he was a special agent.

"You want me to find him so you can kill him?"

He shrugged. "The man is a professional assassin. Did you hear about the gringo that got murdered in Mexico City?"

"Si," she said.

"He did it."

"It's done now. Too late to stop him, no?"

"He's a contract killer. He could come back here. He might kill all of you to cover his tracks."

"He left no tracks here," she said. "But if I see him, I'll be glad to call you."

She went back behind the bar. Only after the man left did she take Ricky a fresh beer and refill Chris's drink. Then she put the card the man had given her on the bar.

"Gentlemen of the gringo squad, here is your new assignment. Is this man real? He claims Drummond is a contract killer."

As her regulars looked at the card and began tossing out ideas and plans, Raquel smiled. Things had changed in Merida. No question about that. After they vetted him and the situation, if the man turned out to be CIA, if he was telling the truth (fat chance of that, but...) then she would call him. Not that she had any idea where Drummond was, but this Munrow... well, he was definitely cute.

THE END

Thailand

. . . .

This story is fiction, although it is true that Thailand can follow people home, or wherever else they go. In our case, I met up with Lee and Gigi at Elephant Bay, on Koh Chang Island. The idea was to finish the final draft of CRYPTO CITIZENS. I was struggling with some parts and we needed face time.

I caught a flight from New Mexico (via LA and Shanghai) to Bangkok and a shuttle to Koh Chang. There we worked and played. It was a time soaked in Thai whisky, relaxed by massages, and embroiled in the chaos and pageantry of a number of exciting Muay Thai matches.

I was studying for my black belt in karate and took advantage of getting in some Muay Thai training and we got the novel done.

In the evening, sitting on the bungalow porch and looking out at the Gulf of Thailand, we came up with this story. Wherever I go, I think about the other people who have gone there and the ones who live there. As writers, Lee and I can't resist turning our thoughts into stories.

And now this story follows us everywhere.

Ed

"Means must be subsidiary to ends and to our desire for dignity and value."

— *Ludwig Mies van der Rohe*

I stood at the buffet at the hotel, staring numbly at a bewildering array of food. So much of it was strange, exotic, and, for me, a little unsettling. I suppose it wasn't exotic for the place. After all, I was in Bangkok, Thailand, trying to sort out breakfast on a gorgeous morning.

Some of the offerings... well, I wasn't even sure what they were. Bowls overflowed with strange, prickly, bright-colored fruits (even purple) and porridge dishes arranged with bowls overflowing with odd bits of things (seaweed?) that seemed to be condiments. There was an orange juice, labeled 'blood orange juice' that did look disconcertingly like blood.

Looking at it all made me shudder. I want my breakfast to be comforting, not an adventure or some grand experiment. All that choice and strangeness made my stomach tense.

Fortunately, the hotel also offered an entire table of more familiar offerings. As I heaped my plate high with scrambled eggs and bacon, rolls, and potatoes, I thanked my lucky stars that I'd insisted we stay at a five-star hotel. When we arranged the trip, Jake had tried to talk me into letting him book us into a local hotel.

"It would give us a chance to experience something more like the real thing—the real Asia," he said.

That kind of experience, being immersed in an entirely new world, a different culture, sounded dreadful. The only exotic experience I wanted was one that would make me, a rather finicky and particular Westerner, comfortable while away from home. Despite the higher cost, I'd insisted on staying at the Marriott. "I want clean, white sheets on the bed, well-appointed rooms, and familiar food," I told him. And I'd gotten it, even if a lot of unfamiliar food was along for the ride.

As I turned and headed for a table, Jake staggered into the dining room, looking the worse for wear.

"Hey, sleepy head," I teased.

"Right," he said. "One hell of night."

"That's one way to describe it," I said.

The day before, we'd met with an Australian businessman named Ralph. After discussing business, he had insisted on showing us the town. As his notion of entertainment mean a tour of sleazy bars and nightlife, and as much as Jake had drunk, seeing him up and about this early surprised me.

"You could've slept in. Our flight back home isn't until early this afternoon, and the hotel isn't even 20 miles from the airport."

He sat down, looking at me oddly. "Typical that you'd know that and not much else about Bangkok."

"The distance to the airport is important," I said, once again struck with Jake's knack for making me feel defensive for using common sense.

He didn't hear me. His attention had shifted to the important task of waving an empty cup at a waiter patrolling the dining room with a silver coffeepot. "Help," he said. "Desperate man here."

The man smiled and came over to fill his cup. "Bless you," Jake said, taking a deep swallow, then shaking his head. "I have bad news."

"News? You just got up."

"From last night. Seems I lost my passport."

His odd grin made me wonder if he was teasing me. "Don't make a joke like that."

"It's not a joke."

"How did you manage to lose it?"

"The way a person loses things. You put it down somewhere and forget about it." He cocked his head. "In this case, I'm pretty sure I left it in the taxi that brought us home last night."

"What makes you think that?"

He shrugged. "Because I'm sure that's where I left my jacket and I had my passport in the pocket. *Quid erat* something or other, as the Romans are supposed to have said." He squinted. "Last night I spent an hour tearing my room apart, and it isn't there."

"What do we do now?"

He stole one of my rolls and nibbled it. "Eating breakfast comes to mind. And then... you didn't happen to write down the number of the taxi, did you?"

"No. Why would I? I barely remembered the taxi ride." I'd been too worried that the taxi was taking us to the wrong hotel.

"Because you do shit like that. You keep every damn receipt and write down all sorts of things."

"For tax purposes."

"Whatever." He waved a hand. "It was worth asking."

"I wasn't in top form. It was late."

"Past your bedtime."

"I was tired, and you were drunk."

He sighed. "So, even if that's where it is, safe in some taxi, we can't get it. Now, all that matters is that I don't have a passport. Happily, I have my wallet, and I have a photocopy of my passport tucked away in it."

"You can't fly home with a photocopy," I said. My stomach was tighter now than when thinking about the strange food. Even the eggs and bacon smelled wrong.

"But it will simplify getting a new one."

"What the hell do we do? That's an official document and you can't fly without one."

"We? You are good to go. Best thing is, you stick to the plan. Catch the plane back to California and take care of business."

"And leave you here?"

"I talked to the airline this morning, and I can reschedule the flight for a small fee. No big deal. I called the embassy this morning and learned from their recorded message that I need to show up at their doorstep at 9am Monday morning."

"You want me to leave you?"

"I have to do a bunch of paperwork, but once I do, they will issue me an emergency passport. I think the gist of their message was: 'Don't go home without one.'" He laughed.

"That sucks," I said.

"I screwed up. It isn't such a big deal," he said, reaching over to steal a piece of bacon from my plate. "It's all fixable. Just a glitch. I know you hate glitches, but shit happens." He pointed a finger at my plate and made a face. "You do know you are in Asia, right? The food here is incredible."

"I like bacon."

"They've got stuff here that you'll never see at home. To learn about it, you actually have to eat it."

"You seem to be enjoying my bacon well enough." His criticism made me snarky.

"I'm starving. When I finish my coffee, I'll wander over and get some stir fry and other delicacies. This is to hold me over. It would be poor form to starve to death on the trek to the buffet table. The hotel management would not approve."

I watched him, wondering how he could take the idea of losing his passport so calmly. "Why is it that I'm more upset about this than you? You losing your passport, I mean."

That got me another laugh. "Because you always get upset when anything changes or makes you alter your plans. You don't like things that take you out of your comfort zone."

"And you do?"

"Not always, but in this case, I see it as an unplanned adventure. That's why your job in the company is to make sure the plans work out and mine is to bring in the business."

That was true. Jake was the idea man—the big picture guy who sold his vision to clients. We were partners in San Mateo Sparkle; we ran teams that cleaned high-end homes and offices. Well, I ran it. While Jake helped clients decide it was a grand idea to pay us high fees to have their places reliably cleaned to perfection, I dealt with the gritty detail. I pulled the resources together, arranging things to make it happen.

Even after years of working together, I'd never understood Jake's cavalier attitude about things going wrong. It didn't bother him. "You lost an important document. That was careless of you."

"Yup, it was. But, c'mon, Billy boy. Lighten up. The way I see it, that means I have to extend my trip a few days. That's not a disaster. The sinking of the Titanic, or whatever ship actually sank... now there was a disaster. But no lives will be lost correcting my mistake. I'll shell out a few bucks and while I wait for the bureaucrats to do their thing, I'll see a little of Thailand. I'd love to go to the floating markets."

I'd read about them in the guidebook and stared at the pictures. "Why go to such unsanitary places? They do have supermarkets here."

He laughed at me, raising my hackles. I wondered if Jake was telling me the truth. He'd wanted to make this a ten-day trip, but I'd insisted we keep it short. "We only need to be there long enough to meet with this Ralph and hear his pitch," I'd said.

And that's what happened. Ralph had a manufacturing business and wanted investors for expansion. After meeting him, he gave us a tour of the facilities. Then he'd taken us out. By that time, I'd learned more than enough. I wanted no part of Ralph's enterprise and I was ready to go home.

"Unsanitary?" Jake was laughing. "That's become your favorite word for everything here. It's what you said about the place we went to watch the show last night."

The memory of the crowded night market, ringed with sex shows made me cringe. "Please never mention that back in the US. If Doreen knew that we'd let your creepy Australian pal take us to one of those, I'd never hear the end of it."

"My creepy pal? Ralph is a businessman who wants us to invest. He was entertaining us in the local style."

"It was disgusting."

Jake shrugged. "The eye of the beholder and all that. Besides, you can blame it on me. Doreen knows I'm a bad influence."

"And that so-called business of his?"

"I know you are uncomfortable with the idea."

"Not just the idea, it's the place itself."

He shrugged. "It's a business."

"And I don't see how we could manage the operation from California."

"We wouldn't. Ralph has been running the manufacturing operation fine without our help for several years. All he wants is someone to fund his expansion and help find new clients that want to subcontract toy manufacturing."

"And it's a dump—a sweatshop."

"He complies with all the local regulations that he can't bribe people to ignore."

"That's no answer!"

He grinned, letting me know that he brought up the issue of bribery to taunt me. Jake considered my attitudes puritanical.

"So tell me how we would keep an eye on things from halfway around the world? We couldn't even be sure he kept honest books."

"He's honest."

"You just said he bribes officials."

That earned me another cavalier shrug. "That's the way business is done here."

"Which is a good reason for not doing business here," I said. "Besides, neither of us knows the first thing about manufacturing. We run a service company."

Jake just grinned. "You make problems where there are none. Shit, subcontracting is a service business every bit as much as what we do. And when it comes to manufacturing, Ralph knows what he is doing. We'd be investing in a profitable, ongoing operation."

"But why do that in Asia?"

Jake gave me an incredulous look. "Why? Because that's where this opportunity is. We can't invest in his manufacturing operation in San Jose because he doesn't have any there. US companies subcontract to low-cost Asian operations. An outfit in San Jose couldn't be competitive."

"Your sarcasm aside, it's a serious question. If you want to invest in another business, to diversify, I understand, but you know I'd be more comfortable with a smaller return on something closer to home."

Jake sipped coffee. "That's my pal Billy boy. Always ready to do something new and different as long as it's exactly the same." Then he smiled. "Just teasing, buddy." He always said that when I refused to go along with one of his plans, so I knew he was disappointed. My hand was resting on the table and he tapped the back of it. "You go home and forget about Ralph. I'll tell him that San Mateo Sparkle will stick to its core business in its hometown."

"Are you willing to let it go? If it's such a great opportunity—"

He shrugged. "Don't sweat it. If it makes you all jittery—" He stood up. "Your comfort is important to me."

"Since when?"

He turned toward the buffet. "Yesterday morning I saw something on the buffet called dragon fruit. That sounds intriguing. I need to explore."

I remembered it. "Weird looking stuff." I sighed. "But then you like taking risks," I said.

"Someone has to," he said.

"I wasn't talking about the damn fruit."

He smiled. "I know. And, as far as eating dragon fruit goes, given that, at a minimum a few million people have eaten it and survived, I don't see much risk there."

I watched him go to the buffet and fill a plate with all sorts of things I'd never seen before. Part of it was probably to taunt me. When he came back and sat down, I looked at him. "So, we agree we aren't investing in this company?"

His head bobbed as he chewed some kind of dumpling. "That's what I said."

"And you—"

"While I get a new passport, you go home and dream of van maintenance and cleaning teams and how we will adjust the cash flow to pay the payroll tax—all the things you enjoy worrying about."

His surrender, coming so easily, made me nervous. Jake had an affinity for Asia, and he'd been excited about this company—so excited that he'd made me come look at it.

"And you are going to go sightseeing while you wait for your new passport?"

Jake shook his head. "Don't trust me, Billy boy?"

"You've been known to go off on your own. I want you to remember that we have a business back home to run. And there are a couple of small outfits we were looking at acquiring—failing competitors. We were collecting data. If you want to expand—"

"I'm sure Betty will have incredible analytical summaries waiting for you when you get back," he said. "Feel free to take the appropriate actions. You and Betty have my blessing."

Betty is my twin sister. After college, she managed an office, quitting when she married Jake. That didn't work out well for a number of reasons, mostly because Betty is like me and Jake is... well, he is Jake.

For instance... being in our family meant spending every summer at a family gathering near Omaha. My parents had a place on Lake Carter, and Betty insisted he come along. It's likely our family's carefully planned vacations would have been enough to put the end to that relationship all by themselves.

The marriage lasted a couple of years. They never fought, just found life together a tiring tug of war. They had a son and Jake felt an obligation to stay married, but Betty, as conservative as she is, is also pragmatic. "It didn't work out," was her only comment.

After the divorce, they stayed on good terms. Meantime, our business grew like crazy, and when their son was a teen, Betty wanted to go back to work. Jake agreed, and we brought her into the company part time. I trained her to run the shop. Naturally, as it was a system I designed, and she is my sister, she fit in perfectly.

"You aren't comfortable going back home without me," he said, his mouth full of noodles.

"I worry about you getting involved in something here."

He waved a hand. "The world is filled with amazing things," he said. "I can't see turning a blind eye to them. And if they are a little risky, well, someone has to test the waters. But I won't obligate you in any way."

"I just worry."

"Of course you do. But think of it this way—if I hadn't started the cleaning business where would we be? Not here, for sure. And at the time, you thought it was silly."

The summary had enough truth to it to sting, although Jake's version was, as usual, a rather biased and narrow account. "If I hadn't insisted that we stop hiring illegals to do the work, we might be in jail."

Jake's eyes glistened. "Maybe. Or maybe we'd be even richer now." He sighed. "Besides, that wasn't you—it was a condition your old man put on loaning you the money."

I coughed. He was right. I wanted to make it seem I'd been noble, but it was my father's idea, and it was a practical matter, not idealism. He didn't want us getting shut down.

"It was the right thing to do. And as times and enforcement changed, it was a good move."

That earned me a grin. "Maybe so. What matters is that once you came on board, we built this business into something good—together, as a team, buddy."

"And why change things?"

"I've always thought my crazy ability to pick the risky ventures that could work and your ability to make them work would be unstoppable." As I let the obvious attempt to flatter me do exactly that, Jake looked around the room. "Look. I can go see live tigers and crocodiles at the Sri Racha Tiger Zoo," he said.

"What?"

"A zoo that specializes in tigers and crocodiles. I've never seen live crocs."

"I didn't know you wanted to."

"It's down on the Gulf of Thailand, to the south—a beach area. Ralph told me that it's only about 60 miles from here." I laughed, and he stared at me. "Tigers are funny?"

"No, but the image of you sightseeing at the zoo is."

He grinned his evil grin. "Depends on the sights there are to see. A croc might be worth the trip."

I remembered about his distaste for the family vacations. He'd told me, sarcastically: 'I need a vacation from the family vacation.' And now he'd go sightseeing?

"I can't see you sightseeing," I said. "You'd be bored."

He shrugged. "Well, I suppose I'll have to stay in Bangkok until I get the embassy drones started getting me a new passport. I can't expect they'll pop a new passport right out of the printer. It will take at least a couple of days for them to process things. I might not be a sightseer, but I can't just sit in a hotel room and watch television. I'll poke around. Ralph might have some ideas."

"I'm sure he will." Most likely none that I'd like. I looked at my watch. "Well, I need to get packed for the trip back."

"Give me a ring when you're ready and I'll ride out to the airport with you, make sure you get off safely," he said. He winked. "You can leave me any Baht you haven't spent. You won't have much use for Thai money in San Mateo."

This line of banter relaxed me. I knew damn well that seeing me off was just his way of ensuring I didn't go to the wrong airport (there were two in Bangkok) or do something equally stupid. It wasn't much comfort that he was right to worry. Outside of California, away from the family and the routine of running our cleaning business, I was out of my element as well as my comfort zone.

It might sound pathetic, but simply taking the trip had gotten me anxious. As the one running the day-to-day operations for our cleaning company, it was my job to worry that our cleaning crews weren't working to the standard I set for them. When I got back, I'd be phoning clients, making sure they were happy. I'd spend some time going over reports.

The thought of getting back to that made me relax. Once again I was struck with the contrast between my partner, my best friend, my brother-in-law and myself. I was looking forward to catching up on the basic things in life, and Jake, stuck in Bangkok without a passport, seemed happy as a clam.

～

Two roads diverged in a yellow wood,
And sorry I could not travel both
And be one traveler, long I stood
And looked down one as far as I could
To where it bent in the undergrowth;

• • • •

Jake didn't make it back home for another week. During that time he called a couple of times to let us know that some Thai holiday had slowed the paperwork, and then to explain that although his new passport arrived, the airline screwed up his new reservation somehow. "Computers," said with great disdain, made up most of that discussion. "They can't get me on a flight for a couple of days."

I got the impression he didn't mind. "I'm sure you are heartbroken."

"I'll find some way to fill the time," he said.

Finally, on a Saturday, he sent me an email telling me it was all settled. "I've got an airport shuttle picking me up—it's late night arrival. I'll see you in the office Monday."

Monday morning, as I sat at my desk reviewing the spreadsheet I use to track the weekly schedule, my door opened and Jake walked. He was smiling and carrying two mugs of coffee. He held one out.

"Your espresso, sir. Two sugars, one milk."

I took the offered mug and watched a very relaxed Jake slip into the leather chair across from my desk.

"You must want something, stranger."

"Just an update. How's our wonderful world of cleaning?" he asked.

"Everything is on schedule," I told him.

He smiled. "Of course. Silly of me. You are in that chair and Betty is cracking the whip over the crews. All has to be right with world."

I laughed, but even after all the years working together, I still found it hard to know what my partner actually thought about what we did and our relationship. As with his marriage to Betty, the business had us, two quite different people, working hip to hip. I was confident he respected what I brought to the table, but what he thought of me as a person was something else.

"You look happy and relaxed," I said.

Jake sat back, holding his favorite coffee mug in both hands, looking at me over the top of it so I could see, "If you never try, you can't fail!" emblazoned on it in bright red letters.

Doreen had given him that mug at one of the office Christmas parties. He'd laughed when he opened it. I never understood why she picked that gift.

When I asked her what it meant, she'd just given me an odd look and said, "It's a joke."

"I don't get it."

She grinned. "You probably shouldn't even try to understand jokes."

Now that enigmatic slogan stared at me. "Was Ralph pissed when you told him the news?"

I saw surprise in his eyes. "The news?"

"That we decided not to invest."

"No. Why would he be?"

"Because he spent all that time with us and paid for the drinks…"

"Hell no. He knows it's just business. We were an option, nothing more."

He took a sip of coffee and glanced around my office. When he did that, I found myself wondering what he saw. I had things set up for efficiency. Flowcharts and a calendar (I still love paper calendars) were prominently displayed on the walls, along with a large photo of Doreen, the kids, and me at the folk's cabin on Lake Carter.

Jake's office was strange. The only things on the wall were a painting came with the office and a large poster with a photo of a tree-lined forest. Taken in fall, the trees had yellowing leaves. Robert Frost's famous poem, THE ROAD NOT TAKEN, was written over it. That's the poem about a man coming to a spot in the yellow woods where two roads diverged and having to pick one.

He'd had that poster for years. I'd never asked him what it meant to him. It didn't seem like Jake to regret much of anything. He always looked ahead.

"I'm glad you are back," I said now. "We took on both of those failing cleaning services we were looking at and hired several of their people. They are doing well."

His eyes glazed over for a moment, then he snapped his fingers. "Oh, right." I wondered if he knew what I was talking about. "Listen, I wanted to apologize," he said.

"For what?"

"Bangkok. Making you go. The whole thing."

"What whole thing?"

"Asia. Manufacturing." He laughed. "Ralph."

"I tried to tell you I didn't like the idea."

"But you know me… when I sense a good deal, I'm like a hunting dog on a scent. I can't let go of a good deal without a chase."

"A good deal?" I laughed. "Ralph runs a squalid sweat shop. The whole thing seems shady."

"No better or worse than most."

He made that sound like an endorsement. "Investing in it would be a gamble."

He pursed his lips. "Maybe. Some gambles pay off. Doreen said the books were good. Ralph has a track record of making money."

"That doesn't make it a good investment for us," I said firmly. I wanted this discussion to be over so I could put Thailand out of my head completely. I couldn't shake the images of the squalid nightlife.

Jake cupped his hands around his coffee mug, considering his words. "I thought I was being something you'd appreciate—prudent."

"Prudent?"

"I saw an opportunity. I thought we should go see the operation and make an assessment." He gave me a wistful smile. "I guess you made your decision before we left."

The dig struck home. "True, and I don't know what I could've said to make my position clearer. I never wanted anything to do with it."

He waved a hand. "Yes, you made it clear. The thing is... well, for several reasons the idea fired me up. I wasn't in a mood to hear any negativity."

That stunned me. "You didn't want to hear what I thought?"

"Not if it contradicted me." He pushed back in his chair. "You are my oldest friend, and over the years I've dragged you into more than one thing kicking and screaming. You were against developing the commercial end of our business, for instance. But I found us lucrative contracts. Once you saw the possibilities you were all for it."

"But that was—"

He held up a hand. "Different, I know. And I'm not offering an excuse. I'm trying to apologize and explain that sometimes I hear you saying no, and I hear you saying, 'make me do it.'" He smiled. "This time you meant it. I didn't treat your opinion with the dignity it deserved."

"It was a bad idea."

He looked at me. "Perhaps. At least by going over there you gave me the satisfaction of knowing you looked at the business opportunity closely and didn't just dismiss it out of hand."

"I suppose." For him, the outcome was what mattered.

"So, are we good?"

"We are fine," I said, not sure if that was true. "Maybe next time you will listen to what I say."

"I will."

Jake's answer came too quick for that. I've never trusted instant reassurances from anyone. They seem rehearsed and superficial. And now I wanted to change the topic. "Did you enjoy those extra days in Thailand?" I asked him.

A flicker of a smile crossed his face, and his eyes sparkled. "I did," he said. "A lot."

"The place put me off."

He grinned. "You didn't really see the country or meet any of the people. While I was there, I took some time to do that. They were amazing; I found I like the Thai people a lot."

"Really? I found them noisy and pushy."

My comment seemed to startle him, and for a moment, he sat still. "I found that they have a sense of dignity. Being among them made my time there peaceful."

I had to choke back a laugh. "Dignity?" I tried to relate that to my impressions of the country and failed.

"I'm not talking about the tourist touts," he said. "Cheap hustlers are the same, whether you encounter them in Naples or Bangkok. And the street sellers the worst of the lot."

"If you say so." Jake had been to both places. The brief stay in Thailand was my only experience outside of the US. "But dignity?"

He seemed to wake from a reverie then. "Just my impression," he said, standing. "I found being around them comforting, and I needed that." Before I could ask why he needed it, he was heading for the door. "If I am truly back, then I better get to work and follow up and get making cold calls. New business won't generate itself."

"Glad you're back," I said as he headed for the door.

I noticed that he didn't respond to that, but he did pause in the doorway where he turned back to give me a wistful look. "You know, Billy boy, we had a lovely tax-deductible trip to Thailand. There's something you can take off your bucket list."

Then he was gone, leaving me in a cloud of resentment. He knew damn well I hadn't had a lovely trip and that my bucket list, to the extent I had one, was limited to things like shooting par at the golf club or making enough money to be able to afford an infinity pool for the house. Visiting Thailand had been a chore, not some dream of mine. The allure of far-flung places was lost on me.

With the door closed behind him, I thought about that difference.

I was still stewing when I got home.

"I can tell Jake is back," Doreen laughed.

"He is."

"And he's frustrated you. Again."

"Yes. I don't understand him."

"How could you?" she asked. "You two live on different planets. Your idea of a perfect life is his worst nightmare, and his dream world would be a living hell for you."

"That's not true," I said far too quickly. "We both want the same things. Good people all generally want the same things."

"They do?" she asked. Her look suggested that the idea surprised her.

"I think so."

She shrugged. "Well, the thing is you need to accept the differences between you. They define the strength and weakness of your partnership and friendship," she said.

"I'm organized. He's visionary."

She smiled. "Something like that. You know, you and I are rather different kinds of people too... although the differences are less dramatic."

"We complement each other," I said. I knew what she meant. Her spontaneity and willingness, even eagerness, to try something new, often unsettled me. Still, I thought that by working out those differences, we strengthened our marriage.

I found her smile a tad enigmatic. "Maybe we do," she said.

"And I understand you... most of the time."

She kissed my cheek. "You think you do," she said. "That's enough."

I knew and loved Jake, and I think he felt the same. We did not have a single clue into what made the other tick, but in business we made a good team.

"Well, he's back in harness now, and life goes on."

"Okay," she said.

The next Saturday morning, after the kids had gone off with their friends, I settled myself at the dining table to go over the family finances. Yes, there are computer programs that do it for you, but I was old school. It kept thing manageable.

After a time, Doreen grabbed two bottles of cold beer from the refrigerator. I watched her pour one into a mug and smiled when she handed it to me. I took a grateful sip.

"I could do the books, you know," she said as she opened the other bottle. "I'm a trained professional."

I cringed as she took a long drink straight from the bottle. Betty and I grew up with the idea (the fact) instilled in us that bottles were dirty. "You don't know they cleaned them properly," Mom said. Given that firm conviction, anything less than pouring your drink, any drink, into a clean glass was unsanitary, and unsanitary was almost the worst thing in the world.

I'd never gotten used to the fact that Doreen loved her beer right from the bottle. It still surprised and, I'll admit, offended me. The way she'd look at me out of the corner of her eye as she drank gave me the impression that it delighted her that such a commonplace thing upset me.

I loved the woman, but she often irritated me. And yet, it was such a small thing. They usually are!

She nodded as she looked over my shoulder at the ledgers. "You do know that accounting, bookkeeping, projecting fiscal matters is what I do."

"I like to play with the numbers," I said. "I get satisfaction from seeing how we are doing."

She laughed. "Nonsense. It drives you crazy when numbers don't come out right."

"Of course it does. That only happens when I do something incorrectly."

She smiled. "I suppose. Still, I love tracking down the errors."

While she had the training and the experience and had been the company's accountant before we got married, I insisted on doing the accounts at home. That amused her too. She had several regular investors and small businesses that she worked for, keeping books, analyzing fiscal statements, and doing taxes.

"Doing our accounts would be no big deal for me, Bill. But you are a control freak who hates letting the books out of your hands."

I wondered if that was true. "I just like—"

"Being in control. That's why it was Jake's idea to bring Betty into the company, not yours. He asked her about it and she got excited. You just couldn't figure out how to tell your sister no."

"Not really."

"And that's why you don't want me coming back to work."

"I never said—"

"Right now, those numbers have you frowning. You aren't having fun, but you insist on torturing yourself."

"It's not torture."

"So why the scowl? Are we in trouble?" She sat down beside me.

I smiled. "No. Not trouble. Not at all."

Suddenly she laughed. "It's that damn infinity pool, isn't it?"

"It would be great for us and the kids."

Her grin cut through me. "Right. The kids want it. As if they are ever home for more than meals and a night's sleep these days."

I ignored the jibe. "The problem is, they are expensive. We'd have to buy it on credit and the payments would stretch us to the limit."

She shook her head. "That's only because your comfort zone is so narrow, darling."

Once again someone close to me was getting on me about wanting to be comfortable. "What's wrong with wanting to be comfortable. And anyway, this is a matter of being prudent."

"Being prudent, as you see it, defines the outer limits of your comfort zone."

When she said that sort of thing, and she said it often, I found it pointless to ask for an explanation. Not that she would refuse to tell me what she meant. She would try, but her rationale always escaped me.

"We'd be overextended."

She tipped her head. "You make that sound like a bad thing."

"You are just being nasty now."

"Actually, I'm serious. What would happen if you acted imprudently—just once?"

I shuddered. "That wouldn't be sensible. It would be irrational."

"And there's no doubt that you are sensible."

"I hear a 'but' in that."

She sipped her beer. "Have you ever considered that we are where we are financially because we act sensibly and prudent. And Jake, insensible as he is, gets more of what he wants."

That held enough truth to hurt. "He takes risks."

"You get jealous over that fancy house in Half Moon Bay that he and Betty bought, his fancy car, and the expensive vacations he takes."

It struck me, not for the first time, that Doreen admired Jake's sense of adventure. So where did that leave me in her view? Somewhat parochial, I imagined. Not that it upset her. On the contrary, one of the things about her that amazed me was how she acted as if everything that went on was a play being staged for her amusement.

Bringing up the house seemed like a cheap shot. Doreen and I owned our nice house in Hollister. It was a nice area, but nothing flashy. (And nothing like the house Jake had bought and signed over to Betty during the divorce).

"I still don't know how Jake could afford that place," I said.

Doreen surprised me by laughing. "Don't you guys talk? Don't you talk to your sister?"

"What do you mean?"

"Your sister said that when they found it, the place was in foreclosure. Jake made a cash offer. He sold some investment, and that was it."

"Cash?" It was hard to imagine having my hands on that kind of money. "Betty and I don't talk about money," I said. "You must've asked."

"Of course, I did. Tight-lipped Betty never would have told me, otherwise. I know that family trait too."

That she could pry the information loose from Betty came as no surprise. Doreen could make people open up. It never occurred to me to ask such questions. "I have trouble believing he had that much in investments."

She held up her empty bottle. "Wait!" Then she went in the kitchen, coming back with two more, pouring mine into my glass before provocatively putting her own, open, dirty, on the table. "You shouldn't have to believe it. Jake never makes a secret of his investments. You are always mentioning some scheme or another he thinks you should put money into. The problem is that you don't really trust him."

That shocked me. "Of course, I trust him. He's my partner."

She patted my hand. "I'm not saying you don't think he's honest."

"What else could you mean?"

"His judgment. You don't trust his judgment."

"Sure, I do."

She shook her head. "Really. It doesn't seem so."

"Why would you even say that? After all these years—"

Her eyebrow lifted. "Well, I figure that if you trusted him, you'd have gone in on some of his investments. But you don't."

I shook my head, but it didn't make things clearer. "What are you saying?"

"That when he comes up with investment ideas, you dismiss them."

"If one seemed right..."

That had her laughing again. "In all these years, not one, besides the cleaning company, has ever seemed right to you, and never will. And the only reason you are in the cleaning business is because your father invested his money to get you a partnership."

"Because I asked him to. Jake wanted to expand."

"And you've never trusted his judgment enough to put your own money into anything."

As I pondered that, trying to decide if it was true, she pursed her lips.

"Remember the time he came over all excited and tried to get you to buy into that bakery?"

I let out a breath. "A risky proposition. The guy wanted to sell because the big chains were killing his business. There's no way to compete with those guys."

She sighed and smiled. "You remember it that way."

"How do you remember it?"

"The business was in trouble because of piss poor management. If you recall, Jake had me go over the books before he came to you. I saw no problems with their finances, and I told you that. I even told you then that Jake's idea of spinning the business into a boutique bakery for upscale customers — catering, special events, things like that, sounded good."

"That's a real challenge."

"Not for a debt-free business with low overhead. If the owner had wanted to do the work, he could've made it profitable himself."

It didn't pay to disagree with Doreen's fiscal analysis, so I changed tactics. "You need to remember that money was tight for us back then."

"You think it wasn't' tight for Jake? When you didn't go in on it, he had to borrow everything he could to raise the money. Last year he sold the business and made a bundle."

I hadn't known that. "What's your point? Jake got lucky."

Doreen stared at me. "Seriously? Lucky? You think luck is why his investments almost always make money?"

I sipped my beer. It tasted bitter, even from a clean glass. "When you take enormous risks, luck is always a factor. I'm not comfortable doing that."

She sighed again. "That's fine. No one expects you to be anyone other than who you are. I'm just saying you are a control freak. As long as you accept that it isn't a problem. But it means you can't begrudge him his money."

"I'm just not a gambler. I need to know my investments are safe. That way I can sleep nights."

It hurt that she laughed at that. "I hope you know that 'safe investment' is a contradiction in terms, right? An investment is a gamble. The riskier gambles earn the most return precisely because of the risk. But you'd rather stay in your comfort zone without the pool than take a risk."

"Better be safe than sorry," I said.

"I know that's your motto, Bill."

It was only later that I found myself wondering if she'd meant that as a compliment. I tried to convince myself that was how she'd meant it.

After the talk we'd had, Jake never brought up Thailand again. In fact, it seemed that he was avoiding me. That made me wonder if he was sulking. But that was foolish. Jake wasn't the kind to sulk. He'd laugh at what he saw as my foolishness and move on.

As we got our newly acquired crews up to speed, I expected Jake to come in with some new business, but that didn't seem to be happening. Under normal circumstances, he'd swoop into a staff meeting and cheerfully ask how many new clients we could handle. Betty noticed too and made some remark about him being off his game.

When I heard him snap at the receptionist over a minor matter, that made me really start to worry. Mattie was a cute young woman and Jake loved teasing her, being charming and flirting, even when she upset him. She could be careless at times but reprimanding her always fell to me.

His attention was somewhere else. The man who rushed into the office, eager to make cold calls, to chat up big clients, hadn't come back from Asia. He still worked the phone, but the calls I overheard lacked even a little enthusiasm. He had no fire.

When I asked him if everything was okay, he just brushed me off. It went against the grain to probe. Our family had a saying: It's rude to intrude.

But I noticed him taking time off, coming in late, sometimes staying out the entire day.

"I assume he's got a new transitory girlfriend," Betty said. He'd dated frequently since their divorce, but never gotten serious about anyone.

That day I as I stared out my window (daydreaming) into the courtyard, Jake sat on the bench talking on his phone. I could see the frustration on his face. That got my curiosity in high gear, I can tell you. Jake never minded making his calls in front of people.

That night, I shared my concerns with Doreen. "It's like he is still partly there," I told her.

"Where?"

"Bangkok. Asia." I gave her a hopeless look. "Somewhere else. His attention certainly isn't here, not focused on the business. And Jake has always been someone who lives in the moment."

She rubbed her chin. "That doesn't sound like him."

"And I think it's my fault."

"Bullshit," she said. "What could you do that would cause him to change like that?"

I struggled to figure out how to explain. "It's just a theory, but I get the distinct impression that the trip to Asia meant more to him than I understood."

"Like he wanted a major change?"

"Maybe. Or a sign. It could be symbolic. Whatever it was, my unwillingness to take that gamble, to do business in Bangkok disappointed him." I looked at Doreen. "It's as if I shit on a dream that was precious to him and in the process, showed him my true, conservative nature."

"He's always known who you are. If that surprised him even a little, he's dumber than I think."

"But not the depth of my conservative nature. On that trip... it's never been so clear that we look through opposite ends of the microscope. Everything excited him; everything I saw repelled me. I'm thinking he took that personally. It's like I rejected him."

She stared out the window. "A wounded pride, or unhappiness with you might explain him withdrawing and being out of sorts, but it not why he's making secretive phone calls."

"I didn't mean I could explain everything."

"No."

"Another thing... he has barely talked about the days he spent alone in Asia. When I've chickened out on some adventure of his, he's always loved to tease me about what I missed. The time he went skiing in Aspen he came back with hundreds of stories. I expected to hear about the great meals he ate, the fun he had. But he's been cryptic—hardly said a thing."

She put her hands on her hips. This was her stern thinker pose. "Maybe whatever is wrong has nothing at all to do with you or the trip? What if it isn't about you?"

"It is about me if it goes on. It could interfere with business.

"Why do you say that?"

"He snaps at Mattie, for one thing. That's not good. And even though he's still talking to the clients, it isn't the same. He's going through the motions. His heart isn't in it."

"Maybe you are misjudging things."

I doubted that. "The other day, a client called and told him she needed to reschedule several cleaning jobs. But I didn't hear about until she called me to find out what the new schedule was. I stalled her, told her we were trying to work it out. I had to pretend it was a mixup." I pushed my chair back.

"Did you ask him about it?"

"Yes, and he seemed pissed at me for bringing it up. He said not to worry, and she'd get over it, whatever that means."

I watched her consider that. Her look showed concern. "Something is wrong."

"Another thing. You know how spartan he keeps his office. Now he's covered the walls with travel posters of tropical destinations. I've seen him staring at them wistfully."

She raised a finger. "A subtle hint?" she asked, smiling. "If he wants to go back to see more of Asia isn't necessarily a bad thing."

"That's what I thought. Maybe he needs to go back and get Asia out of his system. I walked in and stared at the posters. 'Planning another trip?' I asked. All he said was, 'life is short.'"

"You need to ask him right out. Or bring him here and I'll ask him."

"He'll tell me if something big is wrong."

"Will he? Fuck that. Jake is your friend. If he isn't acting like one, then you need to point that out. Get in his face and let him know that you are concerned about him and are there for him. Surely you can do that, at least."

"I tried."

She smirked. "Really."

"I said he wasn't acting like himself."

"That isn't exactly asking."

"He said it was probably a good thing. Then he smiled and went in the courtyard to make another phone call. He's shutting me out."

She sighed and shook her head. "Don't let him. You need to step up. Ask the damn question."

"You said that."

She held her hands open. "What else can I say?"

My wife can be damn irritating. It's always worst when she is right.

The next morning, I arrived and found his office door wide open. I poked my head in to see him sitting at his desk, smiling at me over his coffee. I hesitated. Despite the smile, despite the hearty good morning he'd thrown at me, I was taken with how frail he looked. I hadn't noticed before.

I took a seat across from him and his eyebrows raised. "Is this the Spanish Inquisition?"

It was his favorite Monty Python routine.

"Not if you tell me what I want to know." That was my attempt to keep it light hearted.

He leaned forward. "I know nothing at all. But that's a secret. Don't even tell me."

I think Jake could deflect an inquisition. I jumped right in. "What's going on with you, Jake?" I asked.

"What do you mean?"

"For one thing, you look like shit."

He grinned and hoisted his mug. "Not fair. I'm only on my first cup of coffee. Life doesn't start until after that. I have come to the conclusion that evolution began with the discovery of coffee. I've let the Nobel committee know of my findings and expect to hear from them any day."

"Well, that's certainly a major step forward for science, but if I ask something personal, will you answer?"

He sat his mug down and looked at me. "Ask me anything, old buddy," he said. Given the circumstances, his sincerity embarrassed me.

"Are you upset with me?"

That seemed to shock him. "With you? No. Why would you ask that?"

I ticked off the reasons on my fingers. "Because you don't answer my questions, because you look like shit even after many cups of coffee, although you keep saying you are fine, and because you sneak into the courtyard to make phone calls."

"Is that all?" he said. Then he broke out laughing. "I guess that does sound fishy as hell."

"I feel you are keeping me in the dark—that you have secrets you are keeping from me."

"If I tell you, the NSA says I'll have to kill you."

"I'm serious."

He sighed. "Okay. Serious it is. I do have secrets from you, Billy boy. Too many. Do you really want to know what they are?"

"Yes. I want to help, if I can."

"Well, you can't and don't want to help with the first one. Secret number one: I invested in Ralph's manufacturing operation."

"You said you wouldn't."

He shook his head. "No. I said we wouldn't. I used my own money and left you out of it—at your insistence."

"And you lost it?" That would explain the way he looked.

He grinned. "Negative. It's already turning a profit." He laughed, and I wondered if it was at my expense.

"That was fast."

"I told you that Ralph had everything lined up. I handed over the money before I left, and by the end of the week he was cranking out toys. With US government putting pressure on manufacturers to get out of China, he's had to turn customers down. He wants me back in Thailand to look at plans for the next level of expansion."

"Next level?"

"We are looking at building a new plant. Well... buying and refitting one near Chang Mai. That leads me to secret number two: I'm heading back to Thailand. Ralph wants me to see the new place."

The knot in my stomach that had begun showing up when I talked business with Jake grew painful. "Does that mean that all this, the cleaning business, isn't important any longer?" Or me, I thought.

He grinned. "Not at all. But I'm looking at winding down my role. You guys are kicking ass with this business. Skipping the humble bullshit, I was vital in getting it here, but you and Betty are the management gurus."

"You are the face of the business."

He held up a hand. "I suggest that we bring Doreen back into the fold."

"What?"

"That woman is bored, and we both know she is more than capable of taking over the books from the outside firm and doing my job as well. Probably better than I can. And I bet she'd jump at it."

My heart sank. He was right. "What about you? Will you stay in Asia?"

He paused, wincing briefly. "No. I have to figure it out."

My heart skipped a beat. Jake was cutting himself loose from the world that I had assumed would go on forever as it was. He wanted out. "You want to quit?"

"Something besides business in Asia needs my attention," he said.

"What?"

He turned his coffee cup. "Pain management." Silence filled the room. "I'm suffering chronic pain. My doctor put me on meds for pain about a year ago. They helped at first, but it was getting worse and the meds made me feel like shit. Part of the reason I wanted to go to Thailand was to visit a clinic there. The doc said they have access to techniques that aren't approved here... yet."

"You didn't lose your passport."

"No. But I couldn't talk you into staying, and I didn't think you'd like me staying behind."

"Did they help you?"

"Not as much as I would've liked. They have other, longer therapies that could do something. I went back on the meds when I came back, but they make me irritable and I can't focus. I'm assured that continuing to take the drugs will make the side effects get worse. I've decided to go back and try a two-week program. So, you see, bringing in Doreen to take over for me is our best option."

I tried to picture the business, my life, without Jake around all the time. It was like watching a friend go off to explore the unknown. I had no desire to tag along, yet somehow felt like I was being left in the dust.

"I don't understand. Doreen can fill in for you, but why not take some treatments and then come back to work?"

He shrugged. "It isn't clear that any treatments will do the trick, and I'm tired of pretending I'm not in pain—not that I've done that well lately."

I couldn't think of a reply, an alternative that I could insist he try. "I'm sorry. You go get well."

"I've got a business lead for you and Doreen to follow up on," he said as cheerfully as if we'd been discussing him going on vacation.

"What is the new job? Cleaning up after space launches?" I asked, my voice dripping with a ton of nasty that I hadn't realized was lurking there.

"Nothing so profitable," he laughed. "I had lunch with a realtor, following up on my idea. She is expanding her business... renting out office spaces." He wrote down a name and phone number and pushed it across the desk. "Give that to Doreen. I talked to this woman briefly and I think she could give us a hell of a lot of business. If I won't be here, it's better if you two make the pitch."

Taking it, feeling the finality of the moment, made me numb.

"While I'm in Thailand, maybe Doreen should give Space-X a shout."

"Space-X?"

"Follow up on your idea about cleaning up after launches. That has to make a hell of a mess. It could be a new specialty. Way to think out of the box, partner."

Jake was right about Doreen being up for the challenge. "I only hate that the reason I'm doing this is that Jake is suffering," she said.

We all felt that way.

She arranged a meeting with Jake's contact, and after a brief conversation, Jake's optimism infected her. "This will be big for us," she said.

"What is it?" I asked.

"Offices," she said. "But this woman is moving fast. She will be a serious player.

When she seated us in her office, it only took a moment to see that Doreen had sized up the realtor perfectly. Her office was as spartan as Jake's used to be, and she was a no-nonsense businesswoman in a hurry.

"I'm glad you called me," she said. "I think we can do business."

"Business is good, then?" I asked.

"It's crazy good. I've had a couple of office buildings for a time, but with the failure of some of the tech companies, I'm expanding. Those startups build lovely industrial parks. Right now, if I act fast, I can get them in foreclosure." She grinned. "They build them, I buy them and rent them out."

"And there is demand?" Doreen asked.

She threw her head back, laughing. "Demand? I've got people screaming for decent, well-managed office space. I'll charge a premium and that's where you come in. My clients want to move into spotless offices and not have to think about maintenance." She shook her head in dismay.

"Unfortunately, some people are pigs, and these spaces need serious cleaning before I can lease them, and when that's done, I need to be able to guarantee routine cleaning as part of the deal."

Doreen nodded. "Of course. That's what we do."

"I'll want a contract that includes light cleaning of the entire complexes three nights a week—empty the trash, vacuum the rugs, clean windows, clean and restock bathrooms—"

"Standard stuff."

"I want a major cleaning, including carpets, once a quarter." She shuffled through some papers. "I've got bids from a couple of companies for the grounds, but if you know anyone..."

"We have a company that does that well," Doreen said confidently. "I'll send you a bid for the entire package." My pulse was racing. I forced myself to be quiet even though my brain was screaming out that doing all this meant adding teams, buying new equipment... and Doreen was simply taking the order as if it was just another house to clean. "My bid will be based on a firm commitment—a one-year contract to start."

The woman nodded and handed Doreen a folder. "This describes the facilities and gives you the square footage. I want an estimate for doing them all and a promise from you that you will expand to accommodate me if I add more. I'm looking at a service bay out at the airport."

Doreen looked at the pages and handed them to me. "I'll need to do a walk-through," Doreen said. "It all looks different when you are there."

The woman nodded. "My secretary has the keys and can meet you whenever you want to check them out."

A quick glance told me this was a massive amount of work. "We will need to add people as well as some more trucks and equipment. We should talk to Jake."

Doreen shook her head. "Are the people available?"

I ran the teams through my head. "If we promote some workers into team leaders and add the new ones into existing teams they can train on site. So yes. I'm more worried about going into debt for the trucks."

"We won't," Doreen said. She looked at the realtor. "I'll get you a bid by tomorrow morning, if that's okay."

"If we come to an agreement, I'd set up a monthly autopay." Then she paused. "Can you accept payment in Bitcoin?"

"We prefer cash," I said.

Doreen put a hand on my arm. "Bill runs our operations. He has an ingrained fear of new financial, like crypto, but I run finance. I'm restructuring things and, while we don't take Bitcoin at the moment, I'd be delighted to set up a wallet. I'll send you the QR code along with our estimate."

For the first time, the realtor smiled. "That's so perfect. I do like doing business with people who enjoy making things happen."

Making things happen—that described Doreen, I thought. And Jake too... the old Jake. For now, Doreen was a wonderful new Jake. She might even be more Jake than Jake. And, like Jake, there seemed to be things she wasn't telling me.

The next weeks were filled with all that goes with ramping up business. It was crazy, and I was glad when Betty came in full time. Working together, we made it happen.

"Jake's back," Betty told me.

"He didn't call. How is he?"

"I don't exactly know, even though he's staying with me. He asked me to get everyone together this weekend. He's being dramatic and wants to tell everyone his news all at once."

Betty doesn't think much of people who are being dramatic.

"And you don't have a clue?" I asked.

"I don't speculate." Her schoolteacher grimace put me in my place. "Just get over to my house Saturday afternoon. I'll make a huge vat of spaghetti and we will send the kids off to eat in the television room."

"Why?"

"Because the television room has vinyl floors and wiping up the inevitable spilled sauce isn't a big deal?"

"I mean, why have the kids eat separately?"

Betty sneered. "Because I'm sure Jake feels the need to be grown-up dramatic over wine or something stronger and they don't really know what's going on. He's going to rent some new movie that Doreen said they are clamoring to see."

With the turmoil at work I found myself looking forward to a relaxing get together and hearing how the new therapy had gone. Seeing him made my stomach knot up. He'd lost even more weight and his pale skin told me he hadn't gotten any beach time.

"How are you?" I asked as we settled into chairs on the patio.

"First—" Jake held up a bottle of a whisky that I'd only heard about. It was absurdly expensive. I couldn't help but think of the cost of each glass as he poured out healthy drinks, neat. "Now, I know I owe you all, each of you, an explanation. You deserve to know what is going on. But first a toast. *L'chaim* — to life"

Not one of us had a snappy reply to that. I sipped my drink, and the others did the same. Jake drank, then took a deep breath.

"The trip I took to Thailand wasn't successful."

"Their pain therapies didn't work?" I asked.

"That's no surprise," Betty said. "If they worked, then doctor's here —"

"When I came back, I didn't come straight here. I made a side trip up to the Mayo clinic in Phoenix. That wasn't productive either, except in confirming the diagnosis."

"I thought it was chronic pain."

He paused to taste his drink again. "Damn that's fine stuff. Anyway, the thing is I've been lying. Now I have to come clean. I don't have a chronic condition."

"That's a relief," I said.

"Is it?" He sighed. "Sorry, I'm being flip. It isn't a relief. You see chronic means 'continuing or occurring again and again for a long time.' I looked it up. That makes this a rare situation because the doctors and the dictionary agree on something."

"So your pain isn't chronic?"

"No. You see, although it does continue and reoccurs, it won't persist for the long time that makes it chronic."

"I told you he wanted to be dramatic," Betty said.

The look in Jake's eyes told me the story didn't have a happy ending. "What do you mean? Tell us the rest."

He cocked his head. "You see, I'm dying."

"That's absurd," Betty said. "You are only in your fifties— a young man."

"A young man dying of colon cancer," he said calmly.

"What exactly did the doctors say?" Betty demanded.

"A lot of shit," he said. "Most of it contradictory or doesn't make sense. But it all comes down to the fact that I have much less than a year to live."

"We need a second opinion," Betty said. "Doctors make mistakes."

He shook his head slowly. "I've already been to three doctors and more specialists. They all speak the same party line."

"Can't they operate?" I asked.

Jake leaned back and laughed as if I'd told a grand joke. "Of course they can operate. They love to operate. They want to remove infected tissue from my kidneys."

"I thought you had colon cancer," I said.

"The fun fact about colon cancer is that it spreads to other organs. They can cut out the bad bits, but it won't cure me." He sighed. "And I tried their poisons the last time."

"You had it before?"

He nodded. "Last year. They did some magic at a clinic here—dosed me up as an outpatient. I felt like shit, but it seemed to work. I went into remission. But it came back in spades. The clinic in Thailand has access to drugs that US doctors aren't allowed yet. That's what this last trip was about."

"And it didn't help?"

"After a consultation and some tests, they said my cancer is too advanced. Their treatment would kill me. Ironically, as I told you I was going for pain therapy, all they gave me was pain pills."

Betty swallowed. "What do our doctors recommend?"

"That I prepare to die. They think I should accept the inevitability of going into a hospice and dying pumped up with a laundry list of drugs and radiation treatments. I think they are full of shit, personally."

"As usual," Betty said, "you know more than the doctors."

"In this case, they are the ones saying they don't know anything. At least I know what I want."

"And what the hell would that be?" Betty asked. I could hear anger, shock, fear churning in her voice.

"I've talked to a hospital in Bangkok. They are developing an experimental treatment that seems to have a real cure rate."

"Real?" I asked. "What does that mean?"

"Greater than zero." He grinned. "That's a damn sight better than the odds I'm offered here."

Betty gave him a look of disbelief. "You want to go to some filthy hospital in Asia and let those people treat you?"

Jake put a hand on hers. "Betty, I've seen it. It is modern and clean and the only place in the world that offers this treatment." He handed us brochures. "I had these printed from their website."

As we looked over the material, I could feel Betty's anger building. "This is just New Age garbage. It's coffee enemas and such."

"The program I'm looking at involves extensive vitamin therapy, specialized diets, and work in a hyperbaric chamber."

Betty sneered. "That's not medicine."

Jake sighed. "No, it isn't. But the doctors here tell me there is no medicine that will work for me, Betty. All they can do is prolong my life—make it take longer for me to die. This Thai hospital offers me some hope and ensures my dignity." Jake pointed to a line at the bottom of her copy of the brochure. "This is the part I like."

Betty squinted to read it. We'd all been after her to get glasses, but she was as stubborn as, well, as everyone in our family. Holding the brochure close, she read the statement: "We promise to do our best to cure you. Failing that, we ensure you a death with dignity." When she finished, she put the brochure down and looked up at him. "Would you like to tell me what in the world you like about that?"

Jake looked excited. "It's something I've thought about a lot. I think it is a beautiful phrase: Death with Dignity."

"A beautiful phrase? You want to leave us and run halfway around the world for a phrase?"

"No. For dignity. I can't stand the thought of letting doctors fill my body with chemicals that turn me into little more than a sick vegetable and stick tubes in me to keep me alive well past my shelf life."

"Don't joke about it! This isn't funny," Betty said.

"No, it isn't," Jake said. "None of it is funny." He touched her hand again. "I'm looking at this the same way I've always approached my investments. I do my research and pretty often turn out to be right."

"That's true," I said without thinking.

Betty glared at me. "We are talking about your life, not an investment."

"Betty, I am dying. The chances of this cure working are slim but, if their treatment fails, I will avoid dying in a hospice, surrounded by the smell of disinfectant and forced to take medicine by the clock. I can't stand the thought of such an undignified way."

Doreen sighed. She was still reading the brochure. "They say they help you die... in comfort."

Betty looked confused. "Comfort. That's why the doctors give out pain pills. When I had my gall bladder surgery—remember how they kept me all doped up. It was glorious."

"I'm not afraid of the pain, Betty. I'm afraid of not feeling it. Living dead to the world isn't living, and it isn't dignified."

"So, you are ready to give up!"

"Just the opposite. I intend to try a Hail Mary play in a Buddhist country and see how that works for me."

"It isn't funny!" She was almost screaming now.

"Betty, I'm going to do this. I'm not asking permission. I just needed you all to know what was going on. I've made the arrangements."

Just as with his investments, Jake had done his research and made up his mind. We could go along or disapprove, but that wouldn't change a thing. What any of us thought was irrelevant.

Betty frowned at me when I got to their house. That was becoming her default expression. "He's in the bedroom packing," she said.

I found him staring at a nearly empty suitcase. "Traveling light?"

He gave me a strange smile. "I find myself wondering just how much a dying man needs to lug around the world with him."

"Enough to have clean clothes for the trip home after he gets out of the clinic, at least."

He gave me a sharp look. "Are you a believer now?"

I laughed. "No, but I think if you intend to try a Hail Mary, you need to take the attitude that it will work. That's what you told me about all the gambles you took."

He nodded. "Who would have known you were even listening when I said that? Okay, then I should pack for a round trip."

"Sure. Even if their treatment doesn't work, your doctors said you'll have as much as a year, and maybe more."

I saw him tense. "Oh yes, but that year is predicated on letting them stick me with needles, on lying in a bed with tubes feeding me for most of that time. That isn't living."

"It is living. None of us want to lose you."

"You have already," he said. "Orson Welles said: 'We're born alone, we live alone, we die alone. Only through our love and friendship can we create the illusion for the moment that we're not alone.' I have no patience with illusions. Your sister is going to have to go on without me and delaying dealing with that won't help her or me. This disease is like experiencing a car wreck in slow motion. It's already happened, but you have to live through it."

"Betty found an article that says the Mayo Clinic is trying a new procedure that extends life for patients with your symptoms."

"I don't want the life of my symptoms extended," He said. "Sorry. Bad joke. She showed me the article. The treatment sounds dreadful." He tossed a pair of swim trunks in the bag. They were decorated with palm trees.

"I haven't seen those before," I said.

He grinned. "Not exactly the thing for Carter Lake, are they? In Thailand, I won't be in the hospital all the time. I've decided to spend free time on the beach. Maybe I can die with a decent tan."

"I see the cancer hasn't spread to your sense of humor gland. But I don't see those trunks doing much to add to your dignity."

He cocked his head. "Well, your sense of humor seems to have improved."

He was right. Black humor had always offended me, and here I was joking about cancer. "I'm in shock. Trying to lighten the mood, I guess."

"Aren't we all?"

"The thing is, I can't come back to this, Billy boy."

"To what?"

"To some incarceration in a hospital. Betty doesn't get it, but I'm at a crossroads."

"That makes no sense."

He sat on the bed. "Look. You know me as well as anyone. Better than Betty. If you had to say what I lived for—being totally honest—what would you say that is?"

"Adventure. Risk."

He nodded. "I've sought thrills. I couldn't have run a business they way you do. The routine would kill me. And there is a dynamic there. How do you think I'd do confined to bed in a drug-induced stupor?"

"Not so good."

"Now, I could run around the world chasing cures. If this one doesn't work, hell, there are lots of them out there, and I can spend my money running from one to the next."

"No. You couldn't."

He smiled. "Exactly. That takes two options off the list. What does that leave?"

"Dying without doctors or cures."

"Right."

"Giving up? That's not your style."

"No. Not giving up. That's a sucker game. I'm talking about embracing the best option."

"Death with dignity?"

I saw my answer pleased him. "Here we are... back to that again. I can give this cure a try, but if it fails—"

"Come back and let us take care of you."

He sighed. "I can't do that, Billy boy."

For once, he made that dreadful nickname sound truly affectionate. "Then?"

"I don't want to tell Betty, but I won't be back. I have to follow my bliss."

"Does that mean you intend to buy Thailand?"

Jake shot me a look, then burst out laughing. "I hadn't thought of that. Good one."

"Then what?"

"You know that from the time I was little, I wanted to be rich."

"And you are."

He sighed. "Did I ever talk about my fallback plan?"

That made me laugh. "I've never considered you needed one. It's hard to imagine you not plunging ahead."

"Well, it's not so much a fallback plan as my alternative goal—the life I'd choose to live, I dreamed of, if my early plans didn't work out. See, I always saw myself as either getting rich or hiding in some idyllic place."

"Thailand, for example."

"He nodded. But without all this. With no investments to think about, no business to run."

"And doing what?"

"Living in the moment."

"The anti-Jake."

That amused him. "To a degree. The anti-Jake in his beautiful, alternative universe." He held up the swim trunks and looked at them as if there was a message in the fabric. "There's something to be said for living each moment as if it is our last. A lot to be said for it. And when I had that dream of peace instead of prosperity, it never occurred to me that I might be spending my money to go to an idyllic place because my last moments were coming at me so fast." He dropped the trunks in the suitcase again. "There's an irony in that."

"And this other life you dreamed of... that's what the poster is about, isn't it?"

He grinned. "You are full of insight and surprise today."

"Two roads and now you wonder about the one you didn't take. That's the theme, right?"

He nodded.

Two roads diverged in a wood, and I—
I took the one less traveled by,
And that has made all the difference.

He twisted to smile at me. "Unlike Frost, when I reached that fork, I took the one more traveled by. I wanted money and success. Now, when I'm forced to confront my life, I wonder what it would have been like if I'd taken the other."

"And where does that road lead that you'd want to go? You love adventure."

"Adventures lie along both paths, I'm sure."

"Are you telling me that after all this time you regret your choice?"

He smiled. "Not at all. It's just that the other represents the great what-if. What if I'd gone that way?"

"We wouldn't have started the business; you wouldn't have married Betty."

"All true. My life would have been different. What I think about, what I wonder is if by taking that path my adventures would have had me chasing peace and dignity instead of money."

"You've enjoyed your money."

"I enjoyed making it and spending it up to a point. But it lost its luster quickly. In the beginning, I wanted Xanadu."

"What?"

"Another poem."

"In Xanadu did Kublai Khan
A stately pleasure-dome decree:
Where Alph, the sacred river, ran
Through caverns measureless to man
Down to a sunless sea.

Suddenly I had an idea. "You should take Betty with you."

"What?" He gave me an astonished look. "What for?"

"She still cares. She'd be there to help you, take care of you."

He stroked his chin. "And Betty would agree, because she'd see it as her duty. But can you imagine Betty sitting in a Bangkok hotel room all day while I get treatment? I can't. First of all, she doesn't believe in what I'm doing. She thinks that I'm throwing money away on quacks. More to the point, without ever seeing the place, she hates the idea of Asia. She'd be miserable there."

I couldn't argue that point. "Then I could go."

That earned a laugh. "You don't like Asia much more than she does. Why should my miserable ending be an excuse to make you suffer any more than her? I'd feel guilty about putting you through that."

"But you'll be all alone."

He trembled slightly. "We die alone, like Welles said. I intend to deal with it"

I wanted to offer sage advice, a bit of wisdom, but none came to mind and trying to force some nugget to the surface made me dizzy. Truthfully, I fancied myself a pragmatic person, and what Jake said made perfect sense. Yet, part of me rebelled against his decision.

"Then this is it? We won't see you again?"

He held his hands out. "Unless the hospital comes up with some high-quality magic none of us can even imagine, I suspect it will be our last chat, Billy boy."

He took my hand. The frailness of his grip shocked me, and I found myself pulling him into a hug.

Jake patted my back. "You are a good friend and a great partner. Betty is lucky to have you for a brother."

I didn't trust myself to say another word. He took up his bag and left. I never saw him again.

After Jake flew out of SFO, Doreen and I took care of some paperwork for his treatment. Our company self-insured medical care for the owners of the company, and I had to authorize payments to the Thai hospital.

At their instructions, I had Jake's doctors send his medical files to them. I took a strange comfort in doing something, however superficial.

The next morning, we had Betty come over to the house for breakfast. While we were eating, she got a call from Jake. I put it on speakerphone. "It was a great flight," he said, sounding enthusiastic.

"Where are you?" I asked.

"I just checked in to my hotel. Tomorrow I'm going to see Ralph."

"What about your treatment?" Betty asked.

"That is scheduled to start in a couple of days. This evening I'm meeting Ralph. We will take care of some business. Remember that once I'm admitted I'll be out of touch for a time."

"If you are going to be out of touch, how will we know how you are doing?" Betty demanded.

"I don't know, exactly," he said. "All I can ask is that you try not to worry. If the doctors have news, if there are promising signs, I'll call."

Betty wasn't appeased. "What if it goes badly?"

There was a long silence. Finally, Jake spoke softly. "Betty, bad news is the most likely outcome. If you aren't hearing from me, that will be because there is no good news, and I don't want to give you any bad news. But don't worry—everything is taken care of."

"What is taken care of?"

"The business—"

"Do you mean money? That isn't what I was worrying about, fool."

"I'm taking care of everything that it is within my power to take care of, Betty. I might take risks, but I try not to leave things to chance." He let out a sigh. "I don't seem to be in control of much at the moment. I thought I knew myself, but I'm learning a great deal I didn't know."

"Damn it, Jake," she said, "you know yourself better than anyone I've ever known."

"Remember when I went to that weekend Buddhist retreat a few years ago."

Betty's lip curled. "Of course. While we were in Omaha."

"They taught that everything you think you know is illusion."

I laughed. "Good thing you aren't a Buddhist."

That made him laugh. "I'll call as soon as there is any good news."

We never heard from him again.

Betty and I got busy ramping up the business to meet our demanding new client's needs. Doreen took over the financials. Combining our efforts, we managed to whip everything into shape.

One day, Betty came in all worked up. "Enough is enough," she said. "It's time to do something."

"Do something?"

"About Jake," she said. "It's been a month since he called to say he was starting treatment. We should have heard something since then, good or bad."

"That long? Damn." I couldn't believe it. "I guess I should make some calls."

Betty snorted. "I did that much. The hotel said he checked out. The hospital wouldn't give me information at all. I called the US embassy in Bangkok. Three times. Officially, they weren't the least bit helpful," she said.

"And unofficially?"

"Some under-something-of-something was nice enough to tell me that he had heard of the hospital. He said it was a reputable place. I got him to call them for me. All they would tell him was that Jake had checked in for treatment but had left long ago."

I sighed. "I'm not surprised."

"You aren't?"

"He was terrified of getting sucked into some system or other," I said.

"Sucked in?"

"He didn't want to start endless treatments that would keep him barely alive, confined to a bed."

Betty snorted. "It isn't as if a dying person gets a lot of choice in the matter." My sister, the stoic, had firm ideas on the subject. To her it was plain as day, a phrase that echoed our mother. "A dying person has an obligation to follow the rules," she said. "He needs to let us nurse him through it." Anything else violated the order of things.

"Jake doesn't see it that way."

That brought Betty up short. "What do you mean? What other way is there to see it?"

That pushed me over the top. "You never understood Jake, but I can't believe you didn't know damn well he had no intention to come back unless he was cured. If he expected to return, he'd have stayed in constant touch. He'd have made arrangements." She scowled, and I decided not to mention that having the disease had reminded Jake of other dreams, reawakened his idea of bliss.

"This won't do," she said.

"What will do? What do you want?"

"You know people there," she said. "Talk to this Ralph person. Find out where Jake is."

"I do know Ralph, but I only met him once. I didn't keep his cell number and can't even remember the company name. I wasn't really that interested. He was Jake's guy."

"Go through Jake's files," she said.

"No need," Doreen said. "I have his number."

We both looked at her. "Why?" I asked.

Surprise crossed her face. "Because I keep Jake's books. I have for years. That's why I know so much about his investments."

"How long has this been going on?"

She laughed at me. "Since he started Campus Cleaners and needed to form a separate company. Who did you think my biggest client is, dummy? I've always kept his books for him."

"You never mentioned it."

"You never asked about my business," she said.

While I stared at my wife, wondering if I really knew her, Betty nudged me. "Call this Ralph. Or just go over there and talk to him. Please. Find out if he knows where Jake went."

"I'll call him," I said.

"I'll book you a flight," Doreen said.

My second trip to Thailand was as uncomfortable and annoying as the first. Being confined with a bunch of other people in a metal tube for 14 hours, plus a five-hour layover in a boring airport in Taipei provided a constant low level of stress.

During the layover, I noted, however, that there were some cheerful travelers—the ones sitting comfortably in first class. They even had their own lounge. Cattle car provided access to little more than hard plastic chairs and a handful of chain food vendors.

When we re-boarded, passing through the front of the plane, I took in the large seats, the drinks in their hands, I decided it would be worth checking into the cost of upgrading my ticket for my return. Jake could damn well pay for it.

When the plane finally landed in Bangkok, I made the long walk of shame through customs and immigration. Duly processed and stamped, I retrieved my luggage, exiting into the hot streets, heading toward the taxi stand. "Hey Bill!" someone called.

I turned to see Ralph grinning at me. "I was watching for you, mate. Come on along."

"How—?"

"Doreen sent me your flight info, mate. Your missus asked if I'd check to see you arrived and got to your hotel okay."

"Thanks," I said. "I appreciate this." His cheerful and friendly manner made me feel guilty about the image I had of him as a sleazy wheeler dealer.

He grabbed a bag. "Ditch the fucking cart. We can talk in my car."

As soon as he headed out of the parking garage, he looked at me. "I've got some news. While you were snoozing on the plane, I called the embassy, just checking in again. I'm afraid they found Jake's body yesterday."

"Found his body?"

"Washed up on a beach in Pattaya."

"What the hell!"

"They think he died of a drug overdose."

"Jake?"

Ralph shrugged. "Whatever happened, they need you to identify the body. I chatted with Doreen and she faxed over a power of attorney that Betty filled out. Your government still has her listed as his next of kin and we saw no reason to bring up the divorce. The idea is you can ship the body home."

Tall buildings whizzed by along the elevated road adding to my dizziness. "Jake, dead?"

"What happened?" I asked he navigated traffic.

He shook his head. "They aren't sure."

"Why was he in Pattaya? What about the clinic?"

"Ah, yes. Jake came by the day he got to town. We took care of some business and then had a nice dinner. He told me about the shitty luck with the cancer and that he was going to the clinic. They had to run some tests."

"Was he depressed?"

"Not at all, the boy seemed overjoyed to be here. Like he was on vacation, you know." He scowled. "A couple of days later he showed up on my doorstep wanting me to sign a few documents and get some notarized. Said that if anything happened to him, I should give them to you, explain as much of this shit as I understood. Then he had me help him convert some crypto into baht. Quite a bit to be hauling around with him, but that's what he wanted."

"Documents?"

"A bunch of business stuff that he said would wrap things up a bit."

"I need to see them," I said.

"'course. He dodged a small truck as he looked over at me. "Straight to my office then?"

I nodded. "I wouldn't be able to rest now, anyway. The hotel will keep"

His office, situated in an old part of town, in a French colonial building, consisted of a shabby suite of rooms. It seemed smaller than I remembered and had a musty, but not unpleasant smell. His secretary, a lovely Thai girl who looked to be about fourteen, sat in the outer room texting on her phone. She didn't even look up as he led me into the inner office and offered me a drink.

"You'll need this, I imagine."

"It's pretty early."

"Early? Think of it as an obligation," he said. "White man's burden and all that shit. If you like, you can blame it all on Somerset Maugham and that crowd. They made the fucking rules, and it's up to us to live up to their decadent image or there will be hell to pay. It's bad enough we are going to drink whisky. Fail to do even that, and the Minister of Tourism will send thugs over to beat us and force those damn gin and tonics down our throats."

The sarcasm, coming on the heels of learning of Jake's death, seemed inappropriate. Yet, in a dark way, I found it amusing. It lightened the dark cloud over me. I let him ease me into a chair and found myself sipping a surprisingly enjoyable straight whisky.

I found such wicked pleasures intoxicating, I suppose. For me, an early drink was a big step on the wild side.

As I sipped my drink, Ralph opened a desk drawer and pulled out an envelope. He held it up, then pushed it across the table to me. "Here's the deal, Billy." He gave me an evil grin. "It seems your so-called best friend has stuck you with the likes of me."

"How?"

"He signed over his shares in the company to you and Betty—half-half. I can understand doing that to his ex, but I thought you two were mates."

I looked at the documents. "This is half the company."

"Yup. Jake loved the business. After the initial dip, he kept putting in money. Worked out well for the bloke too. Business is over the top. Ever since the US got China up its ass, we've been picking up tons of work from US companies that don't want to get shit from the politicians back home for doing business there. We've got several contracts making toys for big US companies and a lot of inquiries. That's why the Chang Mai operation."

"Are you good with this? With us being involved."

"I ain't interested in buying you out, if that's what you mean. You being my new partners doesn't mean shit in terms of the day-to-day operation. Jake's shares have him as a silent partner. Now we didn't stick to that entirely, but he didn't want to involve himself much, except helping hustle new business."

"So passive income."

"And a right nice cash flow it's become. Your Missus sees that it gets paid out regular too."

"Doreen?"

"She's been auditing the books. Part of Jake's deal." He downed his drink. Then he laughed and waved a paper. "I hadn't noticed this before. Jake left me a little something too."

I looked at it and it was note forgiving Ralph of several thousand dollars for a wager on the dragon-boat races.

Still struggling to accept that Jake was dead, this news rocked me. "I don't understand."

Ralph grinned. "I told your Doreen, and she said he did the same with some other companies, splitting them between you and Betty."

"This is crazy." I was thrashing around, wondering how much Doreen knew. And why?

Ralph grinned and held up the bottle. "Looks like you need a little more chaos conditioner." He refilled my glass.

"What happened to Jake after he left here?"

Ralph shrugged. "Here it is... Jake said that this clinic ran some tests and they found they couldn't treat his condition. He didn't like the options they gave him either. Said they were full of shit about letting him die with dignity. No better than the doctors back home. But once he got the mad out, he grinned and said he had a plan. He knew how to find that. We had a few drinks while my legal guy drew up these papers, and then we signed them."

"So where did he go after that? Where was this place that would let him die with dignity?"

Ralph shrugged. "He didn't say exactly. Since I don't expect to die soon myself, I didn't ask. If it were me, I'd be looking to go out having a good time."

"And you didn't ask where he would go?"

"The man went on about animals crawling off to die so they wouldn't be harassed. Sounded like he was asking to be left alone. We went out for a couple of nights, but he didn't seem inclined to want my company after that. Then he said he was going to get a tan." He opened his hands. "Never saw him again."

"Do you have any idea where I could look for him?"

The man shrugged and refilled the glasses. I hadn't realized mine was empty.

"It's early," I said, not sure what I meant anymore.

"Last time he was over here, I took him down to Pattaya. He took a shine to the place. It's only 100 kilometers down the road. Seeing as they found the body there, I'd guess he went straight there."

"What's there that would draw him?"

"The essentials of life: bars, broads, and gambling."

"But he was sick—dying."

"The lad was a fair way from dead yet, though. Said something about the dignity of a simpler life, basic pleasures and knowing where he could find it."

I thought of Jake's description of bliss, his vision of an idyllic place. "What's the best way to get to Pattaya?"

"Rent a car and driver. The buses are nice, but better to hire a driver for a few days and go exactly when and where you want. I know one who has good English. He can translate for you."

"Thanks."

"What should I tell the embassy?"

"That I have to run some errands. I'll be in touch with them when I get back."

He raised his glass. "That's the spirit. Old Jake ain't going anywhere soon. You have time to chase down all the answers you want." One eyebrow lifted. "It's a good place to have some fun doing it."

"The answers I want?"

"The last thing Jake told me was that Billy boy wouldn't be able to resist following his trail. The idea of you tracking him, wondering about his last days, seemed to amuse him."

I stared at the man. Ralph didn't know Jake well at all, and yet he understood some of what made him tick better than I ever would. Dying was as much a game to Jake as life had been.

As I pondered the idea, this time I was the one who refilled the glasses. "To Jake," I said, raising mine.

"To Jake," he said. "Long may he wave."

"What the fuck does that even mean?"

Ralph laughed. "Not a damn thing, mate. Not a damn thing."

Ralph's stream of non sequiturs was making me dizzy. No, I was getting drunk. And for once, enjoying the feeling. "Long may he wave," I said.

The next morning, Ralph came by in the car he had hired for me. The driver seemed fluent in English and, almost as important, the car had air-conditioning.

"Look, buddy," he told the driver. "This man needs to track down a mate from home. Now, he ain't gonna find him, see, cause he's dead and already in the morgue, but he wants to find out where the bloke went. Take him down to Pattaya so he can poke around."

It seemed to make sense to the driver. I sank down in the back seat. The driver put on some Thai pop music, put the car in gear, and by midday we were in Pattaya. Armed with a recent photo of Jake, we methodically went from hotel to hotel looking for someone who remembered him. No one did.

The area consisted mostly of bars and restaurants, resorts, and guesthouses. There wasn't an obvious location for dignified dying in sight. Even the Buddhist temples seemed garish.

I started to wonder if he'd struck off in a new direction. But he'd ended up here, so it was worth pursuing a bit more.

Late in the afternoon we took a break for a beer and a meal. The burly, tattooed bartender, an Englishman with a friendly grin, seemed to be having a slow day. He asked what we were up to. I told him the whole story—a shortened version, but the story.

The bartender laughed. "Jake, you say? Shit, I know him. Well, a guy named Jake came in here a few times. Had a luscious local gal with him too."

I took out a photo of Jake. "This guy?"

"Yeah, that's him. A lot more pale and hollowed cheeks, but that's him."

"Do you know where he was staying?"

The bartender laughed. "That's one reason I remember him. He mentioned that he had found heaven over at the Pattaya Palace. That's not exactly a hot spot and I asked him why not stick around here, closer to the action? We had plenty of rooms and we are in the middle of all the vices known to man. He said he needed a little peace. Said he came here to die."

"That's right."

"No shit? I'm afraid that when he started a little sermonette about dying with dignity, I went off to serve other customers. People spin all sorts of stories in here. I thought he might be after free drinks." He paused. "If your pal really was dying, I got to admit the Pattaya Palace ain't a bad choice for that sort of thing. Perfect for going out quiet like."

"I know this place," my driver said. "It not very high-end."

"What do you mean?" I asked.

The bartender laughed. "He means it's an old school beach place—bungalows, kind of quiet. Even the bar is mellow. The locals don't get why foreigners would stay there. Still, there are some fine girls, good booze, and a nice beach. It's just a bit low on parties and discos for most people" He grinned. "But I guess a man banging a sexy local girl wouldn't need our parties."

"I'll check it out."

"Pierre, a French kid, owns the place. I think his Daddy bought it for him to keep him out of France for a while."

I paid the tab, tipping well, then we headed off. My pulse raced. Finally, I felt that I was getting close to real answers.

We found Pierre behind the reception desk drinking anise. A friendly sort, he poured me one and happily admitted to knowing Jake. "Terrific guy," he said.

"And he stayed here?"

"He and the girl. He bought one of the beach bungalows."

"Bought it?"

"Yeah. My Papa would kill me if he knew. They are supposed to be rentals, but he fell in love with the place. When he offered me more than it was worth, I had to sell it to him. It's been a slow year. Too bad he only owned it for a week or so before he died. Too bad he died."

"Yes."

"I'm the one who found him."

"On the beach?"

"Yeah. I told the girl, but she already knew. She gave me his passport and written instructions telling me to call the embassy. He didn't want her involved."

"What happens to the bungalow now?"

The man shrugged. "Nothing. He put it in the girl's name." I must've been giving him the open-mouthed stupid look because he laughed. "She's there now, I think." He pointed at a thatched-roof hut on the beach. "That one."

I bought beers for the driver and myself, and one for the Frenchman too. Then, with my stomach in a knot, I walked across the sand toward the bungalow to meet this girlfriend. I was trying to picture that. Jake with a Thai girlfriend? And he'd bought her a bungalow?

A slim young Thai woman was sitting on the porch staring out to sea. "Hello," I said.

"You want massage?" she asked, sounding hopeful.

I looked her over and guessed she was in her twenties. She wasn't beautiful, but pleasant enough, with small firm breasts under a thin tee shirt; her shorts showed lovely brown legs.

"A massage?"

She pointed to a sign. "Oil massage 500 Baht."

"No, I was hoping to talk to you about Jake."

"Jake?"

"The man who bought this bungalow."

"Nice man," she said.

"Why did he do that? Buy you a bungalow?"

Her look told me that she had little respect for my ability to grasp the obvious. "So I not have to pay rent. I keep more money from massages."

"Did you ask him to do that?"

She got up, moving catlike toward me, before stopping to put her hands on her hips and look me over. "You are Billy Boy," she said.

"How did you know?"

"Jake tell me. He say, 'After I die, Billy Boy come see you and ask too many questions.'"

That sounded exactly like something Jake would say. "I only ask because I'm trying to understand."

"Understand what?"

"Why did he come here in the first place?"

She laughed. "To get a massage." Then she smiled. "The first time he come to get a massage. Every day a massage. The second time he come back to see me. The last time he come here to be happy and have someone take care of him."

"Take care of him? Are you a nurse?"

She laughed. "No. He not want a nurse or a doctor." Her smiled was delightful. "Jake a smart man. He say a dying man just needs a woman who can make the last days good and beautiful. He ask if I can be nice to him, make love to him when he like, while he can."

"And you agreed."

She stood and motioned for me to follow her. "I show."

An onshore breeze wafted across the open porch and the bungalow had double doors front and back to welcome it. I followed the girl as she moved through the doors as if she floated on the breeze. I drifted in the wake of this insubstantial waif who led me to the seaside where a hammock was strung.

"He like to lie there and look out at water."

The hammock was perfectly positioned to give a man a clear view of the Gulf of Thailand. I imagined Jake there, content. "At first, we just live together, being happy. I fix him good Thai food and bring him whisky in his hammock."

"At first."

She shrugged. "His pain grew bad, so bad that massages, good sex no longer enough to wash it away. I brought him opium to smoke. He like for a time." She made a face. "He had me get other drugs too, but these we put away. For later. He said he wanted to be clear when he meet death."

"Clear?"

"Too many drugs, the ones that took away all the pain, he didn't like. He think they are not a dignified way to wait for death. He want to meet death face-to-face and talk plain."

"And yet, he died of an overdose."

She nodded. "One night he wake me. 'Death came for a chat,' he said. 'We had a long talk and settled things, walking along the beach.' He was ready."

"He settled things with death?"

"Enough."

"I don't understand."

"He had me get the drugs. We walked in the full moonlight to the edge of the water. We lie on a blanket on the edge of the water. It made a gentle sound. I watched him take many drugs—all of them. Then we made love."

"What happened next?"

"He slept. When the sun began to rise, I said goodbye. The Gulf has small tides, the water doesn't come up far, but we were close to it already. Slowly the sea come in I watched it wash him away."

I could picture it. It sounded oddly peaceful, serene. "Yes."

"The next day I tell Pierre that someone find him soon, give him the papers Jake left."

"He mentioned that."

"You want the money now?"

"What money?"

She led me inside to an ancient, intricately carved desk. On it was a carved box fashioned out of some dark wood. I opened it to find it filled with Thai money. While I stared at it, she opened a drawer and took out some documents. "Jake said to show you this. Billy boy will need some of these papers, he said."

When I started reading, my knees grew weak. I sat on the bed, and the girl sat next to me, her body radiating a sensual heat.

The top sheet was a note. "Hey, Billy boy," he wrote, "I'm sure you've been told that I offed myself. That means the insurance company will probably raise hell about paying out. Naturally, Betty is my beneficiary and see if you can't make them cough it up. If not, don't worry. I left her plenty of money and there is a brokerage account with stocks and bonds that is in her name. Doreen knows how to access it.

"The cash in this box is for the lovely girl you've met by now. She was a blessing and deserves every baht and the bungalow too. You should already have the shares in Ralph's company now—you and Betty deserve that too. Let Ralph do his thing and rake in the money.

"I hope you can see with your own eyes that, despite all odds, and Robert Frost, I managed to travel both roads, even if the one less traveled was a tad shorter than I might have liked. Boy, was I lucky. Who the hell gets to do that? Take care, buddy, and I'll see you on the other side one day."

The girl walked up and handed me a cold bottle of beer. I drank thirstily, then I handed her the money. "He wanted you to have this."

Without a flicker of emotion, she put it back in the box and replaced it on the desk. I looked away. The touch of her slight hand, slender fingers on my arm made me turn back. A delicious, delicate, and erotic contact that made me tremble. I looked down at her face and saw a lovely, seductive smile— a smile could change how a man saw the world. "Jake was a nice man," she said. "I miss him."

"Did you love him?"

She shook her head. "I made love with him. I made him feel loved."

It all made a certain amount of sense. There were still blanks, but none this girl could fill in. She had played her role in Jake's exit.

"I should go," I said.

The girl cocked her head. "You could stay. With me. Your friend Jake would not mind."

In that moment, a desire for this creature rippled through me. I swallowed, knowing that if I stayed another hour, I would stay the night. And if I spent the night, I might never leave.

This, then, was the attraction Jake must have felt, the allure that drew him back. I didn't have half his strength. And while this road of Jake's, and the girl he'd followed down it both called to my primal being, I still was traveling another path.

"I must go. My family needs me and to know what happened to Jake. And I have a car waiting."

She stood up, smiling, nodding.

As I turned to go, I saw a copy of the brochure for the clinic sitting on the table. Someone had used a felt-tip pen to underline the phase that meant so much to Jake: death with dignity. Whatever that meant to Jake, apparently, he found it.

At the door, I stopped and gave the girl one last look. She smiled. "I didn't ask your name," he said. "That was rude."

She laughed. "Your thoughts were about your friend, not me. He was important to you."

"More important than I knew."

"And you were important to him."

"Why do you say that?"

"One reason he needed me was that he wasn't strong enough to be around you or his family in his last days. He couldn't stand the idea that you would all be angry with him for not being willing to do anything that would keep him alive a few extra days or weeks."

"He wanted to die with dignity," I said.

"Yes," she said, giving me an enchanting smile that made my heart pound. For a moment, I considered the possibility that she might be attracted to me. That was crazy, of course. I couldn't stay here. I had a wife, children, and business to run. This wasn't even my dream. It was Jake's. I wouldn't be out of his influence for a long time. "Still," I said. "It was rude not to ask. You were trying to help my best friend. I should know your name."

She turned her head and stared out across the Gulf of Thailand for a moment. "My name... Jake couldn't say it in Thai, so he always called me Dignity."

When I returned to Bangkok, Ralph took me to the embassy where I arranged for Jake's last international flight. We talked about things and had dinner and then talked some more. I'd developed an appreciation for the man, and he declared that I was 'loosening up nicely.' High praise in Australia, I assumed.

A few days later, I flew back to the US—traveling first class, just as I'd promised myself. From the moment I boarded, I wondered why the hell I hadn't done it before. What a difference there was. The seats, the service, the food, the VIP lounge in Taipei... everything was amazing.

It seemed odd that I didn't understand the true value of comfort until now. In roundabout ways, Jake's death was teaching me a lot about life.

"You look refreshed," Doreen said when she picked me up at the airport.

"In more ways that you can know," I said. "How is Betty?"

"Reconciled," she said. "She is such a stoic that she could accept the idea that Jake deliberately overdosed on pain pills after the treatments at the clinic failed."

"Good."

"I think the news that Jake left her a wealthy woman was the bigger shock." Then she hit me with that devastatingly amused, sly smile. "Are you going to tell me what really happened?"

There was no point in pretending, and I wanted to talk about it. I told her the whole story. "I'm still digesting it all. I'm not sure I should tell Betty all of it."

"Jake wanted his dignity. She gains nothing by hearing a story she won't like or understand," Doreen said. "And telling the truth, the whole truth, and nothing but the truth is highly overrated. Worst of all, she won't even get the joke."

I let out a sigh. "True enough."

It was also true that the story didn't seem to surprise my wife... well, that didn't surprise me. Not anymore.

"Seems you had a much bigger hand in Jake's businesses than I ever knew."

She grinned. "Jake couldn't do it on his own."

"And you didn't think to tell me?"

She looked at me. "And give you a chance to object? That would have been... undignified."

"I suppose it would have been."

"Can't have that," she said.

"I'm just learning who you are," I said.

I couldn't fathom the smile she gave me. "And how do you like me so far?"

I laughed. "Pretty damn well. It's sexy."

"You are changing," she said.

"I've been told I'm loosing up nicely. And that came from an expert. Do you agree?"

"Is there any question? You flying first class? Lying to Betty?"

"I suppose I am. Jake left a void. Not one that I want to fill exactly. But I've learned that he's been propping me up. His death meant I had to change."

"Or fall over," she said.

"How do you like me so far?" I asked.

She wrinkled her nose. "You are still upright, so I'll call it a work in progress. But you show promise."

"On the way back here, with all that time on the plane and sitting in airports to fill up, I did a lot of thinking. Jake gave me a lot to think about and some of it... well, I have some ideas."

"I like ideas," she said.

"I talked a lot with Ralph."

"Sleazy Ralph? Do tell."

"I deserve that. Anyway, he was talking about opportunities to expand the manufacturing business."

"More?"

"By opening facilities in Vietnam."

"Halfway around the world?"

"They have a good, well-trained workforce."

"Okay, Billy boy, now I'm waiting for the punchline."

"Well, he is busy with the new operation in Chang Mai. He is complaining that even he can't be everywhere at once."

"That tends to be difficult even for Australians. So what does that mean to you?"

"To us. This fall the youngest starts college."

"I just got the bill for the tuition and the dorm."

"What would you think about moving to Asia?"

"What about the business here?"

"I'm tired of the cleaning business. Do you think we could turn it over to Betty?"

"Betty is thriving. She's been fretting about what she'd do when you came back. She is enjoying being in charge. And our new big client thinks she is great."

"Then maybe we should make her CEO."

"Are you sure?"

"I need to make my mark on something. I've spent my life running something Jake started. Now, he got us into this business too, but I'd be tackling new things."

She pursed her lips. "Starting up new operations in a new country would require a huge learning curve."

"That part I do well," I said.

"And it will take a long time," she said. "We'd either have to lease our house or sell it."

"We should sell it," I told her.

"You are being impulsive and imprudent, Billy Boy."

"If I keep being impulsive and imprudent, will you go back to calling me Bill?"

"Deal."

"If we are going to do this, let's cut all the ties we can. We will want to keep our options open over there. Happily, for once, we don't need to worry about cash flow."

"My," she said. "Whatever you found following Jake's trail seems to have inspired you. Care to share?"

"Things came together. And then the whole idea of dying with dignity... I met her."

That earned me a huge grin. "So you said. What's she like?"

"It's what she represented to Jake. Simple, primitive, basic."

"And he needed to die with dignity," she said. "Is she pretty?"

"Not as pretty as you."

"Right answer." She took my arm. "Here's the deal, darling. If we go over there, to Vietnam, or wherever, you have to promise you won't be dying with dignity any time soon."

"You wouldn't be supportive? It's a noble goal."

"Well, someday, perhaps. But you said you were just learning who I really was."

"I think that more all the time."

"Then before we even get to any chat about dying with dignity, I expect you focus on living with whoever Doreen turns out to be."

"Deal, partner," I said.

• • • •

"I shall be telling this with a sigh
Somewhere ages and ages hence:
Two roads diverged in a wood, and I—
I took the one less traveled by,
And that has made all the difference."
— Robert Frost

Acapulco, Mexico

Ed and I met on a traveler's website, and almost immediately began to private message to discuss traveling and writing books together. We had just met the prior month to travel to Cartagena to write our first short story "Invisible Fortune" in the beginning of 2018, and then onward to Medellin to work on a portion of the Bitpats series of novels, but an unexpected opportunity arose — an anarchy conference called Anarchapulco in Acapulco.

Even though it had only been a few weeks since our last trip we decided to do another, the prospects for a good story in a hotel full of insanely rich anarcho capitalists was too good to pass up.

We were immediately attracted, not sexually, but maybe, to a woman, an ex-prostitute and porn star who was selling anonymous shares in a company called Pink Date. A decentralized prostitution app similar to Tinder. Yes, I hate to admit it, but I made an investment, yes I lost all the money, "A fool and his money are soon parted..."

So Ed befriended her, and over a few coffees had an in-depth discussion about her business. Later that afternoon, Ed and I were drinking a bottle of Glenlivet Scotch, discussing what an undercover CIA agent would think of this if he was in attendance. That single malt-inspired conversation became this short story.

Enjoy,
-Lee

WHO OWNS YOU?

This story is fiction. Although the Anarchapulco Conference is real, and real people are inevitably mentioned, the characters in the story and the things they do are solely the product of the authors' overheated imaginations. Any resemblance they have to any persons living or dead, or anything those people might have done, would be a strange coincidence.

Langley, Virginia, USA

"The truth is not always beautiful, nor beautiful words the truth."

— Lao Tzu, Tao Te Ching

You want me to go undercover?" Tyler Blake looked at Ralph, his boss. He realized he was blinking stupidly, but then this had to be a joke. He wasn't a spy. "But I analyze white-collar crime."

The man nodded, and the movement made the fat around his neck bulge out. "That makes you perfect for this assignment. You've got the financial and IT background to understand the crypto shit and that will be an important part of the program, and maybe their plans."

"But I've been working at a desk since I finished training. I'm not a field operative."

"Listen, Blake, this is the CIA, not a social club. We own your ass, and this is your assignment. You are going undercover at this anarchy conference."

"Anarchy conference? They have conferences?"

"Anarchapulco, they call it. They think they are being fucking clever because it's in Acapulco."

"But that's in Mexico. That's on foreign soil." Somehow that seemed to make it worse, more dangerous. "Don't we already have trained people there?"

"Sure. But our agent in that location has the flu. We need to replace him."

"We have one agent there?"

He laughed. "It's fucking Acapulco, Blake. Normally it isn't exactly a hotbed of anti-government activity, but this goddamn Anarchapulco conference being held there is expected to have a couple of thousand anarchists collected there. We need eyes and ears."

"An anarchist convention? That makes no sense."

"Still, that's what's going on and the political freaks will be mixing it up with all those cryptocurrency radicals who want to destroy our economy."

Tyler sighed. Ralph was right that his background let him understand cryptocurrencies, but it probably wouldn't be a good idea to mention that he'd shifted most of his own savings into them over the last several years. They'd been his safe haven ever since he lost his ass with silver. He knew it would be pointless to explain that no one was trying to destroy anything, that it was just a matter of the old economy becoming archaic and unwieldy. He sighed. At least that part of the conference could prove interesting. "I suppose I can go, but what exactly do you expect me to do?"

"Blend in. Schmooze with the ones that seem to be ringleaders and find out if they are planning anything."

"Planning anything? Like riots? The conference is in Mexico, after all. Isn't it their problem?"

"Blake, this antigovernment shit is global. The Mexican government isn't thrilled with these bastards either, but they need the tourist dollars and these people are rich—they're filling a major resort for a week or more. They aren't going to stop it, but they don't mind us slipping you in there to keep an eye on things."

It sounded easy enough. "No actual spy craft needed then."

"Zero. Just make some connections and keep your ears open. How hard could it be?"

When Tyler came home from work, Alice, his fiancée, was there, listening to the radio. A man was rapping out lyrics to a familiar blues tune.

"I got the keys to the Ferrari,
I'm loaded and ready to go,
I'm gonna burn out baby,
the speed limit is too fucking slow."

Tyler flinched, then turned it off. Alice glared at him. "Why did you do that?"

"It's too awful. Why does that man hate Brownie McGhee so much?"

"Who?"

"That's who wrote the song."

She shrugged. "Then this guy updated it, I guess."

"Updated? He ruined it. Why can't he write his own songs to ruin?"

"He's a rap star," as if that explained it. "Why are you in such a bad mood?"

"I'm not," he said, even though he knew he was. Normally he would ignore Alice's dreadful taste in music, but today he couldn't. So he told her. "I'm being sent to Mexico on assignment."

"Way cool," she said, clapping her hands.

"Really?" He told her about the assignment and being sent to Acapulco. "I'll be gone more than a week."

"Fantastic."

"I thought you'd be upset."

"About going to a resort in Acapulco? Great. We'll have a fantastic time."

"We? I'm going on what is the CIA's version of a business trip."

"We are talking Acapulco here," she said. "I'm going. Your room will be paid for. We'd only have to pay for my airfare and food."

"I'm supposed to be working," he said.

"It's a conference. You'll be talking to people, drinking in the bar, things like that. It isn't like I'd interfere with any of that. I'd be out at the pool or in the spa."

"It's against protocol," he said. Even as he said it, he knew he was making excuses. The truth was that he didn't want her going along. "I'm supposed to be undercover. You don't take your girlfriend along when you go undercover."

"I bet you are just saying that so you don't have to take me."

Her words stung, mostly because she was right. I didn't want to take her. "So, call Ralph and ask him if it's okay for you to go. If he agrees..."

"You ask him."

"No. I'm already on his bad side now."

"You are so much on his bad side that he's sending you to a resort in Mexico for a week." She didn't buy his argument at all.

"Exactly," Tyler said, knowing that once again he and Alice were tacitly agreeing to disagree. She wasn't going to forgive him anytime soon. Sometimes it seemed like she thought that because they were supposed to get married in a few months that she owned him. That was bothersome, but somehow not surprising. He needed to change that attitude somehow. He wanted a partner, not an owner, but how to undo what he had let happen?

Princess Mundo Imperial Hotel

Acapulco, Mexico

"Yes, I am 100% anarchist. Anarchy, to me, is a belief that all transactions, all activity, should be voluntary. It is a peaceful philosophy of not forcing anyone to do anything and not allowing anyone else to force you to do anything."

— Jeff Berwick

Tyler Blake stood in the lobby outside of the main salon of the Princess Mundo International Hotel in Acapulco and laughed. "Just blend in with the crowd and see what you can learn," his boss had said. He looked at the people around him and wondered which group he was supposed to blend in with. There were men and women in business suits, looking like they'd dropped in from corporate America and others in suits who had more of an academic air about them; there were refugees from the beach in shorts and tee shirts, two women in slinky dresses and platform heels smoking cigarettes and watching the crowd looking like they'd been zapped in from a disco somewhere, and a guy wearing a rainbow-patterned sarong sort of thing that showed incredibly scrawny arms and legs. Still others dressed in an odd assortment of vendor giveaways—tee shirts with company logos, hats...

Blend in, indeed.

Tyler had chosen a middle path, wearing a short-sleeved shirt, and cargo pants. He'd hoped to be inconspicuous, but no one was. As he began working the crowd, introducing himself briefly, chatting with people, he found that how he was dressed didn't seem to matter to any of them. And they were a mixed lot... farmers and entrepreneurs who had invested in cryptocurrency, business owners interested in reducing regulations, conspiracy theorists, anti-vaccine people... a strange mix of true believers of all stripes. As he looked at the literature and eavesdropped it was clear that the attendees of the Anarchapulco conference were only united in one or two ways: they resented government interference in their lives and they had come to party.

Along both sides of the hall, vendors passed out literature and talked about products. The literature was often political, primarily anti-socialist articles, which, according to this group, seemed to include a variety of US government programs; the products primarily associated with cryptocurrency in some form or another. A new crypto tied to silver competed for attention with one that promised secure communications. Another vendor sold hardware wallets.

"Hemp and Cannabidiol–CBD oil," a long-haired guy looking like he just popped in from the sixties said, pointing to literature on his table. "It's a pain reliever derived from cannabis. The government doesn't want you to know these are good for people and the environment." This guy, at least, was more what Tyler had expected.

"I can buy that legally," he pointed out.

"Sure, but the prices are jacked way the fuck up because of government regulation. People who need CBD oil can't afford it."

"You want to subsidize it?"

The man laughed. "Right. That's a government solution, dude. Just set it free." He waved his arms to indicate a bird flying.

Tyler noticed a familiar face on a man standing next to him. He turned and held out a hand. "Mike Maloney, right?" The man nodded and took his hand. "You helped me understand the danger of fiat currency way back."

"I'm glad I could be of help," he said.

"I got into silver and kept buying. Of course, at $45 an ounce I took a bit of a bath."

Maloney laughed. "Who didn't? When there is market manipulation all the best theories fall apart."

"That they do."

Other people approached, taking Mike Maloney's attention, and Tyler drifted about, wondering at the amazing people who were there. He saw Roger Ver, whose videos had convinced him to try cryptocurrency when silver and Bitcoin were both $23 investments, as was another precious metals advocate who was taking a closer look at cryptocurrency, David Morgan of the Morgan Report.

Inside the salon where the speeches were being given, he found more tables, more vendors. A Canadian company mining gold in Mexico, Mexican Gold Corporation had a table across from a company using computers to mine crypto that was announcing a new facility in Iceland. Another wellness company, focused on the things the governments were doing to the water supply, sold filtration systems, and passed out information on the dangers of fluoride.

Some of this seemed rather out there to Tyler—fringe stuff, yet harmless. Ralph had made it crystal clear that he wasn't there to learn about the harmless loonies. No, he was supposed to get the scoop on serious conspiracies and frauds.

"International fraud, most of it digital is growing, Tyler," his boss had said. "This conference is putting the political crazies in touch with the guys who are pushing technology in ways we can't control it. I want to know what they are talking about and who is doing the loudest talking."

"Doesn't the agency already monitor all these people?" he asked.

"Shit yes. And the chatter is all over the place. But you have a finance and tech background—enough to pick up on the threads of things and see where they lead. You need to identify the code words, the key concepts we need to scan for."

And so, here Tyler was, staying in a five-star resort on the taxpayers' dime, trying to filter through the chaos of complaints about government intervention. The irony wasn't lost on him that without the anarchists, he'd be at home, dealing with snow in wintry Virginia.

The tricky part of his job certainly wasn't finding suspicious conversations. Hell, the 'plots,' as his boss at Langley saw them, were all over the place. All you had to do to get involved in discussions of political intrigue was to say hello in a bar.

The problem was... most of the schemes he overheard or was told outright were not, in any way, shape or form, illegal. For some things that were emerging, such as the myriad applications of tokens and blockchain, there weren't any laws concerning them at all. The people at the IRS might see them as ways to avoid taxes, but even they hadn't agreed on a clear definition of what cryptocurrency was—securities, real property, or money. So, there wasn't much to report.

Besides, Ralph was mostly concerned with the political, the radicals who wanted to be able to travel without passports, or other nefarious things. Yet, as he sat in on lectures, as he drank with people in the bar during breaks, he began to realize that almost without exception the 'anarchists' he was meeting weren't plotting anything. They were individually and, at times collectively, seeking out ways to be left alone. Some of their methods might be sketchy, or even marginally legal, but there was no insurrection intended.

"Blockchain frees us from the central control of the government," the communications people told him. While Ralph and his superiors would fear that, and certainly hate it, it was hardly a revolution. More of a sidestep around things, like dropping out and moving to Tahiti without telling anyone.

Tyler found himself liking these people. Well, some were crazies of course, but harmless enough. Many were good business people trying to make money—and they seemed to be doing that. And the vendors were like vendors anywhere. They had a product that they thought suited whatever the hell demographic this was.

One vendor caught his attention. Two attractive women were running a booth wearing black tee shirts that said "DateChain" on them. It was, he learned, a start-up.

"We are having our initial coin offering in a couple of months," a dark-haired lady told him. She had a name tag that said 'Tara' and appeared to be in her late twenties or early thirties.

"Coin offering?"

"We are using blockchain to provide a secure escort service," she said, sounding very matter-of-fact.

"Escort service?" That caught him off guard.

She nodded. "Worldwide."

"But that's illegal," he said.

She laughed. "You must be American. In many places it's a perfectly legal activity," she said with a smile. "In others, only solicitation is illegal, not prostitution."

"But your website..."

"We aren't located in any country. We are in the blockchain."

"But you have to based somewhere."

"Sure. But there are countries that officially recognize and permit both prostitution and cryptocurrency. That's where our servers are; so that's where we are."

Tyler scratched his head. "But..."

She handed him a brochure. "Go to the investor's website and read up. Think about the company and come back with any questions." She handed him a business card. "Tara Hutchins, President, DateChain."

Tyler looked at her. "It's your company?"

"Partly. I'm a founder and president."

"That's surprising," he said.

"Why? It shouldn't be the least surprising. After all, escorts are, have to be, business people."

That made a lot of sense. "But a company is rather visible, isn't it. I thought you'd want to stay below the radar." Radar, meaning people like him who were paid to notice.

She shrugged. "We are changing things. Asserting our rights."

"Your rights?"

"The right to ownership of our bodies and lives. Why should a government have the right to say what a free individual does with her own body? They let people get in a ring and bash each other's brains out on pay-per-view; people can screw their brains out and it's fine, but if a woman or a man wants to be paid for providing their body to give another human sexual pleasure, some governments think they have the right to prevent that–to make it against the law. It's the majority enslaving the minority."

"So it's a political statement?"

"It's a business, but there is inherently a political implication to almost every business. In this case, it's the idea that people own themselves. Our company helps escorts work safely. We are doing this for ourselves."

"We?"

She smiled. "I'm an escort," she said.

For reasons he didn't understand, her answer stunned him.

Back in his room, Tyler Blake took Tara's advice. He was an analyst, and she'd given him a lot to analyze. He opened his laptop to research her initial coin offering, but before he could go to the website, he saw that he had an email from his boss.

"Find anything to report?" it asked.

He hit reply. "I've met a bunch of people who don't like to be regulated in any way, and some very new age people saving the world with yoga. Not much else." Then he hit reply. He knew that would inspire a tart response telling him to dig deeper for his country, but that was okay. He could ignore it.

There was also an email from Alice, but he wasn't in a mood to read it. Maybe he'd check it out later.

He went to the DateChain website and started reading. He hadn't paid a lot of attention to ICOs in general. In fact, he realized that he didn't know anything about them. He needed someone to help him understand why they were happening, popping up across the financial landscape like wildflowers. Certainly, they were tied in with the companies using blockchain to do business, but a coin offering wasn't essential to doing that.

Given that the resort was lousy with garrulous experts, Tyler went downstairs to find one. He went into the Starbucks and got a coffee and took it outside to the breezeway where there were chairs and tables where small groups of people were talking while they enjoyed their coffee and pastries or sandwiches. He recognized a young guy he'd seen at the booth for one of the wellness companies that was somehow involved with blockchains. As he walked over to the table, the man smiled up at him and pointed to an empty chair. "How's it going?"

"I'm getting a little confused by all the terminology," Tyler told him as he sat, thankful that the man saved him the trouble of prying. "Your company, for instance... you are going to have an ICO, an initial coin offering."

"That's right."

"Why not an IPO? They are well understood by investors."

The man smiled. "Because when you have an IPO you hold it in a country and immediately become tied up with all their rules and regulations about securities. With an ICO we are free of that. And why would a company making tee shirts in Guatemala and selling them in Ecuador want to get burdened with that, or with US taxes, if you follow your logic and go where the investors are?"

"Okay, I can see that. Tax and regulation avoidance."

The man grinned. "Besides, who makes money in an IPO? Mostly it goes to the lawyers and the bank that underwrites it. And small investors are cut out of the action."

"The idea is to protect everyone involved," Tyler said.

The man laughed. "So the same government that doesn't care if you lose half your pay check in taxes and gamble the rest away in Vegas feels the need to protect you from getting into the early stage of an investment that your instincts tell you is a great opportunity?"

Tyler laughed. "That's not the intention, I suspect."

"At best, all that does is protect the poor while allowing the rich the first shot at real money-making opportunities. Protecting people from risk, protects them from the rewards too. So, in our case, we think average people will see value in our company, and that value can be greater without government interference. The only I way I know of to allow investment and still be free is through an ICO. And as a bonus, with companies like ours, you are protected from the failure of a fiat currency."

"A small investor can buy silver or gold," Tyler pointed out. "They offer protection."

"Only if the government doesn't confiscate it."

"Why would they do that?"

"The reason isn't important, not as important as the fact that they've done that before."

"When?"

"In 1933. Executive Order 6102. Franklin D. Roosevelt decided that hoarding precious metals was making the recession worse. That was all it took. He implemented it under the Trading with the Enemy Act of 1917. So, thinking they wouldn't do it is foolish. A better play is to invest in mining companies outside the US. There are some here, and some that are truly decentralized. Even if the effort to suppress this became global, if they want to try confiscating a real decentralized cryptocurrency, best of luck to them. If they go after the owners, well, it would be like trying to arrest smoke."

As he thought over what the man said, Tyler's cell phone beeped. He glanced at it and saw an Inclement Weather Alert. "Massive snowstorm blankets Virginia." He swiped it away and saw the home page with a picture of the sun, and the notation that it was 78 degrees in Acapulco.

"Problem?" the man asked.

"Just cold weather hitting Virginia hard and making me glad I'm here."

"Wow, Virginia. Home of the CIA." Tyler flinched. "Makes me wonder," the man said,,, "a conference like this going on... how many Feds you think they've sent to keep track of us?"

Suddenly Tyler tensed. "What makes you think they've sent Feds here?"

"They always hate what they don't control," the man said. "I mean, think about the fact that what we are doing isn't legal or illegal. It's something new, something they don't understand. Like I said, they'll have their hands full trying to stop cryptocurrency and business based on blockchain from taking over. They have to know that. So my guess is that the people who still pay taxes are funding a bunch of black shoes to come here for fun in the sun—and there is nothing useful they can learn."

Tyler was wearing sandals and still had to resist looking at his own feet. "Well, they do collect data."

"And they sit around with us. They eavesdrop on the people who came here on our own dime to do business or learn the latest nuances and developments—the way you are. They send spies to listen to people having honest discussions and taxpayers, who can't afford to stay here, pay for it all."

The truth struck home and made Tyler uncomfortable. The man was sharing information openly. Everyone here was. He finished his coffee. "Well, thanks for the education. I didn't think about a lot of those things before."

The man handed him a card. "The investor information is on the website if you decide it might be safer with us than in fiat currency."

Tyler put it in his pocket. "Well, I will definitely take that under advisement."

With new insights spinning about in his head, Tyler went back to his room and returned to the DateChain website. He read with his usual thoroughness and was impressed. The incredibly business-like discussion of what he had always thought of as part of the dark underbelly of commerce struck him as incongruous if not just plain weird. Although it mentioned escorts providing services for their clients, it left the details to the imagination of the reader. The discussion was of how the platform would act as a broker, a go-between that ensured good customer service, a quality experience. Clients had to create a profile and could pay in cryptocurrency or cash. The service provided a date book, much like the one in the major dating services, where a client could learn about prospective escorts in the area.

The most remarkable page, to Tyler, was the one written to explain to escorts how to sign up and use the service. They had to prove they were over nineteen to ensure there was no sex trafficking. Then they created a profile and could list specialties. They'd be able to see ratings of clients provided by other escorts and there were multiple levels of screenings of the clients they could choose from.

The key word that he kept coming back to was 'choice.' The lectures on libertarianism were naturally about freedom of choice, and now he began to see why Tara and her company were here at this conference. He had begun to see that the appeal would be to investors looking for both innovation and a chance to work in the shadows. This business proposal had a definite political dimension to it–the company fully intended to work around the laws of individual nations.

The way they were going about it was clever. Clearly the same approach would work for so many things where crime was relative–the idea that something illegal was a national, regional, or even local proposition. It wasn't something like murder that could be universally frowned on.

With so many places legalizing marijuana and the network of global tax deals so complex, this was fertile ground. This, Tyler was certain, was what unnerved the authorities and was exactly the sort of thing that his own boss wanted to hear about.

The trick was that the company, its formation, was perfectly legal and unless they carried out business where it was illegal, there wasn't much a government could do about it; even then they could only prosecute the illegal activities in their own area.

Clearly the women who were signing up were treating their work as a business. And the ones already on the site, the examples, were beautiful.

The next day, by the time he reached her table in the conference room, Tyler had several questions buzzing in his head. "You've done such a thorough job of researching and planning...why not use this model for a business that doesn't run afoul of local laws?" he asked.

Tara laughed. "Name a business that doesn't run afoul of local laws and regulations. Most just consider it a cost of doing business. Think of the legal battles Amazon and Google fight in Europe and China. We prefer to be more off the radar and decentralized. That way no government can demand we defend what we are doing, which is simply marketing something we own."

"And the escorts that join your service all feel that way?"

"I wouldn't know," she said. "I imagine some of them just see us as a way to reach the right clientele and, not incidentally, keep a larger portion of the fee she negotiates. We take a transaction fee, not the huge cut a pimp or escort service demands. Each person will have her own reasons, her own philosophy. We don't care what that is as long as they adhere to our standards and our business practices."

"I'm trying to understand," he said.

The room was quiet for the moment. Tara turned to the other woman, Eileen. "I'm taking a break." The woman nodded. "Let's go get a coffee," she told Tyler.

The offer surprised him, but then he found himself constantly being surprised in this crowd. He'd expected that he'd be treated as an outsider, that no one would talk to him seriously until he'd somehow proven himself. That was the way covert groups operated. Instead, it was more common to have some business type walk up, offer him a beer, and shout, "Hey, fuck the government, right?"

It had his head swimming.

He followed Tara to an outdoor buffet restaurant where they took a table in the sun and ordered coffee. Nervous blackbirds were dancing around, lurking on the umbrellas of nearby tables and making forays to attack unprotected plates and returning with bits of bread, fruit, or pastries. They looked well fed.

"Why are you here, at this conference?" she asked him.

The question surprised him and his body tensed. Was she onto him? Had his naïve questioning blown his cover? "To learn," he said. "I've heard so much about this movement."

She laughed. "There's no movement."

"No? You get fifteen hundred people to go to Mexico to talk politics and technology and there's no agenda."

She shrugged and put sweetener in her c0ffee. He watched her long fingers holding the spoon as she stirred it. Something about the image transfixed him and it took a few moments to realize that he was trying to reconcile the idea that this woman he was chatting with was an escort and an entrepreneur. Actually, he was trying to reconcile his preconceptions of both. He didn't know any entrepreneurs, and he doubted he knew any escorts. He'd never hired one.

"Are the people who go to computer shows a movement?" she asked. "Are people who share an idea necessarily a movement? It doesn't seem inherent to holding a convention, I'm here because these people are more likely to support my company than investors at large, and a good number of the attendees are filthy rich. Other people are here for much the same reason. If you want to learn about the principles or theories, the people espouse you'd do better to stay home and read their books and watch their videos. They are glad to tell anyone who will listen what they stand for, and why."

She sat back and tasted the coffee. "Should've walked over to the Starbucks next to the main lobby," she said. "This is weak."

Tyler looked at her, wondering. She made it sound so simple. "Okay, forget the others and political agendas for the moment," he said. Hearing himself talking, he realized how far he was getting from the mission he'd been sent to accomplish. Tara and her company might eventually get entangled with law enforcement, and perhaps criminals were involved with the operation, but he was looking for networks of radicals, operatives. This was just his own curiosity.

"There is a theme to most people's motives for coming here," she said. "Including mine. I'm doing what it takes to free myself and the other escorts from the control of pimps, criminal organizations, in which I include governments." She pointed to herself. "This is my body. Like I told you before, it isn't right that they have a damn thing to say about how I use it. If I want to monetize sex, sell my body, that's between me and my client. My company makes it possible to do that more safely and without bribing cops or other crooks."

"If I didn't know better, I'd say you were a tad cynical about cops."

"They've not done much to make my life easier, Tyler. They tend to think they own other people, just as other people in authority do. Not all of them, but enough. It's the way they are taught."

He turned the conversation back to her business, still curious. The more Tyler learned, the more the business model intrigued him.

She laughed. "You are either deciding whether or not to invest, or thinking of applying for a job."

He joined her laughter. "It probably sounds like that."

"Well, if it's your thing, and your questions about financial matters make me think it might be, I want you to know that we need a new chief financial officer for DateChain. The woman acting as our CFO at the moment is part-time. She has a full-time gig at an investment bank. That's worked well up to now, but at this point in our roadmap the investors want to see a real staff. If you think you are looking for a new opportunity and a challenge, send me your resume. As you can imagine, we will have a challenging few years ahead of us."

Two things about that statement shocked Tyler. The first was that someone that high up in the financial food chain had been working with Tara's company, even just helping out. The second was that he found himself actually considering it for a moment, picturing himself pulling this company together, financially. What a challenge that would be, and his experience with international monetary systems, studying the ins and outs of financial transfers, made him an ideal candidate.

And Tara was serious. She was staring at him, waiting for a reply.

"I..." before he got the words out, he was assaulted by a huge splat of bird shit that landed on the leg of his shorts. "Damn," he said, grabbing a napkin and wiping at it, mostly spreading it around. "I'm going to have to go change clothes."

Tara was laughing. "That was priceless," she said. "Listen, I'm leaving in an hour. We've already checked out and need to get back and sort out some things." She stood and put a hand on his. It sat there, light, warm, sending a tingle through him. "Filling that job is important, so if you think you might be right for it and are interested, get in touch. If you know someone else good, have them contact me."

Then she left. Tyler put the charge on his room bill, amused at the idea of the CIA paying for her coffee, then he went to his room and changed.

When he rejoined the conference, it was with more questions than ever, and few, if any, had to do with uncovering terrorist attacks or assaults on the republic that was The United States of America.

At the break, he saw Jeff Berwick, the founder of The Dollar Vigilante, the conference organizers. He walked up to him and shook his hand. "I'm new to this, Mr. Berwick, but it's an impressive conference."

"It is," Berwick said, obviously pleased. "It's growing like crazy. I never imagined it this big and next year it will be bigger."

On the flight back to Virginia, Tyler found himself digesting everything he'd seen and heard. He would have to make a detailed report, and the powers that be would be unhappy that he hadn't uncovered some group planning an armed revolt, so they'd question him.

And when it was over, they'd send him back to reviewing stock trades, spreadsheets, and bank transfers, looking for the evidence of money being used to finance terrorist cells. He sat back in the seat, looking out at puffy white clouds in a clear, blue sky and, for the first time, thought about the people the records belonged to. He was making a career out of snooping into what were largely legitimate transactions, the financial records of people who had done nothing wrong. There was no 'presumed innocence' in his office. Everything was suspicious until proven otherwise.

His plane landed on time, and during the taxi ride from the airport, he thought of the people he'd met. They'd been a cross-section of people, from all walks of life, who were attempting to assert their right to be free. Through political action, through taking charge of their own financial future, through eating right and paying attention to wellness, they were taking ownership of their lives.

And he was the enemy–of their independence, of their financial security, of their freedom to live without scrutiny.

Langley, Virginia, USA

When he got back home, he found Alice waiting for him. Her expression told him that his welcome would be exactly what he had expected, had feared. She'd been mad when he left, and her anger at being left behind hadn't abated. It didn't help that he'd ignored her messages. In the context of that conference, he couldn't bring himself to deal with them, with her issues. Too many new ideas had been exploding in his head to deal with old baggage.

"I hope you are intending to take me out to dinner," she said. "You owe me."

"Why is that?" he asked. For once, her forceful assertion didn't upset him. He found it odd and illogical. "Assuming I had a grand time in Mexico while you dealt with a snowstorm, why does that mean I owe you anything?"

"Because..." She wasn't able to finish the thought. Finally, an idea came to her. "Because I'm your fiancée."

"I'll take you out," he told her, "because I want to eat out and so do you. I don't accept that I owe you a dinner or anything else."

She was silent, but something in her eyes told him she wasn't satisfied with his attitude. At some point, the relationship with her had gone terribly wrong; only now did he begin to understand what it was. "You're mad at me," he said.

"Hurt and upset. Not mad. You don't act like you love me."

"Doing what someone tells you to because you are afraid of upsetting them isn't love. Demanding that another person think only of your happiness, even when it costs them their own, isn't an act of love either."

"You went off without me."

"Yes, I did."

Her look changed to confusion, and he knew she was wounded. He didn't want to hurt her feelings, but he no longer was going to let her dictate how he felt and what he did. And, if she was hurt, at least it kept her quiet that night.

When they got back to the apartment that night, she came onto him, using the sex card. Because the idea pleased him, he made love to her but found it remarkably unsatisfactory.

His entire existence with Alice was unsatisfactory, and he saw that it was nothing he'd ever sought; he'd just let his life happen, let it evolve. That had to change.

The next morning he learned that his boss Ralph was as disappointed in him as Alice. "You didn't bring me shit," he said. "There isn't anything actionable in any of it."

"Was I supposed to make something up? None of the people I talked to or overheard wanted to do anything to damage the US government. The most they wanted to do was withdraw from its control; they wanted to assert their ownership of their own lives."

"And how is a republic supposed to function if everyone does that? That undermines the system."

"The point is, not playing the game isn't illegal. If someone goes to Amsterdam and smokes pot, it isn't illegal."

Ralph's face grew red. "Damn it, you know what I mean."

Tyler looked at him. "Actually, Ralph, I don't think I do. In fact, I'm not sure you know what you mean. I get it that it frustrates you that these people aren't doing anything illegal to accomplish a goal you are against, but I don't see what we are supposed to do about that."

"We aren't cops, Tyler. We don't enforce the laws. Sometimes we break them to keep this country safe."

The idea startled him. "Really? Then who are we keeping it safe for? The people you want me to find things on are citizens too. If we have a democracy and they all voted to abolish the government then from a legal point of view, that's the will of the people and we'd be out of work."

"That's just hyperbolic political rhetoric," Ralph said. "They just want to run things."

"You mean like the Democrats and Republicans?"

"Don't be a wise-ass, Blake. Your career is on thin ice as it is. Go write a full report and give me something I can use or you will be counting paper clips for the next 20 years if you have a job at all."

Back at his desk, Tyler took out his notes and read them over. There were things he could take out of context that would please his boss, but as he read over them, he pictured the people who were talking, remembered who and what they were. Ralph wanted him to construct a context that would allow them to be investigated. That had to change too.

He switched on his computer and typed: "Report on Anarchapulco 2018. Met some fascinating people. Had a good time. Drank too much. Ron Paul's speech was pretty cool and probably rather subversive, although everything he said has already been published in his books and other speeches. The resort was lovely, but overpriced; the trip was a waste of taxpayer money."

At the bottom, he typed: "P.S. I quit."

He picked up his personal phone and dialed a number he'd memorized. "Hello, Tara, it's Tyler Blake... from the conference."

"Well, well. That was quick." She sounded happy to hear from him.

"I just sent you my resume. I'd like to talk about the CFO job you mentioned."

"I'm actually reading it now, Tyler. Very, interesting background. Given your current employment, now I understand why you were interested in movements that might be meeting in Mexico."

"And I learned there weren't any."

"No? You seemed to feel differently in Mexico."

"There weren't any of the kind I was sent to find. None worth mentioning in my report. As a result of that report, I need to warn you that my current employer isn't likely to give me a recommendation. And I just quit."

She laughed. "They didn't like what you learned."

"Not in the least. They expected certain results from me." He shrugged. "I didn't come through."

"Well, I'm not likely to call human resources at Langley for a reference. But what happens if I don't hire you? I feel like I've led you on."

"Not at all. If this doesn't work out, then I'll have to take my freedom elsewhere. There are tons of start-ups. None as interesting to me as yours."

"What makes my company so attractive?"

"I think that the legal and personal freedom aspects will make for an amazing challenge that would be fun to tackle."

"Fun?"

"Yes. I've decided to start having fun."

"Good for you. So, are you ready to travel? Starting now? We need to set up some business centers in Europe."

He thought about Alice for a few, long seconds. He thought about the things in his apartment... his possessions. They meant nothing. "I'm ready. I don't have anything keeping me here."

"And you can help secure our records?"

"My current employment has given me a reasonable amount of experience in keeping financial and any other records away from prying eyes."

"You know the pay will be small to start. We are putting the money in the business."

"The pay isn't important. I'm counting on getting tokens and I'm pretty sure they are going to be worth a bundle very quickly."

There was a pause. "Are you sure you want to be a major player in a business that is actively looking for the shadowy areas of international law? You do understand that, right?"

"I've given it a lot of thought and yes."

"Then you are hired." The sigh of relief that escaped his lips surprised him. "I'll send you an e-ticket and we will meet in London in two days. We have an investor meeting there."

"Fantastic."

"And congratulations."

"Thanks. I'll do a great job."

"Oh, I know that. You'll work your ass off for us. I meant congratulations on deciding you have the right to own yourself."

A sudden rush of happiness ran through him. "Thank. It feels fantastic," he said.

"Then I'll see you in London."

As he hung up, Ralph stormed into his office waving a printout. It was the report he'd filed. "What the fuck is this, Blake? What the hell is going on? Is this some kind of joke?"

"You always said the agency owned me, Ralph. I just reclaimed the title to my life. Now I own myself... for better or worse."

"What the hell do you mean?"

"It's all about freedom, Ralph."

"And you were sent to protect America's freedom."

"Real freedom is all about ownership, Ralph. Think about it. Who owns you? If the government or the agency owns you, you aren't really free."

"You were infected by those fucking communists."

"Communists don't like free individuals, Ralph. Neither does the agency, so I'm quitting."

"You will regret this. There will be a black mark on your record."

Tyler doubted it very much. "Maybe I will, Ralph. But if I do, at least I'll regret making my own mistakes, not that of a faceless agency." He took out his ID and slid it across the desk. "You'll want these."

"You're quitting right now? Today?"

"There's no time like the present." He stood, feeling oddly lightheaded. The feeling would pass, of course. Reality would descend on him to remind him that he hadn't solved all of his problems, that maybe he had made his life harder, but that was all right. It was his hard life—he'd own it for good or evil.

The first task was to face Alice and tell her the truth. He needed to tell her that she didn't own him, that he didn't recognize her claim on him. He would tell her that he was packing to leave forever. However that went down, he was going to London, to his future. He wanted to take a look at the company's organization and its books so he could see how things needed to be structured... He was thinking of ways to do international business via blockchain and keep the organization off the radar—all radars except that of investors, clients, and escorts.

There was so much to do, and every bit of it exciting when you knew who owned you.

THE END

Did you love *Time and Place: Six Travel Stories*? Then you should read *Crypto Shrugged* by J. Lee Porter and Ed Teja!

The financial world is changing.... where is it headed?

Emerging technology provides the means to free people, but also to control them in new ways. Nation-states struggle to adapt in battles increasingly fought in a digital arena and across the globe. Those who would prefer a borderless world and freedom struggle to assert their right to privacy and distribute their operations as they see fit, free of interference.

In Ayn Rand's Atlas Shrugged, Galt's Gulch was a physical place where the best minds could retreat — withdraw their skills and support from a corrupt system. Distributed ledger technologies such as Bitcoin provides a cyberspace that means there is no longer a need for a utopian land to escape to.

In this book, the movers and shakers, the ones who create the technology, the ones who implement it, the John Galts of their age, decide to use it for their own ends. What if they make their transactions invisible? What if they choose their location, their profession, the people they work with based on shared values and merit without any concern for government sanctions or rules?

And what happens when increasingly incompetent and anachronistic governments try to use blockchain to preserve their status — and their crypto shrugs?

About the Authors

J. Lee Porter is a former IT specialist, programmer and data analyst for banking, security, and government agencies. He left the IT world behind on July 4th, 2016, declaring it his personal independence day to travel the world full time in search of inspiration for his writing.

@JLPorterAuthor on Twitter

Ed Teja is a writer a poet, a musician, and boat bum. He writes about the places he knows, and the people who live in the margins of the world. After being friends with tech giants, pirates, fishermen, and a coterie of strange people for many years, he finds the world an amazing place filled with intriguing, if sometimes crazed characters.

@ETeja on Twitter

About the Publisher

www.nomadicgiant.com

www.ingramcontent.com/pod-product-compliance
Lightning Source LLC
Chambersburg PA
CBHW061549170626
46811CB00001B/143